THE GALAXY GAME

TRILOGY

THE GALAXY GAME
TRILOGY

BILL BLY

To order additional copies of this book, contact:
Xlibris Corporation
1-888-795-4274
www.Xlibris.com
Orders@Xlibris.com
79134

This book is dedicated in memory and devotion to my
late parents, Louise H. and Lloyd G. Bly.
Their flaws were few; however, their kindness, goodness,
dedication to family, and unpretentious personalities,
were abundant, and appreciated by those who loved them.

PART ONE

A Paradise Lost; One Found

Prologue

I, Gordon Paradise, do attest to the veracity of the following events. My story encompasses the fact Ross Red Jacket, a Seneca Indian, and I invented the means to travel within time present. Though it seems impossible and laughable, such events did occur in the late1980s, and only a doubting Thomas would say otherwise. Truth cannot deny our invention, our ingenuity, and our word as honorable men.

Allow me to say that truth is what we live, and life is the time remembered in fragmented moments. These moments, both sublime and troublesome, compose the lives of all men and women. Indeed moments are those things most remembered, and moments connect the dots to our lives, as if our lives were mere puzzles to be completed. Yet perhaps life is a mere puzzle, or game, or a never ending journey?

When all human achievements are accounted for, society will all be amazed that time travel existed within their lifetimes without the national media's knowledge. In fact, Ross and I took pride in masking our discovery, mainly for humane reasons. In our secrecy we would prevent those evil among us to access our device and use it for conquest or exploitation.

We both knew the same Biblical warning from Proverbs 16:32, "A patient man is better than a warrior, and he who rules his temper, than he who takes a city."

To rule one's temper surpasses and overrides the warrior who conquers cities. Yet I would become temporarily, a warrior, and one assisting in conquering a city. Gratefully, those moments were brief and held no glory for me. However, these words of temperance and patience would be our moral guide, though not always achieved, by me and my friends named in this story. However, our actions shown in the story express human actions and histories, and thus, history and conscience become the final resting place of our actions.

"How precious to me are your designs, O God
How vast the sum of them! Were I to count;
They would outnumber the sands; to finish,
I would need eternity."

Psalm 139: 17-18

"All rivers go to the sea,
Yet never does the sea become full.
To the place where they go,
The rivers keep on going."

Ecclesiastes 1:7

Chapter 1

Above eastern Oklahoma a thunderstorm raged an hour prior to sunrise. By now, Duchess, my Welsh corgi had jumped upon my bed to be comforted from the reverberating noise. Awakened now and unable to fall back asleep, I lie on my back thinking of upcoming events. My happiest thoughts rested upon my fiancée, Diana J. Fleming. We'd been apart now three months and her plane was due to arrive Sunday afternoon, just days away. Knowing we'd be together again soon made me smile. Yet I knew we had a difficult agenda to discuss.

With emotional closeness being the epicenter of human love, one may wonder what life would be in times of lengthy separation from our loved ones. Such a time Diana and I had just experienced. This realization made me anxious and my upcoming travel plans might be viewed by Diana as abandonment and folly, considering her recent return from a lengthy trip. With one just arriving, and the other planning immediate departure, creates emotional conflict between soon-to-be married people; this conflict needed quick resolution.

Duchess crept up to me and laid her head on my chest. Doing so made me think she was empathizing with my feelings. Anyway, I'm constantly amazed by the perceptive abilities of animals; their sense of loyalty and compassion. Human loyalty and love seemed too conditional, and with high expectations. Animals are direct. Humans are stealthy and deceptive. However, both Diana and I had seen each other in our worst moments, and still loved one another. Our capacity to fool or deceive the other no longer existed.

I felt we approached marriage with more realization than most couples. Perhaps my statement sounds self-righteous, seen through the lens of emotion rather than the lens of logic. Yet I felt we truly owned a deep perception of each other's feelings and minds that few others knew.

After a shower I dressed and ate breakfast, my favorite meal, and simplicity of organic foods: cereal, soy milk, toast, and juice. Such simplicity streamlined life.

Our forthcoming reunion made me think many things, as if the door to my unconsciousness had opened, though slightly, for memories to surface. I thought of how Diana and I met; my life prior to knowing her, my college days, my teen years and childhood; all remembered in a massive sequence of time etched upon my heart. It was a time remembered and a time forgotten; a life lived with both simplicity and complexity, a duality of human feelings as to create anxiety within me. In sensing this anxiety, I especially felt it when a distant train whistle blew after midnight, while wishing for sleep to quietly arrive; hearing only its mournful sound; not the necessity of a train pulling cargo to needy destinations. I grieved the sound of this loneliness and nothing else. There was no logic to my senses, only the sound like that of a cooing mourning dove; its ability to recreate every sad feeling I'd ever felt. Yes, there was to be sadness in our reunion; that I could not deny. However the greatest feeling was the joy of seeing my woman again. With these thoughts my sadness melted like ice on a summer day. Happiness filled me with childhood buoyancy; an inflated joy known by Thanksgiving dinner on the table, or Christmas morning at age six.

Now my unconsciousness had opened wide, as if the closet hall of my family home had opened and all the coats and hats of beloved relatives were being placed there for safe keeping. My childhood feelings and experiences were set before me in a memory, like tapestry, a tapestry entitled "The 1950s and 60s." We children played games like hide-n-seek, tag, and Red light/Green light. Toy guns were popular then with the boys; and I, a boy, had my collection. Many of our dads had served in WW II. At that time toy guns, or even Beebe rifles, were not frowned upon as they are now. A certain harmlessness or "laissez-faire" attitude existed then.

As children we bicycled all about town or played in the backyard. A certain innocence existed then, it has now disappeared.

In winter we sled the steep hill behind the high school building or constructed snow forts in our yards. We also gathered fresh snow and ate it with maple syrup flavoring.

Yet winter often bored us by Ground Hog's Day. Tired were we of wearing snow boots, heavy coats, gloves and hats.

Spring was a time of hope; and, Easter Sunday provided baskets of green "grass," candy rabbits, colored eggs, and marshmallow chicks. Often we'd visit relatives over Easter break. However, dad rarely took time off from the store, though mom warned him a month early of impending travel plans; she also gave weekly reminders, in other words, no excuses for dad.

Spring meant rain and it rained often. Large puddles were a source of fun, running through them and soaking our trousers with the muddied water, or perhaps splashing others and laughing at their misfortune.

With snow gone, our bicycles were reborn from dusty garage corners and became our constant means of travel. Such fun remains in my mind. Though always wanting a three speed English bicycle, I never owed one; yet pedaled reliable 'one speed' models my entire life. I realized I didn't need to own everything I wanted in life. Some dreams best remain dreams.

Autumn in my youth meant returning to school and viewing colorful leaves in my daily walks. Green leaves turned gold, red, yellow, and crisp orange. So too the leaves were raked and set on fire. The aroma of burning autumn leaves still remain with me, as do the aroma of summer campfires at various state parks. These fires, built of wooden logs and branches, were evening traditions to our camping excursions.

Dad owned a pharmacy; and, in every season I delivered prescriptions all over town. I knew my neighbors well, rare for any child or adult. I knew the misers, the complainers, the happy, the laconic, the ill, and those who thought themselves ill. I knew the grateful and the doubters, the dying and the newly born. I knew the dressed, the half dressed, the intoxicated, the sober and the modest. I saw and heard things others would pass along as gossip. I knew those on time, the educated, the well mannered, the ignorant, the pathetic, the laughable, the scorned, the rude, and those consistently late. Such knowledge was never translated from the Greek, nor learned at any grade school or graduate college. I knew people and their actions and reactions as a language all its own. Test me on this secret language and I would be at the top of my class.

Now that I have spoken of myself, allow me to introduce myself. I am Gordon Paradise, age 37, and hail from western New York. My hometown of Glen Iris is a community on a hill overlooking the Genesee Valley. The Genesee River commences in northern Pennsylvania, flowing north to Lake Ontario. In fact, it's one of the few rivers to flow north in the entire nation. Its 120 mile journey takes it through small towns, past former Iroquois Indian villages, flat hayfields to rocky cascading falls and gorges, where white water plunged one hundred seven feet in unceasing fury, called "the Middle Letchworth Falls."

My town was quiet, yet steeped in traditions. The fox hunt was one such tradition, at least for the upper class, a British tradition at that. The hunt was both ludicrous and unique. Even George Washington was fond of the fox hunt. The land rich gathered on Saturday mornings in autumn upon the grassy fields north of town, and sipped martinis from thermos bottles. These bottles shone brilliantly in the fall sunlight, and the community's elite were fond of their drinks. Those who rode and pursued the long tailed foxes eventually chased them down only to do the same the following week. Any reason for a party would do; any reason for tumblers of martinis and whiskey sours. To drink was to live, and some of the living pursued their beverage habits daily. Yet that is another story, but not another country. The soused shall inherit the earth; yet it will be their delusion.

My parents were unpretentious people. Dad ran the local "Paradise Pharmacy" and kept long hours. Though a businessman and pharmacist are considered unique in the eyes of the community, the land rich and wealthy always looked down on dad and considered him, and all retailers, servants. Dad spent long hours in the store and had little time for socializing outside the store, meaning the homes of local friends and neighbors. Actually, more socializing took place in any local store than any private residence in town, and therefore you learned as much news as the local newspaper printed. At the end of his day, he and mom ate dinner and sought total seclusion for an hour or two watching television in the living room. We children stayed out of the way and did our homework in our rooms, or spent summer evenings amusing ourselves collecting lightning bugs or playing softball. In autumn we played football; in winter we tossed snowballs at each other.

Mom kept the store's business ledgers, and worked diligently to provide our meals, and kept our home well cleaned and organized; hence, she discovered and enjoyed her multiple roles. We four children kept her busy; yet rarely was our life a paradise, rather it was chaotic from both noise and endless activity, otherwise called "perpetual motion," a phrase first used by our cousin from Pittsburgh.

Quiet time was television time. But I often chose reading. Television was an occasional diversion. Often I felt I had time to waste. Childhood, I believed, was a huge plot of time that never ran out, like a river never fully emptying into Lake Ontario. Childhood was a bridge over this timeless river. It was an aqueduct to the future, one where I'd always be living on

Second Street; where mom always cooked, cleaned, and kept the pharmacy's finances in line; with dad always filling prescriptions at his store. No other reality seemed possible.

Mom believed in the well-rounded person. We children worked, played, fought, read, biked, and made peace after fighting. Later we recycled all the actions and feelings of the previous week. Mom also volunteered at church weekly, and daily walked to the store to visit dad and review the accounts. Some customers rarely paid but expected constant attention and favors, as it were an honor to serve them. To live a Christian life was mom and dad's ongoing goal. Their unspoken rules were: "Honesty in business, kindness and charity to all," sounds Lincoln-like, and, "To live as a Christian is the most difficult lifestyle." To "Live a Christ-centered life," became our model; our mantra. We read the Holy Bible growing up and were told "Don't forget your Heavenly Father." But I didn't forget Him, I just didn't understand Him! I didn't fully comprehend the sacrament of penance until college. However, I'm not blaming my Church. My mind and heart weren't ready to comprehend until my attitude toward God changed. This change occurred during college, when I commenced reading the New Testament. Now I understood. Prior to reading scripture my understanding of sin was minimal, my main sins being lustful thoughts about girls and some profanity. My first initial, "G," I felt stood for guilt. Yes, those immoral thoughts during my teen years produced much guilt, and I am prone to guilt as water is prone to freeze in winter; as rain fell in torrents during summer. I knew not where such thoughts generated from, other than the mind. The "mind" was everything and it surely held the soul. For the thoughts of the mind created the actions that became sin, or better yet, the actions that produced kindness and generosity. The mind and the soul seemed as one. As for the heart, do not forget the heart, it too was the instrument of the mind, though philosophers said the heart was its own country; its own domain. Perhaps it was and my immaturity had not realized the subtleties of the heart or mind. Or was it that I lived too much in my thoughts and not enough by intuition? Was not personality the determining factoring as to the logical and intuitive?

What did I know, I was just a child? Yet such thoughts stimulated my imagination. Contemplating the unseen presence of God was good, and at times scary and mystifying. How does a ten year old relate to eternity? How does diminutive intelligence grapple with infinite knowledge? How does a pebble relate to Mount Everest? And, what does the mountain care what a pebble thinks? As if a pebble had thoughts!

I pictured God as an old man, awesome and bearded, and I still do. Even the Psalms call Him awesome. Yet with and without these thoughts and feelings, there was work to do.

As mentioned earlier I worked for dad delivering prescriptions, and I was paid for my work; to paraphrase Holy Scripture, 'the oxen shall receive their fodder; the vineyard workers receive their wages.' The money earned was parentally directed to a savings account. Spending was a luxury; savings a necessity. With this attitude in mind, I saved up a sizable amount by the time I finished high school. My brother and two sisters saved their earnings too, working for Dad, or assisting neighbor's in their summer child care and babysitting, or mowing lawns.

Having parents who grew up during the Great Depression, one learned the value of money and the value of the simplest of meals set before us; neither was taken for granted. Some cynics predicted the depression would return after World War II; yet, fortunately, they were proven wrong, though the 70s were the closest economic hardship the country had known in decades.

Since we all worked at dad's store, we vowed never to enter the retailing profession. Yet my brother Thomas opened his own bookstore in Buffalo, and sisters Pamela and Libby became pharmacists at Rochester's Strong-Memorial Hospital.

All my family stayed in the western New York area. Yet one summer after my college sophomore year, I took six weeks to travel with friends and discovered Tulsa, Oklahoma. College friends touted its warm winters and minimal snowfall. I was willing to try something new. After graduation two years later, I moved to Tulsa. Certainly Tulsans spoke differently than I; yet I was not harassed or made fun of for my dialect, rather, I was accepted.

West Tulsa possessed many hills. I lived among the back roads of these hills, and many a sunset and I kept an appointment, similar to Thoreau's life style, as I marveled at the orange and purple clouds of the closing day. The sunset looked back at me and probably laughed at my puny white color and utter insignificance. However, I cared not if the sunset laughed. We were friends; besides, I was pale white and puny in comparison.

Mornings and evenings exuded peace and beauty, even in the hot summer days when most of us lived close to air conditioners. These tree laden hills lent a breeze occasionally, and this breeze allowed my human life to be united with something outside myself, something bigger and grander. There I'd sit on the back porch and watch the sun's light spread color over the blue canvas of the evening sky, with an unseen breeze rushing over me like a handheld fan—perhaps the hand of God; His hand providing delightful coolness to the heat of a summer's evening. One more day in the sequential creation of all the days He'd created. God and Time were one; God and creation were one. God and I were close, with oneness, simplicity, and love.

Chapter 2

Winter had its pleasures, too. My frosted living room windows looked out upon open fields dusted with new fallen snow or tree branches bent heavy by major snowstorms. These things provided more visual enjoyment than all the television programs ever aired. On such frosty mornings I trekked among the fields and along the edges of snow laden forests to renew myself on a rare Oklahoma winter's day. It refreshed me and provided time for independent thought and spiritual reflection. Perhaps I was a partial hermit; yet knew no hermits or what they did other than pray. However, the oneness of time, or the oneness of an entire year, seemed to grow in my awareness as seasonal continuity became one unfolding message never ending. Rather it modified itself over and over, regardless of human or animal presence. For my thoughts could not make a snowstorm end or a rainfall begin. My action could not bring sunrise or my inaction allow the starry heavens to appear. My deeds were not influencing the natural forces, and my words were meaningless to the clouds. In this realization I felt comforted. Yes, I felt better than a handful of medicine might make me feel, because I realized I was not in control.

The Good Lord was in control. He made the snow fall with such gentleness that only a Russian ballet could be compared to it. God alone made the storm clouds send rain upon Oklahoma's wheat fields and grasslands. Only He could produce a tornado that twisted about in power as to destroy a few barns, yet leave an entire neighborhood untouched by 150 mile winds. His touch alone made the full moon a mystical experience for every loving couple to gaze upon with endless fascination; holding each other with a love He alone gave them to share. God Himself saw to it that His grand creation would be enjoyed by conscious and living humans. For is a snowstorm just a storm to nature? Inanimate nature knew nothing of its power; its grandeur. To a man and woman, a child, or the forest animals, only they could grasp the beauty or danger of the storm. Yet the human realm could appreciate the waning moon or the myriad stars of the Milky Way; only a human mind could grasp Niagara's power or the elegant simplicity of an opening red rose bud. And are not humans one of a few species with color vision? Prove me wrong if you can; yet only the human mind acknowledges and notices the swirling pattern within a sunflower. Look at its sublime pattern, the mathematics alone is beyond my comprehension. In fact, that one plant has enough seeds to grow a hundred more plants, all basically the same, the following summer. Does not time and eternity play with us daily? Are we too blind or too busy to see creation? Thoreau was right when he states in *Walden*, "The mass of men lead lives of quiet desperation."

We are desperate to deny that our lives possess anything more than superficial experiences. We live on the outer edges of our lives and willingly do so for lack of thought. We develop apathy between the ages of 12 and 22, and its chief characteristic is the unwillingness to embrace every moment as unique. Moments renew themselves into various versions of life, thus they do not reappear as the same exact moment. Thus life was renewing itself in similar and familiar ways; yet retained uniqueness. We the created, unwilling to think of our Creator, do ordain and proclaim our laziness, our thoughtlessness and lassitude, in the battle between good and evil in our lives. We do so willingly and will continue doing so for generations. We will refuse to think the full moon beautiful; rain will just be rain, fog will be a bother; and snowy ice a nuisance. The heat or cold will be our main source of complaints, and our neighbors will be held at arm's length so as not to offend our sensitive nasal passages. We too will retain our family prejudices towards other races, faiths, and mental acuities. We will continue to laugh at failures, and feel envy toward the wealthy. We will hold in esteem large saving accounts and well planned stock portfolios. We will scoff at the dreamers, the poets, and children's imagination, whether true children, or the inner child of adults, who retain natural curiosity. These shallow and apathetic people will be part of all cultures, and therefore halt progress in the creative dimensions; for their goal is simply money; its power and prestige. The wealthy will rule the masses, and the rich will want it in hard cash. The powerful will elect officials, and many elected shall be mere puppets to the empowered money people. Yes, the weak shall inherit the earth, but six feet below, trampled on by the land-rich gentry and the arrogant who know what's "best" for society. The misfit will remain the misfit, and thus be cast out into the night, wailing and gnashing his teeth. The individual will count for little. But the individual is like an uncomfortable chair or community eyesore, or the person along the parade route who proclaims, "The King has no clothes!" Beware of these people, the "crackpots!" These are the people who make for change, and few like changes. "Life is good," the crowds say, "life is comfortable. We know the pattern; now leave us alone to experience the pettiness of our lives."

However, the individual becomes God's greatest creation, though the masses will be blinded by their self-righteousness. The masses will not realize the significance of one lone person who trusts his or her own Creator. In that faith, the individual possesses more power than he or she realizes; acknowledging singleness of purpose with dignity.

Chapter 3

I stand six foot two inches tall, with brown hair and blue eyes like my mom; yet my height was from dad.

A while back I concluded my scholastic studies with a PhD in physics. My specialty was electromagnetism and quantum theory. I gave homage to James Clark Maxwell and Einstein; Heisenberg and Faraday. I owed much to Newton, Galileo, Copernicus and Kepler. Then there was Hubble and Hawking, a rich intellectual basis that gave me pride and humility of my own abilities.

Hobbies are centered on my personality, I'm drawn to reading fiction, biographies and history, I collect clocks and have been obsessed with the concept of time since youth. First book editions are also a collector's item for me, also, Corning ware and Pyrex, and glass insulators too. Glass fascinates me for its utility, as well as for its aesthetic quality.

Regarding time, what is it? This question was asked by me in grade school and never did I receive a satisfactory answer. I still ask, "What is time? Is it a substance, a particle, an illusion, a passage, a measure of radioactive and organic decay?"

Even before I reached school at age six, I marveled at grandpa's pocket watch. I also examine watches. Mom wore a dainty gold timepiece; dad's timepiece encircled his wrist with a leather band. The leather band eventually gave way to the metallic twister-flex bands popular in the 60s.

Dad preferred silver watches; mom liked gold. In grade school I collected watches and clocks, both working and nonworking models. My walls soon were crowded with the onset of a growing clock display. My parents were amused by my avocation.

My mechanical ability was first noted during these years. Non-functioning timepieces were converted to working ones by my diligent work. It proved satisfying.

I had few girlfriends in my youth; I was socially retarded. With age, things improved in this category. Yet I still regret being unable to reach out to Susan Kingsley, a beautiful and action-oriented classmate, a true 'womanly brave heart,' who 'liked me a lot,' as I heard later by way of the student grapevine. Not until months after my graduation with my B.S. in Physics, did I experience my first love. However, like most first loves, it disappeared within two months and made for memories more ideal than real; more painful than pleasant.

When I met Diana Fleming, at a party I nearly neglected, on Oklahoma's Grand Lake shoreline, the best of times were beginning. By the way, the lake property was owned by the Lanier's, and Dr. Lanier was my mentor.

So let me say that being in Oklahoma, thirteen hundred miles from my hometown, allowed my life to mature. Until this time I believed I lived an extended childhood, and sought friends and relationships that maintained my naiveté, all of course, unconsciously.

Two years ago I concluded my Doctoral thesis and have since been fully engrossed in my current project. If I hadn't been a recipient to part of my deceased uncle's estate, I would have been unable to maintain my private work. Yes, Uncle Waldo passed away two years ago. Mom's rich brother divided his wealth among us. My portion assisted me at a critical point of scientific research.

"Thanks, Waldo! I always enjoyed your company."

Coincidentally, a good portion of his wealth came from investment in the petroleum business here in the southwest.

To inherit money is nearly everyone's dream. I admit to fantasizing about it growing up. Finally, it happened. May I use it wisely! Money either builds us or destroys us. Rarely is its effect neutral. When I say "builds us," I intend to say that helping others through our charity builds society. Scripture tells us to tithe, I agree. Wealth is neutral. It's the individual possessor of this wealth that makes it good or bad. Money has value because people place value on gold, silver, or paper. Yes, colored and printed paper; who would have thought that folding money would overtake our society? Certainly not President Andrew Jackson, coins were reality to him.

Has plastic access to credit taken over? Either way, access is access; and, either way you have it or you don't. Like appearance, you either have physical attractiveness or you don't; it's one extreme or the other, as I mistakenly thought so at one time.

I suppose the term middle class developed in this fashion. Most of us are somewhere in the middle, probably the monkey-in-the-middle. Sure, money or mouse, chimp or chump, Darwin or creationism, which do we choose? Money or poverty; death with wealth is still death; poverty with death is still death, too. We, the working, seek its power to buy our homes, our cars, our futures, our backyard barbeques, and nice vacations to Las Vegas, or to pay our child's private schooling. Money is neither good nor evil. It's only good or evil with what the owner does with it. Am I sermonizing, or do I prefer simonizing? All joking aside, The Sermon on the Mount was not about money, it was about human behavior. Yet even our beloved churches and charities operate on money. The rich shall inherit the chancery, the cathedrals, and five star hotels. Yet the faithful know one thing and know it well, money is just a temporary thing. It does make for beautiful churches, and allows for the poor of north Tulsa to receive food; the hungry rural Oklahomans to receive assistance. Money equals food, equals medicinal purchases, provides housing, allows scholarships, and as stated, money is neither good nor evil. Only human action or inaction makes it so.

With my inheritance I chose action, scientific action now achieved. I will now speak of my work. My travel concept is unique; and, I first proposed the idea in fourth grade. My classmates laughed and my teacher, Miss Browning, frowned. In junior high I once again proposed the idea in science class. Classmates mocked me for weeks afterward, and my teacher, Mr. Markus, shrugged his shoulders and said, "Maybe." In high school the reception in physics class was greeted with silent stares and a few snickers. My teacher said, "Only in your dreams, Paradise."

He was skeptical of new thought and probably still is twenty years later. Yet I don't fault teachers. No one thought my idea of time travel probable, just mere fiction.

Actually, my concept was simple; I wanted to travel within the present moment. I wanted to travel not to other countries, but within our galaxy. How basic could my travel instincts express it? I chose not to travel time past or time future, as portrayed by H. G. Wells. Rather I wished to partake of the present moment. Metaphysically, to paraphrase Thoreau, I wished to bathe my intellect in the river of time. Why was this dream, this fantasy, so laughable to others? Small minds and stunted imaginations, I guessed.

Yet it hurts to be laughed at and hurt I did. Yet giving up was not in my vocabulary.

As my maternal grandmother used to tell us," Believe in yourself and trust in God." Also she'd say, "Work diligently, save your money, and avoid fast women." I never knew what she meant by "fast women," nor would she explain it to me or my brother, Thomas. For many years we both guessed they were women athletes. Tell me, how was a ten year old boy supposed to know?

To our sisters, grandma warned also of "honey-tongued men who tell you everything you ever wanted to hear." It was years before they understood her warnings. We miss Grandma Grace, she was fun. She would even play in our squirt gun wars; few grandmothers would allow themselves such silliness or spontaneity.

Mother apparently heeded her mom's advice regarding men. Dad was rather blunt in speech and not prone to hyperbole. He was honest to a fault and worked constantly. He was a war hero, though never spoke of the medals given to him. Like all veterans who earned medals, the 'real' heroes are the friends buried who never lived to see age 21, let alone 65.

Mom's brother, Waldo, followed grandma's advice too, "Work diligently and save your money." Waldo ended up quite wealthy. Yet his diligence for labor became an obsession. Actually Uncle Waldo was a "workaholic." Work was his life and he never married. I suppose money was his mistress, a heartless one at that. Rumors had it that Waldo gambled too. However, no one ever spoke openly of this affliction. Such matters were swept under the emotional carpet of our lives. Submerged in all families, live guarded secrets, and invisible; yet always present. These secrets were swept beneath unseen emotional carpets; these carpets cover the past and present perfectly, while waiting for the future to yield familial truth; truth that rarely made its appearance known.

Dad never gossiped, especially about family. He told us he learned long ago a hard lesson about what gossip did to others. Apparently he was made the target of vicious gossip, and both he and a friend suffered with vicious lies. Dad reformed at an early age and never partook of gossip again. Gossip leads only to pain, like a cross of despair, with the pain both vertical and horizontal in its feeling within the mind and body.

Since words are easily fanned into a fiery blaze of half-truths, the knowledge of my time journey was kept secret. "Come, my Way, my Truth, my Life," so said Ralph Vaughn Williams in music inspired by a George

Herbert poem, such a way as to measure my life; such a means to measure personal strength, and to realize an old truth I dreamed possible.

Currently I am in the process of concluding experiments that will allow me to engage in travel activity never before achieved. To say that I'm excited is an understatement. To say I'm scared is an understatement as well! My heart feels both tension and excitement. My mind is in overdrive every evening, and I find it impossible to fall asleep quickly, rather, it takes hours. Adrenalin keeps me going daily; otherwise I'd collapse into exhaustion's black hole. Insomnia has been a curse; yet the pharmaceutical industry was offering new therapies.

My travel concept seemed unique, and in college a few true believers came into my life. Ross Red Jacket, my lab partner, was one such disciple; Dr. Lucas Lanier, a physics professor, another. My faith in a Heavenly Father was enhanced by their friendship and support. Their encouragement at the right point of time allowed me to forge ahead, to make things happen. Now I was taking charge, no more passive waiting for me; no victim role to cry over.

The results of my idea and its subsequent use would help us earth-living creatures. How it would help I wasn't exactly sure; yet that concern would resolve itself later. My natural inclination was to override selfishness and benefit the human estate. In other words, achievement was not for self-glorification, rather it was an altruistic move to assist humanity. However, I was not so naive to realize other humans would use new technology to deliver destruction upon others.

Allow me this fantasy: The Nobel Prize and being rich. Alright, both are ego-oriented and somewhat selfish. Fame is the prize; riches for its peaceful uses. As for riches, I was taught to be a wise steward. Ownership and wealth are not to be life's rudder. Christian stewardship might be defined as investing in others before securing one's own needs.

My forthcoming adventure would make me part Huckleberry Finn, Lewis and Clark, Columbus, and Moses. These figures, four real, one fictional, would be role models in my mind's eye. They existed as self-history, if only in imagination. To me, time existed in our lives as a road or river, especially a river, influenced no doubt by the image of the Genesee River flowing through my hometown.

"May time's river be kind and may I swim it safely; may I experience its force and return to tell about it." These thoughts rippled like waves against the shore of my mind; my hair being tall grass; my ears rocky pinnacles;

my eyes two lighthouses; my mouth a cape of hope; my tongue, a net cast out; my teeth, sharp rocks.

My friend, Ross Red Jacket was a genius. He was also, as family oral tradition stated, a direct descendent of the famous Seneca Chief, Red Jacket, to whom President Washington gave a gold medallion Red Jacket hung around his neck. Thus, Ross had significant family history; both he and I were from the Genesee Valley. He claims his ancestral home was only miles from my home in Glen Iris, located on the Genesee River. During the American Revolution, General Sullivan had orders to burn pro-British Seneca villages of the Genesee Valley. Thus, Ross' ancestral village was burned; Sullivan hoping thus, to break the will of the Seneca to assist their ally.

However, only Ross' Ohio relatives, also Seneca Indian, were forced to Oklahoma by political pressure in 1829. The Ohio Seneca were given a small part of the Cherokee land, thus the Cherokee were once again diminished by Jackson's Presidency. The New York Seneca arrived of their own free will, and their Indian license plates, called tags in Oklahoma, were listed as "Cayuga-Seneca," as they had banded together centuries earlier, and thus became one, not two tribes, to the government. As for the Mohawk, and other tribes of Iroquois Confederacy, they have minimal-to-no presence in today's Oklahoma.

Therefore, we both arrived in Oklahoma of our own free will in different decades. Ross' family arrived in the late 1940s. He soon found himself mastering electronics in grade school, and much later, computers, mechanics, and solar energy, as if five grad students were rolled into one person. He was tall and a full blooded Seneca Indian, his jet black hair was combed straight back. At one time he wore it long down his back; but, he's since cut it shoulder length. Possessed of classic Indian facial features and skin tone, he spoke rarely, and had physical endurance surpassing mine a few times over. His help was priceless in launching my dream from fantasy to reality.

Another friend mentioned was Dr. Lucas Lanier. He, too, was brilliant and his primary goal was educating, and his flair, his passion, and his dedication influenced me deeply. He was of medium height, wore glasses, somewhat stout, and his balding head was bordered with gray hair around the ears. He laughed easily, spoke in parables, and allowed students the freedom to err without guilt or shame heaped on their foreheads. His models were Einstein and Edison. Like his models, he allowed himself to act child-like. This behavior is distinct from childish! God's creation still awed him; a monarch butterfly was always beautiful, a sunset startlingly unique. An elm tree delighted him; an eagle flying over the Arkansas River west of Tulsa thrilled his child within. He was like a grandfather to me; I felt no problem in my attitude.

When I first proposed time travel to Dr. Lanier, he did not scoff at or ignore my idea. Rather, we discussed it as if we were planning a trip to Texas. His open-mindedness permitted self-discovery by his students. This meant learning from mistakes, and challenging rules. However, he insisted the student know nature's rules before attempting to break, bend, or defy them. Thus he was the perfect college professor and mentor for me, before and during grad school.

Ross and I met each other in Lanier's class at The University of Tulsa. Though my undergrad work was complete from my native New York State, I met Lanier in his office at T.U. having heard so many positive things about him. It was then I asked to audit his undergrad classes, before deciding upon my Graduate school's location. Ross was a senior when we met in one of the classes I audited with Lanier; it was as close to a spiritual, let alone scientific, experience I ever knew. I was enlightened now as St. Paul must have felt on the road to Damascus. The Biblical description of scales, had fallen from my eyes, just as they had for St. Paul.

Lanier generated in me such enthusiasm, I chose The University of Tulsa as my grad school, majoring in physics and engineering.

Thus with Lanier in my corner, I had access to expensive research equipment and to other educational institutions. Through his recommendations, I attended summer independent studies at Princeton, MIT and Caltech. These studies made me grateful to Lanier for his intervention, thus allowing me to enhance my knowledge of science. Hence, I was truly blessed and fortunate to know him on a personal level, for few students obtain such friendship and support from their teachers and professors.

During a graduate school vacation, another true believer entered my life, this time in the form of Miss Diana J. Fleming. She touched my life with love and inspired me to succeed. Diana is a tall, gorgeous blonde with hair reaching halfway down her back. She's a shapely and lovely young woman, an executive in the energy business. She plays tennis and golf, rides bicycle along Tulsa's River Park Path, owns a telescope to view stars and planets from her balcony, and enjoys fine food. Blues and jazz make her mellow; sentimental movies make her cry. She owns a cat named Miss Kitty, and a huge fish tank deserving a salute from Chicago's Shedd Aquarium. In it she recreates the underwater beauty of Cozumel. Oh yes, she's a skin diver and loves the sunny beaches from Florida to Cancun; to her a quiet evening at home is reading F. Scott Fitzgerald novels, drinking gourmet coffee; and enjoying oriental or Italian cuisine.

A night out finds us anyplace from Michael Fusco's; The Warren Place at The Doubletree Inn; the Polo Grill, Bodean's, or The Chalkboard, this was our routine and enjoyment, as these restaurants represented to us, the be Tulsa's best. We also enjoy Braum's ice cream and any frozen yogurt shop.

Diana's hair appears as spun gold and whiter teeth no dentist could improve. For smiles, some people are blessed with charismatic smiles, and Diana was blessed; a smile as only Leonardo painted them.

Am I in love or not? Any more compliments and I'll find myself engraving her biography upon Steuben Glass.

While thinking of love, for it is both bitter and sweet, I was moved to write this poem:

> Tell me love; tell me again how you feel.
> Tell me the secret of your heart.
> Ask for my love, ask often.
> For I shall speak love as gardens speak flowers.
> My heart blooms as a rose garden, a red rose garden at that.
> For red is the color of my true love's heart; my true love's lips.
> The sunlight never fades upon her face and sunlight creates
> A richer beauty, an intimate portrait painted in light; by light.
> Ask me how I feel, and I will show you sunrise's colors;
> I will show you the starlight just after sunset.
> I will kiss your lips as the moon kisses evening clouds;
> I will caress your skin as stars caress the night sky.
> Beauty shall live within you, around you, and near you.
> The hours will have no reason to exist, other than allowing
> Me to love you. Passion, stay close to me; stay close
> And whisper cool breezes to both her ears and mine.
> Let us live and love as I listen to her heartbeat;
> And her everlasting breathing; passion's breath,
> Then I'll know our love shall remain eternal.

Writing poetry touches me as no other literature. Poetry is Pablo Neruda, Whitman, Eliot, James Wright, Robert Frost, Yeats, Tennyson, Shelley and Keats, Dickinson, Bishop, and Moore. Poetry makes life sublime and emotional. Only those with a sensitive heart shall know poetry, the insensitive dismiss it. I dismiss them.

To travel in time a device or machine is needed. After sixteen dismal failures, number seventeen proved successful! I called the equipment "Translator," for it translated, so to speak, from earth to another realm of galactic existence.

The "translation" occurring was meant for an earthly animal, specifically mammal, to be transported from earth to another planet within the galaxy.

I chose to call my successful device "Translator 17," or simply, "Trans-17." Ross and I chose to send a couple of hamsters through "Trans-17" to test its abilities. Like I said, sixteen attempts failed. And yes, some hamsters died in the attempt. Poor brave friends! Let me add by saying these mammals did not suffer.

On a morning in 1989 we placed two hamsters, one called "Ginger," the other "Fred," in what was the seventeenth effort. We believed that "Fred" and "Ginger" would return healthy. Our device allowed release somewhere along the time warp that was comparable to earth's benign environment. Our computations prevented a living creature from being released into a hostile environment, e.g. Pluto or Venus! On Pluto you'd freeze instantly; on Venus you'd be vaporized.

So at 8:49 AM on a Tuesday, as spring weather allowed azaleas to bloom in Woodward Park, while rosebuds and Bradford pear trees illuminated the day with their joyous colors, two hamsters were placed in Trans-17 and sent to an unknown locale. Only when the time warp "reverberated" or "returned" to today's frequency, would we once again see our hamsters.

Built into our equipment was a "bio-meter" for access to the health of the animals. This bio-meter would also keep tabs on me, the human "animal," who would eventually use Trans-17. This monitoring system told base-control that the time traveler was alive; the status of his health, such as, blood pressure, heartbeat, and metabolism. Therefore, each hamster was wearing a small patch to measure these physical entities and return the information by way of the time warp "river," to earth-base here in Tulsa County.

To think imaginatively, without considering academic consequences, freed us to develop the theory and subsequent apparatus that time travel required. Yes, one must enjoy traveling to enter Trans-17, and I for one enjoy it. Meeting new people and seeing novel landscapes fascinates me, though actually, I'm more of a homebody. Yet to occasionally travel is a delightful treat, like a Hershey candy bar or orange juice-yogurt smoothies drink.

We began with the idea that time was like a river; time present was fluid and attainable. It existed, yes; yet humans measure only its passing, not its presence. Therefore, alternative energy states were researched. We saw the natural world with three states of matter: solid, liquid and gas. Time was of course, none of these; however, it was a cousin to the dimensions used to measure gas, liquids and solids. Einstein told us that time was a dimension. Since dimensions exist as molecules or atoms, time was then an atomic presence, and henceforth, measurable. We explored the plasma state of matter and determined "time" to be related to it. And yes, length, width, and volume were measured by their atomic makeup. Do you understand my reasoning? A foot long piece of oak wood was composed of molecules; molecules are naturally, composed of atoms. Therefore, this twelve inch slice of wood was measurable, and hence, quantitative in nature. If molecular substances containing three dimensions could be measured, time being a dimension, could also be measured. Logic's conclusion, as shown by Aristotle, was undeniable.

The major difficulty facing us was "translating" solid molecular material, i.e. hamsters, into the fluidity of time. This formidable task was approached by Ross and me with the eyes of children, our "child within," so to speak. To choose seeing the world through the innocent eyes of children rather than the tired eyes of adults is the beginning of genius. For adults, there is a right way and a wrong way. Yet all options were open to us. Success is 99% hard work and 1% intelligence! Here I'm paraphrasing Thomas Edison, my boyhood hero. He believed that failures should be viewed as a road to success. Failure showed what didn't work, and therefore, led you to what did. To view failure in a positive fashion kept us going. However, look at our society. Failure is seen as if the person is retarded or inferior. I'm disgusted with that attitude. Even Jesus himself was not successful converting each person He met. Remember the parable of the rich man?

Viewing failure as a vehicle to arrive at success, Ross and I found our way. We ruled out sixteen methods that were milestones or road signs to the end result. Number seventeen gave me the greatest moment of my life's quest for time travel! Ross too felt fulfilled in our results of thinking, thoughts, and feelings; all activated by the gift of the human mind. However, feelings expressed our enthusiasm; thoughts expressed human achievement, as granted by the "light" of insight, a gift provided by Our Creator.

However, before I relate that final result, I digress in memory and wish to state my disinterest in earth's present moment. I was not interested in being taken from Tulsa, Oklahoma in time present to Paris, Rome, Cancun, or Sydney, Australia. The beaches of Hawaii, beautiful as they are, were not my destination, nor the rainforests of Brazil. The heights of Kilimanjaro did not beckon me to its thin air, nor did the banks of the Nile River call out to me. What voice I heard, or feeling within my conscious soul, was to witness a world unseen, the realm of the Milky Way, dark and hidden, light years from earth; a Milky Way candy bar could not be as sweet tasting as my own curiosity felt within me. The flavor of discovery was like honey from the comb; its aroma, natural and pure. The universe was free from manmade pollution, its planets still pure, free, and inviting like Eden. If indeed other Eden's existed, let this paradise unite with God's unspoiled Paradise, made in His image and guarded by His angels. Allow me to find earth's galactic twin and drink of its water and walk upon its carpeted grassy lands. Allow me to smell flowers never before experienced on earth! Allow me to see colors foreign to the Americas! Allow me to witness birds in their unknown plumage. The myriad stars of heaven held out their hands, hands of energy, and fingers of light to lead this poor earthling to heights unknown even to the Incas of Machu Picchu.

Being a praying man, I offered this prayer to my Lord, "Dear God, heavenly Father, the night sky is filled with stars, may they be a friendly playground! Dear Sir, allow this inhabitant of 'spaceship earth,' to be a human voyager among the cosmic islands of your creation. Am I to be another 'Adam'? In your hands Lord, I am your servant; your humble ambassador to the cosmic spheres. Amen."

The answer to my prayer would be forthcoming.

This journey was to be mine to complete, not for ego's sake, but for humanity's benefit. Here I am a scientist, poet, an amateur historian, a philosopher, and a man of European ancestry. Like Columbus, I sought another route to the mysterious world beyond view. Within me, genetically speaking, was all my ancestry, the flaws and favorable characteristics of a multitude of people, spanning generations, with whom I'm related. Ross' ancestral heritage existed within him as well. Are we favored by our heritage, or does it make any difference? I state, and state firmly, our genetic heritage provided, at least, 90% of our intellect and character. With intellect and character, who could ask for more? Only one was left, the precious gift of faith, an attribute inherited spiritually, not genetically.

This whole concept of travel and exploration excited me like caffeine to coffee drinkers, or love to newlyweds. Ross was cool and unemotional. Excitement to him was watching an Indian pow-wow at Mohawk Park, or resolving a mathematical dilemma. He was admired by Dr. Lanier and me for his grace under pressure. His stoicism seemed classic Indian. Naturally he, too, wanted to time travel, and his time would arrive, no pun intended. Yet my time was now! Perhaps Diana would come along on some future trip with me? Again, the answer would unfold before me, in God's time and grace.

Chapter 4

Two weeks to the day that Fred and Ginger disappeared into the time warp, they reappeared; hale and healthy under the protective transparent dome of Trans-17.

I was outside the barn mowing the lawn when Ross burst forth from the barn door and motioned me downstairs. This was the most excited I'd seen him. Yet once downstairs, Ross said nothing; his action was typical of Seneca Indians, laconic and prideful. He merely pointed his arm as if it were an arrow, to the scene of two hamsters scurrying beneath the dome. Ross' entire face expressed joy in his smiling silence.

I shouted in joy and shook hands with my colleague. Then we took the hamsters from beneath the clear dome and placed them in their old playground area. They drank water and ran inside the "wheel." Later they curled up in the corner, snug within a shredded newspaper nest, and slept for hours.

Though the hamsters returned safely, the risk imposed upon my pet hamsters might have ended their lives. Therefore, hovering over me was the risk that time travel might kill me. In view of this death threat, I chose to get used to my upcoming risk as something to cope with, refusing to be risk's victim and realize that daily living is itself a dangerous risk. Plugging in the electric fan, or getting in and out of the bathtub, posed possible death or injury. One thing I knew, I did not want to replay Natalie Woods' death or the electrical demise of Thomas Merton.

Death is not to be feared, as much as to recognize it as a partner with life, a silencing partner at that. We have no choice in natural death, it awaits us all. Feelings of fear are legitimate; however we do not have to live in gut wrenching anxiety over our eventual parting, nor do we need to court death. Some live on life's edge, this lifestyle I reject. Am I being judgmental? How can my galactic journey not be on the precipice overlooking an unseen canyon? The paradox bothered me. Normally I'm a cautious and conservative person; yet another side of me sought adventure, novelty and discovery. Yin and yang; hot and cold; day and night; rock and sand; male and female; predator and prey; fire and water: I lived among all things and took them in stride.

Self-realization presented a debate I could not win. Valid points said "No;" other points said, "Yes." Feelings and facts played within my mind, like a container of oil and water, never the two shall mix.

Noon, now all morning had passed. The facts presented themselves as plausible and possible. The feelings fluctuated between fear and eager anticipation. Fantasy staged itself as one man, I, Gordon Paradise, changing history. Was I ego centered?

My rational mind battled the irrational. My lustful, selfish side argued against good intentions and charitable concerns. Yet these conflicts were nothing new. Every day a battlefield of conflicting armies fought within my consciousness. Feelings and urges were controlled by self-discipline. Without self-discipline, self-destruction rules human nature.

Growing wearisome of thought, I chose to go bicycling. Behind grandma's old couch in my screened back porch, I lifted my bicycle through the backdoor into the yard. Doing so barely interrupted the nap Duchess took upon the couch. She was at peace.

A fury of energy released from my tense limbs as I pedaled over the old county road near my home. This road leads out to untouched land that looks as natural and virginal as it must have been for the Indians who once lived here. Just to be outside in this sunlight, with a cool breeze to my face, was therapeutic. Stress evaporated and I felt great. Riding bicycles reminded me of my childhood in Glen Iris, and I smiled. I rode for hours and returned home refreshed.

After my shower and a brief dinner of leftover spaghetti and bread sticks from The Olive Garden restaurant, I walked out to the barn and the secret stairway to my laboratory. Ross was still there, adjusting Trans-17 and working over his computations on our IBM computer.

"Well Ross Red Jacket, what have you got to say for yourself tonight?"

"Ah, Dr. Einstein, how goes the war?"

I knew what he meant by his words, the war within me.

He looked straight at me with an expression demanding an answer. Before answering I sat down, only after retrieving two cans of Dr Pepper from the refrigerator. Doing so I tossed a can to Ross, purposely activating the carbonation, and he grabbed it midair as I flung it to him. Immediately he pointed the pop top at me and released a vicious spray of soft drink all over my face and shirt. My trick backfired! While laughing at my dilemma, he didn't see me vigorously shake the can in my hand, releasing the top, propelling its twelve ounce content all over him. We had a great laugh. Moments later he tossed me a dry towel.

"Well Gordo, what's your answer, I'm tired of waiting?"

"Waiting, I exclaimed. "The hamsters just got back today!"

"That's right, and the next train out is four days, maybe five. "What?" I was dumfounded. "Departing so soon? You don't give a guy much time."

"Time's on your side, Paradise," he said.

"Reminds me of a Rolling Stones' song," I replied.

"It is a song by *The Rolling Stones*," he stated jokingly.

I sat down and put my head in my hands, amused by the rhetorical nature of my comment.

A few minutes went by and I said in confidence, "I'm going Ross, time to pack. Tomorrow, I've got to pick up Diana at the airport and explain my entire trip to her. We were planning on marrying when she returned home. She'll not be too happy now."

I walked out of the lab, upstairs to my backyard, then into my home and began reviewing my written packing list. However, I felt as in a daze, overwhelmed by my forthcoming departure.

An hour later I spoke to Ross by my direct phone line to the lab.

"Ross, how about we invite Lanier and his wife over for dinner tonight? This way we can celebrate the safe return of Freddie and Ginger."

"It sounds fine to me." Ross stated; then asked, "Is it all right if I have some people over too?"

"Sure, call Knotty Pine and have them fix up a bunch of barbeque beef and chicken, and have one of your Indian friends pick it up."

"Why not ask one of your white friends?"

I chuckled at his humor. "I'll ask Lanier to get it." Ross said, "Lanier's fine," then hung up. He called in the order of BBQ beef, chicken, beans, potato salad, okra, and bread.

As the sun began dripping behind the distant Oklahoma hills, the food arrived with Dr. Lucas Lanier and his delightful wife Helen; what a great couple they made. They always smiled and laughed at the silliest jokes.

They drove a ten year old Lincoln and grew roses and irises as hobbies. Dr. Lanier was an amateur photographer and Helen collected Indian art, as well as lithographs by Charles Banks Wilson, a great Oklahoma artist, still very much alive, and creating excellent paintings, lithographs, and drawings. The Lanier's' were also thrilled by the wooden sculptures created by Willard Stone, and had collected three pieces, purchased directly from Mr. Stone's home-studio in Locust Grove, Oklahoma. They also purchased sculptures from Willard's son, another great Indian talent,

They were also saving to purchase a Charles Banks Wilson oil painting; yet also desired to purchase a Thomas Hart Benton watercolor. They had visited Benton's home and barn-studio in Kansas City, one of their favorite vacation spots, along with Naples, Florida; Carmel, California; Santa Fe and Taos, New Mexico.

Lanier was ecstatic when we told him the hamsters had returned. Helen was filled in on our doings and applauded us. Dr. Lanier proceeded to photograph Fred and Ginger, with us placing them on our shoulders and in our hands.

Lanier was also proud, his friends and former students, Gordon Paradise and Ross Red Jacket had done the "impossible." What the world deemed as impossible was proven possible.

My imagination viewed the process as tapping into time's river like a great gristmill utilizing a stream. Time, a wild river or untamed force, was less so now. I, Gordon Paradise, with the help of true believers, felt the laurel of achievement placed upon my head.

As our guests, Willard Red Jacket, and others arrived, we enjoyed our outdoor fare of delicious corn chips, barbeque, beer and soft drinks. We also played some backyard volleyball, men versus the women. The women won. Helen owned a dynamite serve. Who would have thought a senior citizen with so much "vim, vigor and vitality?" These words were an old Dr Pepper advertisement, nearly a century old, but remembered by many.

After the game, Ross began a huge bonfire of scrap wood and aged logs. Before long Ross began fueling the fire with old furniture and wooden crates from the barn. By this time Ross was pretty well tanked. He easily consumed a dozen cans of Bud Light and began his own pow wow around the flames. Soon his Indian friends joined him, hollering some ancient tribal chant.

Above us the sky exposed thousands of its stars. Here on earth we stared into their cosmic fiery blaze, and a thought of the momentary fire before us, contrasted with the hugeness of red giant stars tucked light years away in the vastness of creation.

Photographing the dance was Lanier's pleasure; and, Helen, seated on a lounge chair, clapped on the sidelines next to me.

Near midnight, Ross collapsed, Willard, the protective brother, dragged Ross to his own truck. With the help of another guest, Willard placed Ross face down in the backseat. Needless to say, the party was over. Lanier and I then helped a half-asleep Helen to their vehicle, and together they disappeared into the night. I was left alone, except for Duchess, who sat beside me gazing into the blackness along this old county road.

It was nearly noon before I awoke. Within the next hour I fed myself, the dog and the hamsters. My scrambled eggs, toast and Florida orange juice, hand squeezed, tasted wonderful. As I said previously, breakfast is my favorite meal.

Later I read for awhile, then Duchess and I took a walk down the same road our guests had departed from the night before. What a sense of space and freedom to walk this road and have no one around.

Yet, was I too greedy for solitude? Was solitude a narcotic? Was being alone a means to avoid others? Some of these feelings seemed accurate; yet I did enjoy people. I enjoyed Diana's company a great deal. In fact, I looked forward to the companionship and love life that marriage offered. My single days were numbered, and all-in-all, it felt satisfying.

Returning home the phone rang as I entered the back porch. "Hello"

"Gordon, it's I."

"Ross, are you feeling alright? You passed out last night."

"Was I dancing around a fire, or did I dream that event?"

"You were dancing."

"Good, I do remember some of last night. But who took me home? That I don't remember."

"Willard did—as he's done before."

"Yes, for a kid brother, he's alright. In fact, he's becoming my body guard and chauffeur all in one." He paused and then asked sheepishly, "Did Lanier become angry at me for being drunk?"

"No, he didn't say a thing. I'm sure he knows you well enough to realize you consume large amounts of beer at parties. He did not judge people whom he respected, whose intellectual gifts were from God. He knew the difference between a common drunk and a genius with alcoholic tendencies."

"I'm glad to hear that Gordo, Yet let me ask one more question, was he taking pictures while we danced?"

"Yes, why not take photographs?"

No reply.

Again, in a quiet tone he asked me, "Do you think I'm an alcoholic?"

His frankness caught me off guard, and I hesitated in answering. Then with a frank reply, I finally stated, "Probably."

He then changed the subject abruptly. "Willard and his girlfriend Pam have me fixed up with a blind date tonight."

"Who is she?" I inquired.

"Some Cherokee woman from Tahlequah is all I know."

"It's about time you started being around women again. You've been too preoccupied with work, you need female companionship."

I could tell by the barely audible groan that my comment was not appreciated.

Then I wished him well and hung up. Talking about his date made me desire Diana all the more. Yet tomorrow would be our day. She arrived at Tulsa's airport mid-morning. We've been apart for months because her job kept her overseas, as well as New York City. My loneliness at times felt like a sword piercing my heart. Yet another jab of pain was evident. How does one relay such momentous news without sounding grandiose or delusional? Actually, why would a man about to marry the love of his life, want to depart? Was scientific curiosity greater than the emotional and loving life of the newly married? If I chose science over marriage, what does that say about me and my priorities? If I chose marriage over science, does that make me an exploration coward or a hero to Diana? I didn't know the best answer. Neither choice was totally satisfactory. Science or marriage, explorer or husband; what would my former college classmates choose? Does it make a difference what my former classmates thought?

Ross and I had discovered time travel. Do I ignore it, or "go for it?" Too many questions unravel wisdom, and it was wisdom I sought.

Chapter 5

A professional woman, Diana worked in the upper management for the Blithe Petroleum Company. Her education was an MBA from the University of Oklahoma, and possessed a sharp business acumen. Her other Masters degree hailed from Oklahoma State University, in computer science. Besides, she had family in both Norman and Stillwater, so each degree provided family relationships to prosper.

She had climbed to the top of Blithe Petroleum's Tulsa office using her intellect, not her body. Speaking of her physical presence, Diana is tall, slender, with the most beautiful blonde hair. Her blue-green eyes shone like crystals, and she owned the most delicate hands and feet I've ever seen. She was of German and Scotch-Irish descent, and had a sense of humor to balance her intense devotion to work.

She was born in Tulsa in the mid-fifties and attended its finest high school, Bishop Kelley. An honor student as well as a good athlete, volleyball and basketball were two of her favorites, along with swimming and track. She enjoyed horseback riding and reading books by authors like Pearl Buck, Edna Ferber, the Bronte sisters, and Jane Austen. As for male authors, she enjoyed Fitzgerald, Hemingway, and Sinclair Lewis. She rarely read contemporary authors, why I wasn't certain. Her reading was retroactive, deceased authors were preferred, and as stated, both male and female. However, she preferred female authors.

I noticed long ago the tendency of each sex to read books written by people of their sex. It was easier for a woman to relate to women authors; men to relate to male authors. It was a literal sisterhood, or brotherhood, depending on whether you're a woman or male reader. It was, once again, a psychological and unconscious drama being played out. Thus it was neither "right," nor "wrong," in my opinion. It was human nature being itself. Do not the intricacies of the human mind exist in transcendental realms of their own?

Yet another part of her personality was her nature to succeed, and thus prove herself to her employer and her parents. Her perfectionism and "workaholic" attitude bothered me. She had a secretive nature to her that kept deeper feelings hidden from others. Was she always honest with me? Did she love me with the intensity I loved her? Yet in her flaws I saw my own defects; realizing this behavior was the probable cause why her shortcomings bothered me.

Feelings of insecurity rose like a thermometer's mercury, partly from anxiety over my time travel, and the fact of having to tell Diana goodbye just as she was returning home after a lengthy separation. However, who first said, "life isn't fair," stated it accurately.

Walking to the refrigerator, I poured myself a tall glass of ice cold water. I sipped it with immediate satisfaction, water being my favorite beverage. Returning to my living room, I picked up my Holy Bible and opened it to Ecclesiastes.

> "There is an appointed time for everything.
> And a time for every affair under heaven,
> A time to be born and a time to die;
> A time to kill and a time to heal
> A time to plant and time to uproot the plant;
> A time to tear down and a time to build.
> A time to weep, and a time to laugh;
> A time to mourn, a time to dance.
> A time to embrace, and a time to be far from embraces.
> A time to seek and a time to lose, a time to keep
> And a time to cast away.
> A time to rend and a time to sew, a time to be silent
> And a time to speak.
> A time to love, and a time to hate;
> A time of war and a time of peace."

I reread these lines from Ecclesiastes, Chapter 3, several times over. It all dealt with time, the present moment in our life. How appropriate that I had turned to these words. Each reading gave me insight and wisdom. The Bible comforts and gives peace to its readers, like me.

These thoughts filled me with confidence as I stood to look at myself in a mirror. My six foot two inch frame, medium build and blue eyes, stared back at me.

"Is this the face of an explorer? Did Columbus or Marco Polo look as naive and wanting as this face?" I asked out loud?

Then I remembered most travelers are beset with anxiety, even the great ones. All too easily I realized I might be torn to shreds by Trans-17, though knowing the hamsters returned safely comforted me.

Prayer comforted me too. I needed to trust my heavenly Father, for it was His wisdom that allowed completion of Trans-17. He would guide and protect me in my journey; He'd always be next to me, even in deepest space.

Outside again, the sunlight bathed my face in warmth and it felt peaceful and a grand way to experience life; to feel the elemental force of nature surround me as I walked. In this activity I was looking at the greenness of earth, and I thought of time travel, with lush, unknown planets to explore. Like Columbus, I believed other lands existed at the end of my journey. New people would greet me. My trip would find doors opening and exiting to unknown planets. I knew that Trans-17 was able to allow me access to hospitable places. Otherwise, with no environmental control, I'd land upon a deadly place in an instant. Calculations, educated guesses, and God Himself, made me believe that I'd be taken to life-supporting places.

Chapter 6

Diana's plane lifted from Houston International heading north toward Tulsa. As she stared outside the window, within an hour she looked out her to see the serpentine movement of the Red River, the geographic divider between Texas and Oklahoma.

Staring out the window she thought back over her life. It was in 7th grade she realized physical beauty had its benefits—popularity and attention; yet she knew if one banked their future on beauty alone, disaster usually followed. Most likely this realization was born from her Aunt Karla's experience. Karla had gone the beauty route and wound up miserable, divorced and destitute. Karla's life was a mess and Diana did not want to follow the dysfunctional pattern, especially when she realized Karla was a mere twenty-two years older. Aunt Karla rejected education, thinking her curvaceous physique and glowing blonde hair would open all the world's doors. Diana, however, embraced education with a passion, pleasing to her parents; yet her obsessive drive in school concerned them frequently. Perhaps their own workaholic tendencies were reflected by their daughter's hard work and long hours studying?

Education then was her trademark. Though Diana preferred physical beauty to its alternative, she aimed at being a powerhouse of academic achievement. She studied late into the night; she watched little television and read school assignments with diligence. Her school essays were written and rewritten; and, she studied French as if she were bound for Paris. She enjoyed history, and researched her class work as if the Free World might one day seek her advice.

As for English classes, grammar was like a wild horse, something to master. Science, mathematics, and driving class were also mastered by the beautiful blonde in the front row. During her senior year she became infatuated with poetry—both American and English. As for American poetry she read Whitman, Dickinson, and William Carlos Williams. As for English poets, she enjoyed: Shelley, Keats, Wordsworth, and Shakespeare.

In college she was introduced to Pablo Neruda, the Chilean master, who at that time was recently deceased. His work proved a revelation to her. South America became appreciated and real to her because of Neruda. Before Neruda, South America was a mere land mass south of Central America; now it possessed a literary beauty previously unknown to her.

In college she made Phi Beta Kappa. Her achievements gave her confidence and self-esteem. Yet too much confidence generates arrogant pride, and this was a flaw. However, this attitude was never a problem for her. She did possess excessive pride; it was not a Fleming character flaw. Though she saw what excessive pride did to other young women, it grieved her. However, Diana did not live life with many doubts, unlike her fiancé, Gordon Paradise. She was a believer in self discipline, and practiced it diligently. Oh yes, she owned a few flaws, however, all humans do. Perfection then is not human, but divine in origin. However, like all humans, anxiety was a natural emotional response, as she soon realized, while the concept arose within her conscious mind.

Being an academic wizard was not advantageous for her social life, either as a teen or coed. In fact, most men were intimidated by her appearance, "too beautiful," and by her excellent grades, "too smart, a brain." Sadly, these two factors kept potential girlfriends away too. Yet one special friend, Ariel Armando, a bright eyed Italian-American girl from St. Louis' famous "Hill" area, became Diana's best friend.

Diana and Ariel developed a close friendship their freshman year at Westminster College in Fulton, Missouri, her Dad's hometown. Yet where is Ariel now? Is she happy, is she married, divorced, or raising children in her native town? They were once close, and then time and distance erased their bond.

Dianna found her thoughts returning to a July Fourth picnic at Grand Lake nearly two years earlier. Since that weekend, she and Gordon have been nearly inseparable. Never had she known male companionship as sincerely and sweetly as with Gordon Paradise! Soon they were to be married. Their engagement took place last autumn in Eureka Springs, Arkansas. He proposed after a delicious filet mignon dinner. At that moment he offered her a blue diamond that sparkled as sunlight upon a lake. Never had Diana felt as needed, so wanted, as at that moment. Human love certainly was the opposite of corporate relationships. Her love for Gordon calmed her in the stressful world of the oil industry, and anyone allowing love to take priority in their life, deserves respect.

Yet with these thoughts of delicious love and their impending wedding, a problem loomed overhead like the sword of Damocles. A promotion was offered, and like all advancements, a price was to be paid; the sword overhead had to be dismantled. The promotion became available just weeks ago. Her supervisor, J. Thomas Reed, had accepted a European management position. Therefore, his Houston position was vacant, and half a dozen able executives placed themselves in the "running," including Diana Fleming. However, the position meant moving from Tulsa to the subtropical Gulf coast, and what's wrong with that idea? Nothing, Houston's a great city. Yet it was enormous compared to Tulsa, with excessively numerous fast drivers, and prone to hurricanes.

At this point in her life she wanted it all: the expensive cars, diamonds, executive privileges, her BMW and condo, and Gordon as her husband. This woman was on her way up the corporate ladder, an unseen entity; yet one sought by the ambitious, and at times, the devious. She was in former category.

However, her stomach felt queasy; she had no wish to overtake Gordon in the process. She drank from her bottle of cherry Emetrol, easing her nausea. Besides, how does she tell him if Blithe Petroleum offers the job, she's moving to Houston? The final decision lay in balance between her and an eight year veteran executive. She had four years with the firm and the recommendation of Reed himself.

Again she asked herself, "How do two people live in separate states and maintain a marriage?" Diana read articles of couples who do exactly that, live long distance marriages—could she and Gordon make it work? Yet those articles seemed two-dimensional. In reality, there were actually four.

Finally a decision was made, and corporate chose Diana over others who were older; with more experience. Her promotion caused one executive to retire early out of sheer frustration and humiliation. A few others were jealous, and the rest waited for their turn. This event occurred just 48 hours previously, and the competition seemed to be ongoing; yet the decision had been made, but had not connected to the reality of her consciousness. She lived then, in temporary denial of her promotion, and this denial was likely a means to ignore the actuality of her newest success. The human mind lives a life of its own, thus a person acts and reacts to the workings of the mind, or denies reality all together; either for hours or days; worse yet, a life time. How fragile the human mind!

In the corporate world, when "things" happen, they occur quickly. Other opportunities awaited them, and their response was healthy. Jealously is not a healthy emotional response, it is self destructive, a self inflicted time bomb ready to explode when least expected. However, Diana had no control, nor wanted it, over other people's responses to rejection, or what they perceived as rejection. As stated, openings occur often, and behave as spontaneous corporate combustions. Patience pays off emotionally and physically; it possessed a reward all its own

As the plane began to descend towards Tulsa International Airport, she felt excited at seeing Gordon again. Since her Tulsa-based parents were on vacation in Arizona playing golf and sight-seeing, she'd be greeted only by her fiancé, and that was fine!

Her tension increased as the plane lowered its landing gear. Her flight had been smooth and she was grateful. Extra doses of anxiety were not needed at this time, and turbulent flights induced anxiety.

"Alright, she thought, another flight survived. Now let's get off this tin can and onto some real food. Peanuts and diet drinks bore me. Let's have some red meat and potatoes like mom used to make," these were her private thoughts. Now the country girl was coming out of hiding. This side of her personality stemmed from her two sets of grandparents, one set living in Eufaula as restaurant owners, and the other set, wheat farmers living near Enid. A few cousins lived in Stillwater and Sallisaw, while her aunts and uncles resided in Norman, McAlester, Ryan, and Bixby. Her family created a living mosaic across her native state, her beloved Oklahoma. On a map, Oklahoma appeared as a giant sauce pan, and what a history the 47th state had created in that giant pan!

Homemade, homegrown foods were her first thoughts, and then Gordon came to mind. Talk of priorities, food was always a priority! However, Gordon was emotionally satisfying, as food was physically. How glad she would be to see him again. Missing him had created a desire within her, one sublimated until they were married. It was their pre-nuptial vow.

The passengers filed greedily from their seats. She waited until an elderly couple behind her had made it to the aisle. The man beside her spoke a few profane words under his breath at the slowness of the passengers, in short, he had places to go and calls to make.

She thought him typically impatient of most airline travelers and said to herself, "All we do is rush off the plane in order to be the first to the suitcase carousel, only to wait another 20 minutes!"

I arrived early to greet Diana at the airport. Today I wore Polo cologne, one of her favorites. It was a sunny day, the kind of day we both enjoyed. My ride over was pleasant, and Duchess, sensing something special, waited for my return, not with anxious anticipation, but a meditative nap on the back porch's couch, once owned by my maternal grandparents.

My excitement reached peak level as I drove toward the airport in my '88 Taurus, sky blue with dark blue interior. Blue was my favorite color; red was Diana's favorite. Her personal vehicle though was a white BMW; yet she also owned a red Corvette. She drove elegant cars; dressed elegantly, and walked with a dignity she learned in a special etiquette class taken during her High School years. Her parents provided social training to enhance her self esteem, poise, and social graces. An acute sense of propriety displayed itself in her adult life.

My parents would have never thought of such classes for my siblings and me. They relied on basic verbal reminders of what courtesy should mean to their children, and lived their lives as examples of kindness and courtesy. Adult behavior instructs youthful behavior, as it creates imagery in the child's mind that never departs. Thus speech and action mutually teaches children to imitate parental behavior.

Purchasing a Dr Pepper and popcorn before her arrival was an attempt to calm my nerves. Little good did it do, eating was often a dysfunctional response to the stress of anticipation. Soon the plane touched down and wheeled itself to the gate. Within moments people scrambled off and I waited for her. Then suddenly, just behind an elderly couple and a few businessmen dressed in Brook Brother's suits, there she was, waving at me!

"Diana!" I said under my breath. I raced up to her and we embraced with a passionate kiss. Others walked around us and seemed not to mind that we blocked the exit. Occasionally the people of this world will allow a loving couple to bend the rules of courtesy.

As the 1958 Doris Day song says," Everybody Loves a Lover." I believe Allen and Adler wrote that song, as mom and dad listened to Doris Day records frequently, as well as albums by Perry Como, Nat King Cole, and Patsy Cline. I would read the albums and knew the songwriters. During Christmas, I adored Ralph Blane and Hugh Martin's, "Have Yourself a

Merry Little Christmas." Ralph lived outside Tulsa, in the community called Broken Arrow. He was nationally and locally renowned.

Within a minute or two we had walked off to the side of the exit ramp so as to make room for others. I spoke first, "Darling, how wonderful to see you again!"

She smiled her sweet smile and said one word, "Yes." Doing so she grabbed me and we kissed again.

Admittedly I do feel uncomfortable expressing affection in public. Perhaps it stemmed from a conservative upbringing, or the natural reserve of northern people? Seeing Diana after months of separation, made me feel spontaneous and joyful, as if a symphony had been written that only we could hear. Neither one of us complained of our enthusiastic responses seeing one another again; thus enthusiasm breeds enthusiasm, does it not?

She wrapped her right arm inside my left arm and we walked down the corridor past the murals, the phones; then stopping at the snack bar, which was my idea.

"What would you like?" I asked.

"I'm in the mood for a restaurant"

I nodded yes, and we continued walking to the luggage carousel. In moments, baggage's appeared

"Diana, do you still have the red leather suitcases?"

"Yes. Nothing new purchased in that department," she said when her baggage appeared. I bent over to grab them off the rotating slide and placed them on the floor.

They were exceptionally heavy. "Diana, you're still packing as if you're departing for a season" "Yes" she laughed, "just like you!" She was right, I over pack too. Fortunately we were able to tease each other; however I still believe that an element of truth lies within spoken sarcasm. Truth disguised is still true. Yet we play word games and camouflage our feelings. I honestly disliked heavy luggage, hers or mine; we carried the luggage to my car, parked in short term parking close to the doors. Naturally I carried the two heavy items; she carried the two light items. I also held onto the suit bag, so I actually hauled three pieces to the car.

Though my hands were full carrying her bulky luggage, I managed to withdraw my car keys from my pocket, a feat rather self satisfying, considering the juggling act I was taking on in retrieving the keys. Heaven forbid I should drop a suitcase; hades has no fury like that of a woman whose suitcase has fallen upon the airport parking lot, springing open to display a host of garments strewn over the oil-stained pavement. Yet all went well and no arguments commenced due to my clumsiness or misjudgment.

What is happiness? My answer, to be with the woman I loved. Months had passed since I held Diana; kissed and caressed the woman I loved. She felt the same way toward me. However, all communication is not verbal.

"Where shall we dine?" I asked.

"I'm in the mood for the Middle Earth Café."

"Ah yes, one of our favorites."

We drove out and paid our parking fee. We had spent an hour in the lot! Time was not our concern, only moments together. Being together was in one sense, timeless. The Bible tells us that love is eternal, and the last hour made me realize that maxim even more. Being with Diana was eternal, eternal bliss.

Our drive to the Middle Earth Café was sweet. She snuggled close to me, having used the seatbelt in the middle of the front seat.

I sighed, she sighed. We said little, as our happiness required few words. Words would emerge later. Our togetherness was a divine entrée, one to be savored as fine food. Yet not food consumed, but emotional food for the heart. That in itself was pleasurable. Her perfume delighted my olfactory sense, her touch melted my heart. Her hair, that blonde glow of hair, settled on my shoulder as she lay against my arm. Being in love surpassed all human experience 'this side of paradise;' the name of an F. Scott Fitzgerald novel. In fact, human love was the closest thing to divine love God shared with us. Love was a gift from Him; we enjoyed this gift.

At red lights we kissed. Soon we arrived at the restaurant's parking lot. Hand in hand we walked into the unique ambience of this place. The aroma of homemade baked bread filled the brick interior of the Middle Earth Cafe. Its name, of course, derived from Tolkien's trilogy, *The Lord of the Rings.*

We were seated by a tall young woman, rather gangly and wearing granny glasses and no makeup. It was 1967 all over again, though once was enough! She wore faded blue jeans and a peasant blouse of rose-colored linen. Atop this attire she wore a denim apron. The tablecloths were composite squares of colored fabric, red, blue, black, and green. On the walls hung loosely draped international flags, and from the ceiling, hung tie-dyed cotton fabric of purple and blue, to soften the light bulbs hung from the stucco ceiling and the restaurant's menus were off-white parchment paper.

A few other hungry patrons were already enjoying their meals when we were seated by the window. However the window was translucent, nearly opaque. Therefore one was not invited to stare absentmindedly outside, a rude gesture for either a man or woman.

In the midst of the table sat a wide and well used candle, multicolored with wax drippings like veins. Apparently someone had artificially created a rainbow-colored candle. Like I said, it was the 60s again.

"My name is Starr, and I'm your waitress tonight. Are you ready to order or would you like a few minutes?"

"Do you still serve wine here?" asked Diana.

"No, we stopped awhile back. We serve nonalcoholic beverages now," Starr stated.

"I'll take apple juice on the rocks."

"You order sir?"

"Make mine Pellegrino water on-the-rocks. Six hundred year old Italian water that even Leonardo da Vinci admired in 1509."

"Do you require hors d' oeuvres prior to your meals today?" Starr asked, not even knowing or caring who Leonardo was or was not.

I noticed the fried cheese rolls and ordered those. Diana wanted tortilla chips and hot sauce.

Starr took our order and vanished to the kitchen.

"It's been awhile since I've been here," Diana said teasingly.

"Yes. The waitress though is less strange than the last one we had here. Do you remember?" I asked.

"You mean the one with the four inch fingernails and the beauty mark at the corner of her mouth that appeared as an outline of Nevada?"

Diana laughed hysterically; she was prone to loud outbursts that could be blatantly embarrassing.

"Wasn't her name Witch Hazel?" I asked.

"No silly," Diana giggled, "it was Hazel, just plain Hazel."

"Oh yes, 'plain' Hazel, the Gypsy Queen."

Again Diana laughed loudly and people stared. "Are people looking at us?" she inquired.

"Yes they are, wouldn't you if someone laughed as loud as you do?"

"Oh Gordon, you're being silly"

"Actually I couldn't care less that they're looking. You're a delight to be with; every woman's envy and every man's fantasy."

"Gordon, I'm blushing."

"And I thought it was just your rouge." I said jokingly.

She laughed again.

At this moment Starr brought us our refreshments. The cheese sticks were wonderful. The water tasted pure and wonderful. Yet I also ordered apple juice at Diana's recommendation.

"May I have a few chips?" I inquired.

"Of course darling."

"This salsa is delicious, but hot!" In a moment my tongue exploded from the heat, and I drank my bottled water in seconds. I immediately ordered more water, several bottles in fact, to cool my inflamed tongue.

Then after easing my pain I raised my glass of apple juice and toasted to the two of us. It went something like this, "May our life together bring abundant joy, and may our home never set on fire with salsa this hot."

Diana once again laughed, trying to muffle her loudness.

"Gordon, you're so funny, I love your sense of humor, and your looks aren't bad either!"

I replied, "Thank you," then stated, "You should see yourself when you're laughing so hard. If it were not for my composure, they'd throw us both out for being obnoxious." She knew I was kidding. I laughed just as hardily, and could easily be considered obnoxious by others. I cared not.

Diana then asked, "Is your pain gone?"

"Isn't pain wonderful?" I stated sarcastically.

"Oh Gordon, your pain is my pleasure. No, let me rephrase that sentiment, your pleasure will be mine to give, and your pain will be mine to withhold.

Then I said, "Pleasure is the absence of pain. However, pain is pleasure denied."

"Gordon, somehow you're being naughty and I love it!" she said laughingly.

"I'll drink to all you've said," she stated, and we touched our glasses. We smiled at each other, looking intently into one another's eyes.

By now we ordered our dinners. We decided upon the dinner size mushroom quiche with a side salad, a house dressing with tomato slices and chunky squares of squash, and long leafy spinach. We spoke softly, enjoying one another's company after months of separation. It delighted us to be close again. Just the physical proximity of our beings caused us happiness; that's what being in love does to a couple. We were lost in conversation and adoring looks at one another, when Starr brought us our meal. I consciously chose to eat slowly. My normal eating pace is fast, bordering on absurd. Therefore I went into slow gear and relaxed. Our time together proved luxurious.

"Gordon, this leisurely meal makes me feel as if I were in a hot bath, soapsuds surrounding me, relaxing me. And the music they're playing is divine, Mozart, isn't it?"

"Yes dear, it's Mozart, some piano concerto I guess."

She laughed, saying sarcastically, "Well since piano dominates the piece, I do believe you're right!"

I laughed. Her sarcasm was meant as humor, not as an emotional instrument of degradation. This type of humor I enjoyed, the essence of being able to laugh at oneself without losing integrity. Not all sarcasm is so intended. As I said, some is aimed at humiliating the other; this approach I did not appreciate.

Humor has a way of bringing people together; it eases our loneliness. Such humor was the humor I sought. Diana sought it too, the elusive joy of laughter without judgment or guilt. Humor, like love itself, was pure, like a fresh egg, and life without joy, was empty as broken eggshells.

"Diana, it's great to have you back in Tulsa. This place has been an emotional drought without you. Your phone calls do not equate with your lovely presence here with me. Nothing feels better than being with you."

"Gordon, you're being sweet," gazing at me with those soft blue eyes, touching my hand.

My eyes swelled with tears at the happiness I felt in her touch. My anxiety melted. My future plans of time travel seemed, for the moment, totally unimportant. However, I would need to talk to her soon of my plans. I could not pass up the opportunity, though love, that supreme feeling of emotional ecstasy, was all I wanted to feel. These hours in her company were the best of times. Yet looking into her happy eyes, there were a few times she appeared to have troubling thoughts. Her eyes glazed over in subtle sadness, perhaps tiredness from the trip?

Diana took her hand away from mine and sipped her juice. "Let's go home Gordon, I want some wine, some chilled white Taylor wine from your native state."

"Oh really, when did you start drinking New York State wine?"

"The last few months had me all over the nation, and while in the Big Apple, the restaurants served Upstate wines."

"Do you now prefer them over French and California wines?" I asked.

"They're all good. Besides, my supervisor introduced me to New York wines. He's from Albany and went to school at Cornell. Cornell is close to the wineries. In fact, we spent a weekend in Hammondsport. What a beautiful little town."

"Hammondsport is not far from Glen Iris, maybe 75 miles," I hastened to add.

"Gordon, when are you going to take me there to meet your parents? I need to see them before the wedding."

"Sweetheart, I agree. However, I'll ask them to fly out. I don't see us returning there soon for a visit. Dad's busy at the store, which is nothing new. Besides, the assistant pharmacist could takeover for a week while mom and dad visited Tulsa, though I doubt dad would feel comfortable doing such. He, like me, enjoys being in control, unwilling to let others 'steer the ship' of his life. However, we'll vacation in western New York someday and see it all."

"Gordon, I want us to vacation in upstate New York, and tour New York City as well; to eat at a few restaurants that I adored while working there. Let me tell you, that city has restaurants that make Tulsa, or Oklahoma City, look void of restaurants." Diana said.

"Now Diana, don't put Tulsa and Oklahoma City down. Oklahoma has great restaurants." Then we both started laughing, because here we were raving about one another's native state, and it seemed comical to us; yet we were that kind of couple. Laughter was a sharing of self, it made us joyful to see the other laugh. Besides, it's good for your health. Perhaps laughter was as important to health as frequent exercise?

We drove away from the Middle Earth Café happy people. Good service deserved reward. I tipped generously.

Tulsa's streets were damp; apparently a mild shower had swept through while we were eating. A pleasant springtime evening aroma was enhanced by the rain. Within minutes we pulled up to her Riverside Drive condo, one with an excellent view of the Arkansas River.

I turned to look at her expression as she exited the car, though normally I always opened all doors for her. Apparently, in her excitement, she forgot our protocol; yet at these first few minutes it did not matter. For now she appeared as a smiling, intensely excited little girl on Christmas morning. In her mind, she returned to 1961, age six. Her Tulsa condominium, for a few moments in imagination, became a giant wrapped gift. The wrapping being colored lights, blue, yellow, green, that cast colorful shadows upon her condo's exterior walls. These lights were on every night of the year; yet how wonderful to see her happy and smiling being home. Being a homebody at my deepest child-adult feelings, made me happy to have brought her home to share this moment, and for a few moments she stood and stared at her residence.

I opened the car's trunk and brought in her luggage. The lights inside her condo turned on instantly and soft classic emanated from the stereo. I thought both features creative.

We placed the bags on her divan and she darted about the rooms in eager anticipation of feeling their space. Her enjoyment was a pleasure to witness.

Finally she settled momentarily in the kitchen. I walked in as she asked. "Would you like a mix of yogurt and blueberries or chocolate strawberries?"

"Some of each would be grand," I replied, having recently shopped for these very items and leaving them in her refrigerator. I was given a spare key prior to her departure. Having her key also allowed a cleaning crew to enter every two weeks to keep her condo fresh as morning dew, as I waited for two hours inside on the couch, reading.

"Oh Gordon, you're going to make this woman very happy, you in the kitchen and I on the couch, demanding and rewarding your good behavior,"

Yet I was on the couch; she was in the kitchen. Actually, she did little in the kitchen by way of cooking; she preferred having her own part-time chef. This matter had already been discussed regarding our marriage. Imagine, a part time chef!

"Really, how did this fortunate woman happen to know the true me, and how did she find me?" asked I out loud.

"Well I found you and I'm keeping you. I'm that fortunate woman, and you're the man to whom my devotion will always be directed. You'll be a nation unto yourself, however, one ruled by me with your happiness in mind."

"Ruled by you, a benevolent elected official of the United States of Paradise? Madame President, your pre-made desserts await us. Here we have chocolate strawberries and yogurt steeped with rich antioxidant blueberries. These fruity snacks will allow us to live a hundred years and never look older than we are now." I exclaimed.

"Gordon, you're such a card, and should be 'dealt' with, so shuffle off to Buffalo and bring back some original Anchor Bar chicken wings, and we shall make a deal. When you return, I shall be yours forever."

"That, my dear, will make you, 'Queen of Hearts,' especially my heart, and we shall lie upon a sundeck and build a house of cards for entertainment,

For was it not your childhood delight to build playing card houses; waiting to see how high one could be built before it tumbled to the floor?"

"Yes, you remembered my childhood, how sweet. You'll get an extra strawberry for that remembrance."

"Ah, strawberries with a Hershey's kiss, what could be finer?"

She laughed and said,"How about that thrill on blueberry hill, that song by Chubby Checker."

"A fine Irish song my lass; you recalled it so well," I stated joyously, with a dash of intentional sarcasm.

"Irish song?" I don't believe so. Surely it's all American?"

"Yes, you win again, another chocolate strawberry coming your way," I said.

We drew close and embraced, blueberries and strawberries surrounded us. Being so close to the food, we nearly tipped the whole tray of fruit upon her newly cleaned carpet.

All those in love are like children again, silly. This was our second childhood, one with money. Our third childhood would be raising children; our fourth would be retirement; yet for now, nothing more of the future needed to be thought of, our present moment was delicious unto itself. Thus the carpet was saved and any wrath it may have generated was never spoken. Our moment together was as 'good as gold,' and nothing more was said for quite awhile, Her gentle breathing was the only sound I heard, other than my own heartbeat. Sublime are such moments, or perhaps, in a pun, 'sub-lemon,' yet I kept it to myself. Later on I would laugh, and she would have no idea where such spontaneity commenced. Yet who cared? I liked lemons.

Occasionally we would sit up to drink from the same glass and look outside at the shimmering light upon the river water just outside her condo's window,

"How beautiful," she said.

"Yes," I whispered, "like a Monet painting, shimmering flecks of colored light."

She whispered back, "I feel as if we are in a painting, an evening version of Renoir's, "Luncheon of the Boating Party," do you feel the same way?"

"Diana, that was beautiful," and I leaned over to kiss her lips. Her hair smelled like a floral garden, perhaps as Monet's beloved gardens? Even Renoir painted delightful floral scenes that seemed to emanate true aromatic essences. Ah, the Impressionists!

"Hold me tight, I've been so lonely," she whispered.

I held her closer without saying a word. I obeyed her with an instinct only lovers knew.

A half hour went by without a word between us. The quiet of the moment enhanced our feelings. However I can't say that it was all quiet, we did have a record of renaissance lute music playing over and over. Lute music appealed to both of us, and for all we cared, each melody praised love, our love, centuries after the composition first appeared. Allow me to also say, without self-righteousness, our moral choices made us feel good about ourselves. We knew we could indulge our sensual selves; no one except ourselves stopped us. Our consciences were clean and I realized our whole lives were a composite of good and evil; pure and improper activities. It was always one or the other, good or evil that operated any moment in our lives; a combination of the battle between the flesh and the spirit, well described by St. Paul. That battle he spoke of was ongoing in every human life.

In the meantime Ross was beginning to learn and like this young woman from Tahlequah. Her name was Kogee, a young woman of Creek heritage. (Pronounced: Co-ghee).

She was a shy and innocent woman, 26 years old, never married. She dated rarely, though friends attempted to help her with her social life. However, this is not to say that her appearance, or manner were deficient. On the contrary, she had soft brown eyes gazing from a pleasant Indian face, framed with long black hair. She did not wear glasses or braces, and owned a smile that melted hearts. However she tended to avoid the peer social scene which limited contact with men her age. After graduating from college in Tahlequah, she ended up working as a secretary to a local lawyer. Her mom, with whom she still lived, was a nurse at the Muskogee General Hospital, a half hour's drive to the south. Kogee, whose nickname was "Cookie," was born in Muskogee, as were her two brothers and one sister. However, the family lived in the Cherokee capitol, Tahlequah. Her dad was Cherokee, yet did not live with them. He had moved west to California a dozen years ago to pursue his fantasy.

Kogee and her mom lived alone and enjoyed one another's company. The rest of the family, whose last name was Whitefeather, had married and moved to Oklahoma City, Pawhuska, and Sallisaw.

Kogee's dad was an alcoholic. His alcoholic tendency made life difficult and painful in her formative years. In a way, his departure was an answer to prayer. The physical and verbal abuse heaped upon her mom ended when he left; although his leaving made the family financially destitute. Yet her mom earned an RN degree from Bacone College, thus allowing some security for her children. Her father-in-law helped out his grandchildren and daughter-in-law, lamenting his son's poor life choices. Life is difficult for Indians. They are among the most abused minority group in America. Here they were stewards to the lands of North and South America, and within a few hundred years these Native Americans neared extinction. Few purebloods of any tribe now existed. How do we Caucasians justify ourselves? We can't. Generations of selfish whites destroyed the American Indian with extermination of their food sources; alcohol too took a heavy toll, and the rest died of diseases never before known to the western hemisphere.

However, the Indians must be responsible for their own faults and strengths. They inter-married with non-Indians, and thus, diluted their own race. This action will cause the extinction of purebloods and full blooded Indians, but the tide is turning for Caucasians. Beware, this nation under God is becoming Hispanic. They will be the dominant racial group by 2025, bypassing Blacks and American Indian populations, and surpass the Whites by 2050. Yet there was nothing wrong with this observation, it was just a personal conclusion and made me feel uncomfortable, as most social change made me feel. Change takes time to acclimate to in any society. Hispanics will dominate business and politics by 2100.

Kogee went to public schools and since her name was different, the nickname of "Cookie," fell upon her without her consent. Most nicknames befall the person as a disease. Few such names are appreciated by the recipient. However, this name was quite innocent, and actually a mispronunciation of her name by children of the second grade. It was never meant in a derogatory fashion, as some nicknames were meant to be demeaning.

So all through school the white children called her Cookie, and her real friends called her by her given name.

Kogee suffered a rough childhood; her drunken and abusive dad scared her brothers, sister, and her, with his violence. When their dad attacked their mom, they felt helpless to protect her. He nearly strangled their mom one time, leaving her unable to speak for a week. Nothing they witnessed before or since that horrible incident came as close to murder.

Children of alcoholic families take on roles. Kogee took on the lost child role. She lived in silence and retreated into the woodwork. She found comfort in television, reading, and her diary. No one had access to the diary. In a way she became like Anne Frank, detailing her life on the pages of a notebook, while all fury let loose across the stage of her family life. In a way, she hid from a terrorist, as did Anne, Kogee's dad acted as a Nazi. His heart filled with hate; no mercy shown. Therefore, when her dad, Frank, left home, peace was restored. However, the anger, confusion and sorrow hung in their hearts like a valley between mountains, its peaks too high to see hope on the other side.

Other family members took up their roles as well. One brother became the mascot, the family joker. Another sister became the hero, and one other brother took on the scapegoat title, thus taking all the blame and acting out his rage.

Their dad called occasionally from the west coast. Sad however, when he called he was as drunk and verbally abusive. Yet their mom made each child talk to him because, "He's your father."

"Yes, he was," Kogee said to herself, "but why do I have to speak with someone whose words are slurred and doesn't really know which child he's talking to?" It made no sense. Alcoholic behavior never does and never will make sense.

On the weekend night of the blind date with Ross, she had driven to Tulsa to stay with her friend from childhood, Susan Tiger. That Saturday evening, Ross drove over to pick up Kogee. All four, including Susan's beau, Travis Goodgame, went out to eat at The Knotty Pine, one of Tulsa's best barbeque restaurants. Afterwards they headed into town on Charles Page Boulevard and found a place to shoot pool. They had a lot of fun. Ross clowned around a lot and made Kogee laugh. This was important, as he enjoyed making others laugh and have a good time. He told jokes, as did Travis, and acted silly and childish with the pool cue. Kogee said little, but Susan knew that Kogee liked Ross, and he apparently liked her. All was going well. They played until nearly midnight. Ross had been downing Budweiser's all evening. By now he was quite loaded. His drinking bothered Kogee; yet she wanted to stay with him. Ross suggested they go out for a snack at the Metro Diner on 11th Street. Susan and Travis had made other plans. This would give the new couple time alone. However Kogee did not want Ross to drive, so after a brief argument, and to the surprise of everyone, Kogee ended up driving Ross' truck over to another diner. After arriving, Ross complimented Kogee on her driving. She smiled. Then she proceeded to have him lean on her as they walked into the restaurant. They got a booth by the window and ordered pecan pie and vanilla ice cream.

As they were served Ross said, "Looks like we're in for some sugar overkill this evening, do you mind?

Kogee looked at him with a puzzled look, and then smiled.

Ross made every effort to stir up conversation. The weather, the economy, their mutual friends, Indian pow wows, and food, were all discussed.

Within an hour of being there Ross was feeling more like himself. Most Indians have a low alcohol threshold, his was high in comparison.

"Did you enjoy this evening, Kogee?"

"Yes, I did enjoy it. I haven't done this much in months."

"Did you say you live in Tahlequah?"

"Yes, and I live with my mother. My siblings are married and moved out. I guess I'm waiting for my turn."

"You're so pretty too. I can't imagine why you're not married by now?"

She was immediately embarrassed. When Ross realized what he had said, he apologized. He was a kind person; he did care about the feelings of others, though he rarely showed it.

To change the subject quickly, she inquired to his work and his age.

"Well little princess, I'll answer the first question now and the latter question in the future. I never give my age on the first date." They both laughed.

"I am a research engineer privately employed by a Mr. Gordon Paradise. We pursue strange and unusual phenomena and try to make some sense out of the things we come across."

"A research scientist? she said, I thought you were a college student!"

"Well I was for a long time, yet the Universities finally kicked me out with a diploma pinned to my lab coat."

She giggled at his silly and somewhat zany attitude. It contrasted to the stark seriousness of her home life.

"Mom, she stated, laughs little and smokes like a chimney, a scene from Dante's *Inferno*."

That response made him laugh. They were enjoying themselves with coffee after the delicious pie. He drank the real stuff; she drank decaffeinated. She wanted to be able to get some sleep tonight and go to church late tomorrow morning. He didn't care if he slept tonight or Monday night. He did not allow time to dictate his needs. He acted as to his feelings of the moment and found himself talking more than he had in months. He drove her to Susan's place only to find Travis' Ford pickup still there. It was three in the morning and Kogee was exhausted. Upon seeing the truck she said nothing.

She was dismayed by her friend's probable immorality and wanted a way out. Yet there was no alternative in her mind. Ross walked her to the door and she slipped the apartment key from her leather purse. Ross touched her shoulder and leaned in to kiss her. She let him kiss her cheek only.

That was fine with him. He felt that she was a delicate flower and he wished to protect her from his normal self. He did not want to break the boundaries of decent behavior, as he had done on numerous outings. This time was different.

As she unlocked the door he said, "I'll call you soon. I'd very much like to see you again. I had a great time."

She nodded yes and entered the door. He turned around and vanished in his pickup. It was dark inside; Susan had not left any lights on. However Kogee found a blanket and pillow on the couch, using a small flashlight from her purse. Then she slipped out of her clothes and fell asleep. She too had an enjoyable evening. Now her body and mind found comfort and peace in a good night's rest.

Ross drove the lonely streets of Tulsa and found his way home. His little home was a place near the Tulsa University campus, only a few miles from Susan's place off Peoria and 15th Street. Without much ado he crawled into bed and submerged himself into the mystical unknown called sleep.

Sunday morning and church bells rang and the sun rose beautifully above the city. Only a few clouds in the west prevented the entire sky from being one perfect blue sphere. The dome of blue was a gift from God, for those who think in such terms. However, few noticed the sky at all and stayed inside to read the Sunday newspaper editions; others hurried to church. A few looked heavenward and thanked their Creator for this glorious day. A few even held the hand of their spouse, and a few parents even listened to their children speak from their hearts.

Many were still in bed reading *The Tulsa World* or *Sunday Oklahoman,* drinking coffee or tea from their favorite mug or cup.

It was near noon when Susan awoke and walked into the kitchen. It was then she realized Kogee was asleep on the couch.

"Good morning Susan," Kogee said softly.

"Hello my little Kogee, I forgot you were staying here overnight."

"I see Travis' vehicle, so I surmise he's here?" Kogee asked.

"No, of course he's not here. His gas tank was empty and some friends drove him home around 1 a.m. Then Susan asked, "Are you ready for breakfast?"

"Yes, replied Kogee, raw fruits and orange juice would be wonderful."

Susan hesitated a moment, then asked, "How was your date with Ross last night?"

"We had fun, though I missed you two when you departed, but I still had a good time. Besides, he wants to see me again." Kogee replied.

"Did he drink too much or not?" asked Susan, knowing all-to-well Ross' drinking habits.

"Yes, sort of . . . ." Kogee replied

"He may be an alcoholic." Susan bluntly stated.

"Susan, how can you say a thing like that?" Kogee asked.

"Well maybe I don't know the definition of alcoholic, but he really puts the beer away."

Kogee's face became tense. It seemed impossible that she might want a romantic relationship with someone like her dad.

"What are you thinking?" asked Susan.

"I was thinking about my dad and his multiple problems."

"Why think about him?"

"Because he's a drunk and abandoned us children and mom," said Kogee.

"Oh, I forgot about that part of your life. But hey, Ross is a good man, despite his heavy drinking. He's kind to others and makes everyone laugh. He's by no means a bum. In fact, he's highly intelligent. He obtained a full scholarship to college and grad school. He's a hard worker and thinks intensely when he's in that frame of mind."

"Really, he's a brain?" inquired Kogee.

"Yes, he is. And the man he works with, Paradise, they make a team and are working on a scientific project . . . probably for the government, a 'secret' project of some sort on their part." Susan stated.

"Very hush-hush?" Kogee asked.

Susan added, "In fact those two characters won't admit to anything, not even when working on something new. All part of their being secretive."

"Are they spies? asked Kogee.

"Spies for either for the Red Chinese or Santa Claus, one never knows the real truth until a trial."

With that statement they grabbed pillows and started hitting one another, laughing. They acted like grade school girls again as they pummeled each other with any pillow they accessed. Besides, it was good, clean fun, and made them child-like; it wasn't that long ago and they were children; yet children from diverse family backgrounds and culture, one Indian and one white-Anglo.

Ross awakened around 2 p.m. and went out to eat at one of his favorite restaurants at Utica Square, a 1950s shopping mall, all one story buildings and easy access to any store. The clock near the Post Office appeared with an innocent elegance noticed by all. The mall was not art deco; yet reminded him of that style. He knew not the name of Utica Square's architectural style. It was delightful to view, regardless of any name given to its style. As always, he enjoyed listening as bells rung out on Sunday mornings. The entire ambience enthralled him and all Tulsans; it was his favorite mall. Ross detested the newer malls, all interior based, as if hiding something. However, all of Tulsa's malls were popular, but none as beautiful as Utica Square. Every season provided a new look to Utica Square; each season held its traditions of floral colors and store decorations.

He ate alone and enjoyed reading the paper. He ordered three scrambled eggs, three pancakes, wheat toast, hash browns, a large orange juice, and coffee. This would be his meal for the day. He rarely ate three meals a day if he was by himself. It was rare for him to have dessert, like he did last night with Kogee. He just didn't think about it. His mind usually dwelled on scientific principles and opportunities.

After awhile, Ross drove to Cathedral Square, not a mall, but a garden beside a church on a street lined with churches, hence the name, Cathedral Square. Many Cathedrals were in walking distance of this corner of downtown Tulsa, with its own fountain; its pine trees and firs, and a peacefulness found only on church or monastery properties. Indeed, the Square seemed holy ground to him, and he sat on one of its unique benches with its ornate iron armrests, reading and relaxing, in this season called spring. These two places, Utica Square Mall, and Cathedral Square were routinely visited by Ross on Sunday. In one sense, each location became a church-like presence to his mind; his heart.

As he departed Cathedral Square, after an hour of peaceful relaxation, he drove the streets of downtown Tulsa. Once again he thought of the time warp and Gordon going off by himself. Once Gordon departed, their communication ability diminished greatly, and it generated fear in Ross' mind; the responsibility overwhelmed him. Gordon's journey was a great unknown enterprise; one Ross was to supervise alone, with light years separating the two friends. This "enterprise" felt as a massive chasm in his heart; a broken heart if Gordon failed to return. He wanted to share all his fears with Kogee, but couldn't. Gordon said no one was to know, unless we married them, or became engaged. Obviously, he made the latter option because he and Diana were already engaged. She had to know. No one, not even Gordon's parents, brother, or sisters were going to know of his journey until he returned. And perhaps not even then would he publish his account.

Let me add that Ross was one of the few who called Gordon Paradise, "Gordo." Diana called him Gordon. Others did too. Ross liked the name Gordo; it reminded him of Gordon Cooper's astronaut nickname. He rented the movie," The Right Stuff" every year and enjoyed the part when Gordon Carpenter was called "Gordo." He had read Tom Wolfe's book of the same title.

Ross read a great deal. However, one tires of scientific journals, and when he did tire of journals, he shopped the bookstores of Tulsa. Borders, Barnes and Noble, or Steve's Books on Harvard were his favorites. Steve's however was more personal than any other local bookstore. You would actually see Steve in the store, and one could have a soft drink and sandwich at the row of dining seats at the soda fountain, that composed part of the store's back wall. It had a small town feeling to it that can't be explained, just experienced. Steve's carried a wide variety of books and had author signings frequently. There was no pressure to buy at Steve's either. It was a Tulsa tradition, and one of many Ross enjoyed.

Reading was mental exercise, and it was a part of being a whole person. Ross and Gordon both believed that to be a whole person one needed to relate to the body, mind and spirit. Exercise the mind with thoughtful reading and processing ideas, exercise the body by biking, walking, running, Nautilus training, or by treadmill. The spirit was to be enhanced with church attendance, scripture reading, as well as frequent use of the sacraments.

However, Ross did not go to church anymore, and his faith had no sacrament except baptism. Yet he did believe in a Divine Being, a divine and loving soul; yet church was not for him. He had enough when he grew up and went twice a week with his mom and family. He grew to dislike that approach to religion. He nurtured his soul in prayer to the Great Spirit, probably influenced by his grandfather who combined Baptist and Indian beliefs into one fabric. Ross chose the Indian aspect. Yet he respected those who did attend church. He didn't feel they wasted their time, or that those who attended Sunday church were hypocrites. His spiritual self was a private matter; he would speak of it when he felt absolutely comfortable with those present. If not, this subject was off limits.

Sunday was his ideal for a day of rest too. After awhile he found himself at the pool hall on Admiral and played a few hours. Then he drove home and started reading. He usually read three or four books, an hour on each book, then rotated back to the first book the following Sunday. At this time he was reading "*War and Peace,*" "*Lonesome Dove,*" "*The Grapes of Wrath,*" and Angie Debo's' "*Geronimo.*" His mother asked him to read "*Children of Alcoholics,*" but he begged off. She was reading many self-help books. He wasn't interested, but he was happy for her. She needed help. Her dad was destroyed by whiskey. His dad didn't touch the stuff. Was his grandfather a lush? He couldn't remember. Others might not believe him, yet Ross Red Jacket had earned a full scholarship to T.U as an undergrad, and later as a graduate student.

He, like Gordon, was given summer privileges of educational opportunities at other major universities, again, with the guidance of Dr. Lanier. Would an alcoholic achieve such things? Alcohol did not run his life, he ran his life, his thoughts, and he felt proud, not realizing his denial was a trait the size of Texas, and only humans lived in denial. No other primate needed or experienced denial. Like blushing, it was solely human, to paraphrase Mark Twain,

Ross proceeded to the lab of Trans-17 in the barn behind Gordon's old farm house. Gordon's car was missing. He drove up to the outside swinging door, locked with two padlocks for security reasons. Ross figured that Gordon was at church with Diana. "That's fine; I'll worship God here in the beauty of this day." What a peaceful Sunday it was too. The sky hung overhead, blue sprinkled with white clouds. The solar star overhead shone intensely and warmed this spring day to near summer temperatures. Ross opened the two combination locks and the padlock on the barn door, with its peeling red paint, on hinges a bit squeaky. Having been irritated for months at the squeaky metal hinge, he returned to his truck and retrieved his tool box. Within it he pulled out a can of silicon liquid and soaked the hinges with a hefty spray. Off to the left, a specially built protective room had two more combination locks. He easily performed the number sequence and opened its heavy door only to enter a stairwell, one leading beneath the barn. The laboratories filled the size of the barn's exterior perimeter, and within the lab were closed off rooms filled with equipment. The main section where they worked was actually only a fifth of the entire subterranean space. Naturally they had a library, restroom with shower, telephone, a kitchen and small living room. It was a small apartment for all practical purposes. It felt good to enter this place, to be alone with one's own thoughts and explore with one's intellect the challenge of time travel.

Ross turned on the lights, all solar powered, as was Gordon's own home. In fact Trans-17 operated on photon power also. The sun over Oklahoma shines 300 days annually, thus adequate energy for their needs. He fed the hamsters and turned on the radio. It was tuned to the classical music station. Then he sat in his favorite chair and propped his feet upon the table next to the computer inside the room where Trans-17 was motionless, innocent, and sterile across and against the opposite wall. Beside him sat a box of Wheat Thin crackers. He munched on them and contemplated time.

As he saw it, speaking out loud to himself, "Time, like water, flowed in main channels. The edges of these channels were probably electro-magnetic in origin. They may even be influenced by solar flames and lightning storms. Like rivers of water, branches of water created their own streams along the way; yet along the way to where?" he asked himself, to its conclusion, he surmised, which probably was also its point of origin.

He had begun to toy with the idea of time flowing in a gigantic benzene-ring circle. The beginning and end were never seen, however, that point was unimportant. The fact that time present flowed in one main channel; yet spread its influence in a radical fashion surrounding everything, and was similar, perhaps, to magnetism or gravity. Magnetism spread its holding power all about; yet centralized itself along a core of magnetic iron, or an electrified copper wire. Just as one magnet influences another, Trans-17 was able to connect with the stream of time and become one with it. It wasn't as difficult as one might think. However, in its simplicity lay its complexity. How do you change human flesh into electromagnetic impulses? Both Paradise and Red Jacket used every corner of their minds and imagination to solve this problem. They came to believe, that as Alexander Graham Bell had converted sound, the human voice per se, into electromagnetic impulses, that the human elements of flesh, bone, water, protein, and such, could also be remade or "translated" into similar impulses. After many mistakes, they came upon a winning combination. Yet it still seemed to Ross that something was missing. However, he always felt like this after success. It was a case of seeking perfection. Even if one is "perfect" when completing work, surely there was one more thing? His feelings were not logical; however, his work proved itself a staircase of logic. This 'stairwell,' in fact allowed humans to walk, one might say, into the time flow that unites the galaxy; perhaps the entire universe. Yet start with the local option. How curious to be calling the entire Milky Way Galaxy a "local option!"

Ross thought back to his youth, and compared it to the present moment. Never did he think he'd escape the poverty and humiliation of being an Indian. Now life had given him many opportunities, and he knew The Great Spirit was the giver of such things, these opportunities: his intelligence, his schooling, and friends who meant much to the laconic man sitting inside a private laboratory, where time travel was soon to commence at the human level. His success seemed too good for him, as he never thought worthy of being given anything.

Indians were quickly judged as being worthless and weak; totally dependent on the U.S. Government and its Bureau of Indian Affairs. He knew that the old way of life he once endured, would never again be his to own, as if one really owned that life. Rather, that old way of life, had owned him. It still owned many, and he wished them all freedom.

With education, ambition, and discipline, he had worked his way out of the trap set forth by the White governmental bureaucrats. He, Ross, was independent, and what a feeling this freedom provided a former poor, down-trodden American Indian.

Chapter 7

I drove to her residence, thus to attend noon Mass with Diana. A gorgeous spring day here in Tulsa, spring being one of the best times of year. Joggers ran along the river on the winding path south to 81ˢᵗ Street. People walking their dogs, children flying kites and riding bikes, this was Sunday in the city. The churches I had driven by were surrounded by cars, and filled with worshipers.

I rang the doorbell and within moments she appeared. "Ah yes, my beautiful woman is ready!" We embraced with a small kiss and hugged each other in the delight of being together again. She proceeded then to place her earrings on in front of the golden framed, oval mirror in her living room, near the unused fireplace.

"Imagine Diana, this condo will become our home. The old place I have will be our weekend getaway."

"You think so, do you?" She was teasing and putting on her lipstick, saying, "Well, there are some important things to discuss, but let's go to church now."

I thought to myself, "You're reading my mind. There are some important things to discuss. However, what is it that she wants to run by with me?"

Questions and curiosity may cause uncertainty; now was such a time. However, within moments I walked to the car, opened her door, and we headed to Holy Family Cathedral for Mass.

As I drove I stated, "Friendship can never be taken for granted. Like marriage, it must be nurtured."

"You're right sweetheart, all friendships need nurturing, like ours!"

I looked over to her and smiled. My eyes met hers and we reached out to hold hands. Within a few minutes I parked the Taurus. Then we proceeded up the off-white marbled stairwell, to the church's interior. I enjoying sitting in the front few rows, and we found a spot not far from the marble pulpit. Diana enjoys the front pews too. We spent a few minutes kneeling in prayer. The bell rang and we stood up to sing the first song. As always the choir voices lifted the service to a moment of aesthetic union with parishioners.

After the introductory prayer, and the three readings, one being the Gospel, and the Gospels today spoke of the two disciples who walk unknowingly with Our Lord on the road to Emmaus.

The Pastor spoke, in summary, these words, to the parish,

"Our need to live close to Him, who died for us, is as real as our daily need for nourishment and sleep. So when we live our daily life, we realize it was Him, Our Lord Jesus, beside us, inspiring us, strengthening us; setting our faith on fire. In our daily walk in faith, we recognize Jesus in His body and blood, in the elements of bread and wine, that He gives us food from Heaven at every Mass. And in the breaking of the bread and sharing one cup, those who follow Our Lord, realize He is the center of our weekly journey in faith. There is no other god; the true God is The Holy Trinity, and the Son of God gave His life so we may live, and live life abundantly.

What can be more important in life than our faith, or our burdens of debt, raising children, our employment, and marriages? The answer is simple, they're all important. However, without recognizing Jesus in our daily lives, everything else is diminished, including our faith. We must nourish our faith weekly, better yet, daily. We must be kind to others, live the Ten Commandments, partake meaningfully of the sacraments, and extend a helping hand to our poor, regardless of town or city. Bring food weekly to church, and in that food, we become Christ to others, and reveal we are active followers of Christ, not just lukewarm Christians.

To be lukewarm, or cold in faith, is early death. Make your faith come alive in your actions, your words, your behavior. We are not just to sit here in our pews and be passive listeners waiting for Mass to be over. We must take the Mass with us, in our hearts, and warm the world with the truth of our Catholic faith. To be Catholic is to be universal, so be universally generous to all you meet this week, and be generous in your donations to church, generous in your words to others, and generous in your living the Gospels. In doing so, at the end of the day, we sit, and suddenly realize, as did the two on the road to Emmaus, discover Jesus was present. Yes, He who died, rose again, and lives closely to us, if we allow Him close. It is our choice. Faith is a choice, make it your choice to live and nourish your faith. Faith, it's a treasure beyond any money, any human gift, and any expensive home, or possession, or luxury vehicles we might own. Own, instead, the greatest gift of all, own Christ as Your Savior and Redeemer. His gifts far surpass the temporal things of earth, and believe me, they are temporary. A 42 year parishioner died two weeks ago of a heart attack, right after Mass and his last sacrament of penance prior to Mass. Yet did his Lexus or expensive home save him? No, Jesus saved him, and brought him home. This young man, who died, was a faithful man in this parish. He walked with Our Lord; now he resides at the banquet table of heaven, enjoying the feast and glory of God.

Let us live as if we too might be deceased within a week, in doing so, learn to forgive yourself and others; love your family, give to others, if only to listen; visit the elderly, embrace the orphans; live Christianity in a way that others will say of you, 'Yes, he or she was indeed a servant of the Lord. Their life was devoted to others, and others were blessed.' This, my fellow Christians, is the essence of our glorious Easter season, a season full of joy and peace; a season of giving and helping others; a season of renewal and rebirth. This is our gift given by Jesus' Resurrection.

Yes, His divine Resurrection is our hope, and hopefully you will return next week a better person than you are today, for they who receive much, much is expected. I know we will meet the expectations of Jesus, His Father, and the Holy Spirit. However, don't allow expectations to generate fear, and thus cause a rift between you and God. Pray for His blessing to be your best, to be the best servant His grace provides. We cannot be good without His grace; grace is His power to us, if we ask for it. Please ask for His grace and blessings. Pray daily and own a heart devoted to Him. Now I pray and say, God bless you all!"

After Mass I thanked the priest for his homily and we shook hands, so too did Diana. I realized too it had only been a week since Easter, as I had certainly attended last week's Easter Triduum; yet it seemed lessened by the fact Diana was out-of-town, and I was participating in the liturgies solo. Without her at my side, attending Mass was lessened in my heart. It was not a realization I enjoyed, rather, I was ashamed. Was it co-dependency based behavior, or a sadness of heart? Then I changed thoughts, I could not answer my own question.

Thus, I knew not if the nearly century old Cathedral's stairwell was made of marble, sandstone, or granite, my geology was not well remembered. Yet the stairwell possessed a simple elegance, and many a parishioner had walked those stairs; many a married couple had walked them as well; and the elderly and the young; the singles and the widowed had walked them too. History, as it related to the parishioners, knew each step, and the history was kept secret within the stones; yes, the stones possessed knowledge that would forever remain sacred and hushed.

I even remember seeing the poor and broken spirited sit on those steps, waiting for Mass to end and hoping, yes, hoping some parishioner would extend to them a meal or a ride to the Salvation Army. I, for one, had helped such a person, a middle aged veteran, clinging to crutches and asking everyone who walked by him, for help. All but I ignored him. Yet how easy to ignore the ill, the dirty; the dispossessed, sitting on these steps after Mass, and act as if these needy people existed not, and that our Christian values had been left behind in the pews. Outside the church, real people may need help, and yet most church attendees will not see them, for the homeless and hungry are conveniently ignored.

"Shall we go to brunch?" I asked descending the stairs, and absent of anyone needy.

Her eyes darted in my direction and smiled approvingly. It was a rhetorical question, for we soon found ourselves at Glass on the Green, and had a delightful meal. We spoke of the ice sculptures, and she commented on Rodin's work. I too appreciated Rodin's sculptures; I thought him and Bayre to be the best of 19th century European sculptors. Then we began to speak of art we'd seen at various museums throughout the world. Actually she was the world traveler; my art exposure was strictly in the contiguous forty-eight states.

"Gordon you simply have to visit the National Picasso Museum in Paris. It's delightful, so full of his color and humor. His sensitive portraits, his rose and blue periods fill the rooms with feelings of poverty, compassion, and love, this is his youthful legacy. His cubist work, though, at times was too mathematical, too contrived, but fascinating none the less. And his late-in-life paintings, created in the year priors to his death, were too bizarre; too obscene, to be enjoyed by me.

And the Louvre, all I can say is magnificent, in both its architecture and collection. It gave me such enjoyment to be there for hours gazing at its renowned artwork. Imagine, seeing the 'Mona Lisa,' and the Greek statue, 'Winged Victory of Samothrace," in the same day? And Gordon, the Musee d'Orsay lived up to its reputation of exhibiting the best of French art. I only wished you were there beside me."

"Yes, I'd enjoy seeing Pablo's Museum, the Louvre, and Musee d'Orsay, with you at my side. Perhaps Europe needs to be one of our first vacations after marriage?"

Beneath the table, as I ate a wonderful croissant, she nudged my leg with her foot and winked saying, "Or honeymoon." I nodded approvingly.

Then before I could say anything more, she went into her description of Amsterdam's Van Gogh Museum, now there was a place I eagerly wanted to experience.

"Gordon, Amsterdam's a great place, clean and full of sweet people. And the Van Gogh Museum sent me heavenwards. I spent all afternoon walking by his work. My co-workers, Patty Rae and Janette came along and loved it, and they rarely visit museums. Seeing the museum expanded their intellectual horizons. They lived with Van Gogh's myth of madness. Indeed, Vincent had his psychological problems; yet he had a gift that made his canvasses transform his artistic energy into love and humanity. No mad or insane person could replicate his sense of color, and the feeling he puts into his work. His paintings made me feel the wind lashing the cypresses, and the French sun burning my neck, as I gazed at his depictions of wheat fields and flowers. He overpowers me momentarily, and then brings me back to his scene with a new sense of vision.

The Rijksmuseum too was powerful. It's Vermeer's and Rembrandt's astounded me, and it was only a five-to-ten minute walk from the Van Gogh Museum. We must see these museums together," said Diana excitedly.

"Yes, I agree, but for now I'd rather gaze into your eyes, the fairest paintings."

"Oh Gordon, you're sweet."

"Naturally or artificially? I asked jokingly.

"Of course, my dear, naturally"

"Well, I'm glad to hear that sincere assurance. 'Naturally,' and by the way, pun intended, it helps to be in love. Nothing is beyond that sublime feeling," I spoke.

We enjoyed our meal and talked for hours. We sat there enjoying every moment together. All was peaceful and pleasurable. Our time apart had been too long for each of us; even now the minutes disappeared too quickly.

After eating we drove around town and viewed the flowers. This time of year, a week after Easter, the azaleas bloomed and created a floral mosaic.

"Nature never ceases to amaze me," I said.

"I love flowers too, all flowers, the red ones, yellow ones, the lavender, and pink ones. The tulips are out, too. I have fond memories of tulips encircling the front of my parent's home, forsythia too. Those yellow bursts always pronounced spring. As a child I would pull off the yellow flower, so small and pure, and taste the nectar upon my tongue. I remember that very well," Diana exclaimed happily.

I replied, "I remember the lilacs outside my bedroom window, lavender on one huge bush, side-by-side with another bush of white blossoms. I've had a fondness for lilacs since."

"Gordon, I can hardly wait to visit your hometown someday, hopefully. And is Glen Iris not close to Niagara Falls?"

"Yes dear, it's a two hour drive west. You'll love it, it's powerful and majestic. The surge of aquatic power makes you feel small in comparison."

"Which is the better view, from the U.S. side or the Canadian side?"

"Both views are wonderful. Besides, you get to see the Canadian Falls, not just Niagara, at any location. They're really one falls separated by some land."

"Is it still a honeymoon vacation spot like it used to be?" she asked coyly.

I turned my head toward her and winked.

Chapter 8

Ross was spending time meditating and relaxing there in the cool basement beneath the barn, a room of simplicity and timelessness. Its home-like quality appealed to him.

After reading his four books over a course of four hours, he sat in his chair with his feet on the table, and began to read about obesity in an old issue of *Time*. Reading the article made him realize the need for an invention to dissolve unneeded body fat. Dieting helps; exercise too. However, a certain segment of the human population was unable or unwilling to reduce their adipose tissue. In other words, fat clung to them, and they seemed helpless to rid themselves of its presence. He began by thinking laser therapy.

"Yes a laser inserted into the fat tissue site, with an attached television monitor as an enhanced visual aide, probes the fat cells and dissolves with a "cool" tip laser. A "hot" tip would destroy tissue, but not the cool tip."* The procedure was formulating in his mind while he read the article, all the while remembering the new surgical procedure for gall bladder removal; less invasive and less traumatic were key. It might work. Was there a need here? Are you kidding? The public would knock you over in a fury if they knew how to have their fat cells melted away forever. He believed that if his theory proved successful, he could eliminate the fat cells from ever being a trouble again. Would he be rich for owning the patent? Yes, Ross Red Jacket would be wealthy. This trance-like fantasy swam in his mind like a child in an Oklahoman pond. In fact, the creative mind floats in such trance-like states.

This project would be worked on during Gordon's trip. While he monitored Gordon's journey, he could easily be researching and developing the devices needed to perform the procedure. Then, and he savored the goal, attending medical conventions and displaying his device to surgeons. The doctors would see dollar signs before them when they see this fat reducing procedure, one as easily performed as gall bladder surgery. Patients will be "knocking down" the physician's office door to be the first to have their obesity dissolved by "cool" laser therapy. *(Since writing the 1980s drafts of this novel, "cool" laser therapy has since been created, but not for the procedure suggested in this novel). Not only would he be providing a valuable medical procedure, he would also give hope to the hopeless; many obese people feeling hopeless. Many have tried and failed at a multitude of diets and programs, only to feel as if the world has nothing to offer but failure. In the process, many obese individuals felt as failures, seeing their worth only in relation to the adipose tissue they had or didn't have at that moment. Ross knew a little about the "fat problem." His many family members suffered from obesity. He did not want his potentially successful project to be focused in on the money part. He seriously wanted to help. In fact he wanted to ease the guilt and shame connected with family members, and the "one" with the problem. Actually, as one family member has a problem: obesity, nicotine addiction, cocaine and/or alcohol addictions, all members suffer. Even those related to workaholics, often suffer in silence.

Naturally he was also interested in the financial part. He just wanted the first priority to be humanitarian, not monetary. In this manner he could enhance the American Indian image, an image tarnished by smoke shops and casinos. Imagine, he thought, "A Native American Indian receiving the Nobel Prize for Medicine; being written up in scientific journals, along with pop culture magazines of the day? Surely such publicity would create positive media coverage for the Indians, and for Oklahoma. Was not tourism the third biggest money-maker for the state? In the process he could hire other Indians and guide them into the middle class. Why be resigned to a low income status all one's life? Besides, we Indians were here first. We're the ones who lived on this continent ten thousand years prior to Columbus and the rest of the European scavengers. Scavengers! That term is almost too good. Damn the Europeans and their smallpox!"

His feelings were running hot against the white crowd. Not for the first time, or the last. Yet he realized his anger stemmed from the childhood memories of poverty, humiliation and subservience of his people. The whites destroyed the bison herds, thus eliminating the Indian food supply. The whites also brought diseases heretofore unknown to this continent. Yet to pay evil with evil ran contrary to the lessons learned at his mother's reading of scripture. Though he rarely attended church, basic values taught by the Nazarene still influenced his judgment.

Though we all know that selfishness, greed, lust, despair, and pride can overwhelm the goodness within, these sins cause all kinds of human misery. Misery was one side of the poverty mentality he wished to eradicate. Misery and despair were twins in the human mind. These twins needed extraction, or better yet, eradication.

As Ross pondered these thoughts, he realized that his gifted intellect could be used in a multitude of inventions to enhance the lives of his people. The white man would not be the sole beneficiary to his work. However reality proved over and over, that one must work the white man's "game" in order to function in the middle class, let alone the upper class. Of this class he knew nothing. Every human contact he had was with the poor or middle class. Millionaires, for example, he had never known. Has Gordon ever known one? Had Diana? She came from a wealthy background, at least she seemed wealthy to him.

He also knew Type 1 and Type 2 diabetes must be eradicated. He wished to be the 'Great Spirit's' chosen scientist for the formidable task to cure this devastating disease too many American Indians, Whites, and Blacks carried as a burden, hidden in the recesses of the petite organ called the pancreas. This disease 'state' did not have a star on our National Flag, as did other States. Yes, he knew it was a pun, but a serious one. Consequences of diabetes were harming and killing American Indian men and women at rates unacceptable. No death is cherished; life, yes, human life, was precious beyond measure.

As he sat in the lab with these thoughts churning within his mind, he heard some voices and the upstairs door open. Diana and Gordon were entering. Ross was the first to speak, "Ah, Sir Isaac Newton and his beautiful bride approaches."

Gordon replied, "Dr. Einstein how goes the world?"

"The world drives by in a Chevrolet, and the universe passes it by in a Lincoln Continental."

Sir Isaac Newton and Dr. Einstein were nicknames for these two, and the names were always used in respect. Besides, Newton and Einstein were their heroes. Without them, contemporary science was nowhere.

Ross stood up and embraced Diana before shaking hands with Gordon.

"Ross, it's wonderful to see you again. It's been too long and too many time zones ago."

"Dear woman, you're too good for this guy. You need a genius like me to take care of you. Or is it that I need you to care for me? Well anyway, it's one of those reasons."

Diana smiled and I just shook my head. Ross had a way with words at times that made you want to disown him. Yet it was all in jest, or was it?

"What's going on with you these days?" asked Diana.

"I'm just thinking about the varied ways to help others and make a few dollars too. The bills don't go away. Besides, I'd like to have a larger home and lab someday."

That was the first time I'd heard him mention either one of those goals. I immediately approved.

"Good idea Ross, a home would be just the thing for you. Then you can pay more property taxes to Tulsa County." said I.

In good faith, Ross replied, "It would be a desirable goal owning a larger home, and filling it with the woman of my choice."

Diana inquired, "Are you dating anyone?"

"Yes, a young woman from Tahlequah; Indian too, named Kogee; perhaps the perfect woman for me, what do you think Diana?" Ross knew that women enjoyed asking that question, "Are you dating anyone?" There was a sense of driven purpose behind a woman's question regarding dating.

"Is she good looking? inquired Diana.

"As beautiful as you Diana, in every way I compare two women."

"Laying on the compliments a little thick Ross?"

"No, just saying what's on my mind."

At that pronouncement I was amused; smiling. Diana appeared embarrassed, red as an apple. Yet we always seemed to be playing word games around each other. Sometimes I feel she, and people like her, commit that "act" in order to disguise true feelings. At times I wondered if Diana really liked minority groups. Sometimes I felt that everyone had a bit of racial prejudice in them, even I; Ross too. Find someone who did not, and I'd probably think they were saints or liars. The two extremes were just that, extreme behavior and attitudes. I for one felt that extremists, even in causes I believed in, were potentially dangerous; sometimes, the most needed of all Americans. Extremism, even in the cause of freedom, life and liberty, may take us down dangerous roads, or perhaps, save us from internal tyrants.

My thoughts were racing. First I'm thinking about racism; now I'm thinking political extremes. It was only recently that I realized my racing thought patterns and actions. I realized these racing thought patterns were actually suppressed anxiety feelings regarding time travel. My compulsion to do things immediately will be a challenge to Diana in our marriage. However, all marriages face challenges, or live in denial. The conflict would either harm or strengthen us. This feeling began to pervade my thoughts, standing there among the three of us.

Ross showed Diana around the lab and took her to the kitchen for a soft drink. Diana noticed changes in our equipment; however, she had no idea of our recent time travel success. Ross sensed I had not talked to her about my upcoming journey. Therefore the topic of time travel and the subsequent machines setting about were off limits for conversation, at least for now. My talk with Diana needed to occur soon, very soon. But for today I wanted to enjoy the peacefulness of a Sunday afternoon, the Second Sunday of Easter.

Walking into the kitchen, a small boxed area with a table and three chairs, "one for solitude, two for companionship, three for society," thus spoke Thoreau, one of my favorite writers and conservationists.

Ross poured a diet Dr Pepper for me, a Classic Coke for Diana, and Miller Light for himself. Diana asked, "Do you have any caffeine-free Coke dear?" "Yes, it's in the refrigerator somewhere."

I opened the door and pushed some things aside before finding a few 12 ounce cans. We both like diet/caffeine-free Dr Pepper or Coke.

"Well," she said. "I'll drink this cup first, and then switch to the other."

"Now Diana, if you don't want caffeine, just pour it out. No big deal," I stated.

"I don't like to waste anything dear, you know that."

"Sweetheart, it's just a carbonated drink."

She raised her eyebrows, somewhat exasperated, "All right, empty this and refill with my real choice."

Ross spoke up, "Diana, I wished you had spoken up when I was pouring."

"I didn't want to rock the boat." she said.

"Diana, we're not in a boat." I exclaimed in place of Ross responding.

"Please, Gordon, you're making too much of this whole thing."

"I want people to state what they really want and not play games with their feelings, even on such trivial matters. Besides, caffeine makes you hyper and nervous."

I felt overly protective of her, and then said, "It might keep you awake tonight."

She changed the subject quickly saying, "Ross, drinking beer so early in the day, you should be ashamed."

"Diana, relax, don't bug me. I'm on an intellectual roll. I was thinking up some great medical advances before you two love doves waltzed in."

"Oh really, like what?" she asked.

"Well, beautiful lady, what problem do many Americans have and seem so frustrated about?"

"Paying their bills," she responded.

"No," Ross stated. "Let me be more specific. What physical defects do 40% to 50% of Americans possess that they desperately want to rid themselves?"

I was thinking obesity or heart disease, but let her speak.

"I'd say . . . obesity."

"Yes, my dear, fat tissue."

"And what do you propose as your therapy?" she inquired.

"Dissolving adipose tissue by means of a laser is my newest idea. My concept is a simple and novel technology; no one is offering it; and, I'm sure it's as safe as delivering a baby or removing a gall bladder."

"I'm impressed," Diana exclaimed. In fact, I was too. I didn't realize he was thinking about anything other than time travel.

Her statement pleased Ross immensely. He thought a lot of Diana, and was perhaps jealous of her devotion to me.

"The way I see it Diana, Ross went on, it's simply a matter of what my grandpa said, 'Give the whites what they want in way of merchandise, and you'll sell them every time.' And this was from a man who had a store on old Route 66. He's dead now but he ran a successful general store up near the Missouri border. I spent summers with that wonderful old man, and he was a lot of fun. Grandfather taught me a lot and let me run the cash register, order supplies, and clean up the place. When you're a kid it seemed like fun. Now I realize it was just plain hard work; yet I was with him and that was the best part."

I had heard this story a dozen times before, but she had not. The story offered a positive message and a proud memory for Ross.

"Ross, if this idea takes off, you'll be rich, famous, and have every obese woman made thin will fall in love with you."

Ross grinned, "I like all three categories, especially the last one. Perhaps I need a squaw to fill my tipi."

We went through about four to five cans of soft drink between us, while Ross downed three beers.

Ross just sat there grinning and feeling good. I put my hand over Diana's and sat there still and quiet. We spoke only occasionally and small talk at that.

Then in about a half an hour Ross began telling us about the woman he had been seeing lately. He was nearly done with his fourth beer when he asked Diana to get another. She did and popped the top for him too.

"Thank you woman, you're too good for any of us. You're an angel from heaven visiting us mere mortals on planet earth. Surely your visit is a gift from the Supreme Deity?"

"Ross, are you drunk or paraphrasing Shakespeare?"

"A little of both," he bellowed. Then he belched and laughed hysterically.

"Ross, your compulsive actions are beginning to show," I said.

He stood up to order more drinks, as if he were at a bar, not a laboratory.

"Ross, haven't you had enough?" Diana asked.

"Enough of what, beer? I don't think so my dear. Besides, don't be judgmental, I don't need guilt poured over me."

Was that phrasing a conscious pun or a subconscious realization? she wondered.

"I'm not judging you, besides; I'm one of your best friends. I was merely expressing my concern," she said.

Ross quickly replied, "Let me see, my best friends are Augie Busch and the brewers of St. Louis who work for him. Ever been to St. Louis? I toured that brewery like I owned it. In fact, I've consumed so many cans of Bud and Bud Light I'm an honorary stockholder in Budweiser. In fact, I've a season's pass at Busch Stadium. Those Redbirds are the greatest. Every time they're up to bat I pop another Bud and salute them."

"What do you do when they're in the field?"

"Well, I start walking to the beer concession and prepare for another batter up, or I give $3 to the guy who hawks that golden brew."

Then he leaned over to Diana, "Now would you please get rid of this two-bit mechanic and move in with a real man? Then when you've done that, get your man another cold Bud."

Diana shook her head and said emphatically, "No way, Jose."

"My name's not Jose, its Martini and Rossi," said Ross. "Get it, I just made a joke, Martini and Rossi, ever drink that stuff?" Ross was beginning to slur his words; his mind seemed diminished of its typical intelligence, and he began making comments and using profanity that were embarrassing to Diana and me.

We were both disgusted with him. No way was he drunk from the drinks he had in front of us. He must have been drinking off-and-on all day.

"I'm sorry, Diana. The more he puts away the more profanity he uses," I sadly spoke.

"Sweetheart, you don't have to apologize for him. He's the drunk, not you," she emphatically replied.

"Yes, but I feel responsible for his actions. I sense I have to take over his life when he's drunk by apologizing and making excuses for him. It seems this past year his beer consumption has risen geometrically in relation to the work we've been doing," I stated.

"Do you realize your talking about me as if I weren't here? Talk about being rude," Ross replied angrily.

"Ross, we didn't join you to hear profanity and see you drunk. I apologize for speaking as if you were not here. However, in one sense, you weren't here. You were in alcoholic la-la land."

Diana moved quickly to change the conversation's direction and tone, and she did it with the diplomacy of a true manager.

"And what have you two been working on?" she asked inquisitively.

I replied, "This is not the time for me to relate all that's been happening, but we do need to have an afternoon or evening to talk things over. What I need to say is beginning to feel like a water balloon ready to burst. My mind, like that balloon, is ready to explode. In fact that's probably how the universe began, God's creativity began so magnificently and ripe for action, that the 'big bang' of creation exploded and commenced its inevitable essence of being."

"Your cologne, she said, smells delightful. You should wear it more often. Forget the universe's creation, I had no part in that, I want to be part of you. Forget this 'essence of being,' it's too intellectual."

With those words we embraced and kissed. She led me to my back porch couch and we spent a few joyful hours there. While beneath the barn in our lab, Ross kept drinking himself into a stupor. The next morning I found him asleep on the floor. Knowing he was too heavy to lift, I let him stay there. But I cleaned up the place. I wanted him to at least wake up to a clean room. What else do you do for a friend? Even if I do feel used afterwards, I knew nothing else. Only later did I learn about co-dependency and enabling.

Being with Diana, in the closeness of touching, kissing, and laughing, made me the happiest man in Oklahoma. Lying with her on the couch was plain and simple joy. However, I had been forewarned that romance before marriage is different than after marriage. Now I wasn't sure. It was difficult to believe that life together would not be better than now. As a future married man I looked forward to sharing everything with Diana, every word, every thought; every loving moment would be treasured as a Duke treasures his Duchess. Yet we were committed to moral behavior, even in a world that preached paganism in commercials, magazines and movies. We did not see ourselves as superior to others, only living in a realm of priority carved out thousands of years ago upon tablets on Mount Sinai. We did not preach morality, we lived it. There was no sanctimonious air about our choice either.

I drove her home, finding it to be nearly 1:15 a.m. She was asleep. Besides, she had a few personal days to use or lose, so there was no need to arise early. She could call in a personal day in the morning, then return to sleep. Actually, I decided to leave a message on her supervisor's voice mail and requested a personal day for Diana. Certainly, Diana would not object to my pre-emptive move? Or would she?

I then decided to sleep on her couch. She remained asleep as I placed her onto her bed. Her shoes were removed and I placed a blanket over her, and obtained her rose and blue striped Mexican blanket for myself. The night slipped by us quietly and peacefully.

We awoke the next morning around 10:00 a.m. and I fixed eggs for us. Diana toasted raisin bread and made fresh squeezed orange juice. Our repast was pleasant, especially as I reminded her I had called in a personal day for her to her supervisor's workplace telephone.

Within an hour a call arrived. It was work, with a recording acknowledging Diana's request for a personal day. Thus, work and the employee had followed corporate protocol. Yes, protocol, everything related to work must have every action recorded, justified, and filed for future reference. No chances for error allowed. Lawsuits were made of errors, ones overlooked, ignored, and conveniently forgotten. Thus it cost money to err, whether it is employer or employee. It was a game, oh yes, a serious game; one held to scrutiny by multiple attorneys in dark suits and blue ties.

We took a walk afterwards and enjoyed the spring morning. Such moments made life seem sublime and transcended the banality of routine experience. Sunlight drenched everything, the buildings, the streets, the church spires and stained glass windows, the restaurants, the very clothes we wore, our eyes and skin. To feel the warmth of light proved a great happiness. This warmth augmented the pre-existing warmth of love and communion we felt for one another. Such moments appear rarely in our lives. Again the seemingly banal things of life fill our senses with the sublime and beautiful. Only when our life is condensed and placed aside, as in a play, do we go out of ourselves and feel the ecstasy of life around us. To paraphrase Thoreau, many of us go around half asleep; you can read the original sentence in his, *Walden.*

"Therefore, if today my life is a play, may Act One never end? May this day become the best of all days; my wish, and my ideal. May this moment supplant all others," spoke I in a renaissance mood; she thanked me for my sentiment.

We were together and our feelings carved the day into a sculpture of human joy. No other days were needed in my opinion. This day sufficed unto its own. May God grant us this one wish! May He bless this day as He blesses our lives. Could heaven be more perfect as this morning? Having experienced nothing as wonderful, I could not fathom anything greater. Yes, human experience limits our perception of heaven. Yet this quality of humanness, the knowing act of human consciousness allowed me to think such things. Consciousness was a God given gift.

I then spoke a prayer, "Thank you Heavenly Father for this gift of life and self-awareness. For within this gift was the present wrapped in the being of Diana. Her golden hair was the bow, her clothes the wrapping paper. Her smile, yes, her smile, was the card inviting me and acknowledging the gift. Could I be happier? Could I want more?" I continued, "Lord, freeze this moment, forever! Hear my prayer; let us soon be one in marriage. Let me dwell in the land of clear blue eyes; let me explore the mystery of her womanhood. Let me listen and share the thoughts of her who will be mine. Do not allow time to steal us away from one another. Let nothing come between us. Amen."

Even in the knowledge that things would soon change, this knowledge I suppressed in the cavities of my mind. To remember what I planned to do, and acknowledge that I would be on a journey, a dangerous and novel sojourn; yet one I might decide to disengage from altogether.

Her hand in mine; her words for my ears only, and her touch, only mine to know. I was beyond myself and relished every moment.

Chapter 9

My neighbor Anne had recently lost her husband. A policeman, he had died in the line of duty during a Bank robbery. Nearly a year had gone by and she was just beginning to feel like herself again. The numbness of losing a loved one was healing over. She found herself in a support group and even 'went out' with a few men. After fifteen years of marriage to the same man, dating again felt scary. Yet the men she went out with had been bachelor friends of her husband, Tony. They knew her and she them. It was the safest dating scene. She went out with one policeman friend who took her to nice Tulsa restaurants, and kept her informed of the newest department events. His late wife, Karen, had died of cancer, it hit quickly and within five months she was laid to rest at the cemetery at 51st and Memorial. Being Roman Catholic, Anne's husband lay at peace in Calvary Cemetery, located in south Tulsa. At times it seemed morbid to center social time on deceased loved ones; however that's the way the living felt most comfortable. Clinging to the past inhibits moving forward. Neither wanted to move ahead, the past, literally dead and buried, felt safer. Even her dates with the police focused on Tony and his life.

However, at a support group meeting, a man in his early 40s challenged Anne when she kept speaking of her late husband. This man was not new to the group, but he had been quiet until now.

"Dear woman, the past is hanging around your neck and mine, like garlic. No one dares get close. If they do, we ward them off. Yes, we all hurt; we hurt like hades and are all scared of changing. Here we are safely clinging to the deceased as if they were the only human beings with whom we could have possibly found happiness. We place this person on a pedestal, yes, we place their dead carcass, forgive the phrase, on an altar for the living. Yet we, the living, are not buried with them. We remain living. Emotionally we buried ourselves with them, but our bodies won't let us forget we still live. We eat meals, we drive cars, pay our bills, cry, and laugh, cry again, speak on the phone, and go to work. Yet we still worship at the altar of the dead. Fear keeps us in this morbid celebration. We live our entire life now around the deceased. I, for one, am tired of worshipping my dead wife. I have got to get moving again, to love again. Anne, please accept an invitation to dinner with me this weekend; during this dinner we will have one rule, neither of us will mention our deceased spouse. They would want us to go on living. They do not want to be worshiped as deity. They had plenty of faults, as do we all here in this room tonight. I cannot go on pretending life has come to an end. I must accept the desire to move ahead, even though my heart aches, and my mind and body exhausted from insomnia."

Leaning forward, finished with his statement, with hands to his face, Anne walked over to him and whispered, "I accept your date." He looked up at her and smiled.

The group leader made a few comments about the stages of grief and how the fifth stage was acceptance.

"Once at this level, the individual makes a break with grief and remakes their life. No longer do they live and breathe sadness; acceptance says that life continues. Thus life acts as a river meeting a huge rock midstream, there is a way around the obstacle of our loss, though it's not easily found or acted upon., Yet we must act, and not wait for 'something' to happen. If we wait, we play a victim's role, a convenient avoidance method chosen by many out of fear or ignorance of choices."

The group leader verbally 'applauded' the gentleman's non-threatening confrontation of Anne, and how difficult it must have been for him to stand up and speak his mind, or more accurately, speak from his broken heart.

The gentleman who spoke so eloquently was named Philip Taylor. He and Anne decided to slip out to a restaurant after the group broke up. He took her to Brownie's on 21st and South Harvard Avenue for coffee and pie. Anne chose hot chocolate and apple pie. He took black coffee and pumpkin pie à la mode. She passed on the ice cream, not wanting to appear greedy for sugar and fat laden foods! She wanted to make a good impression. They talked until after 11 p.m., separated and drove away. He lived in a well-to-do south Tulsa neighborhood. She headed toward the west. Overhead stars shown in the blackness of space pointing the way, or so she felt, toward home and something new in her life. Strange how words said a certain way at the right time could change people? Timing was the key. She also felt she had made a new friend, and did not want to bore him, nor appear unintelligent.

Anne married a few years out of school and never had children with Tony. Her only schooling after Will Rogers High was secretarial school. Yet that was years ago. She was caught up in church activities and taking care of her home, and, oh yes, her mother-in-law had lived with them until her passing away three years before her husband. That episode in their life went on for a decade. In one sense, her mother-in-law was their child. Dementia and a stroke ended her human life, though not her spiritual existence. Mortal human life proved finite and brief; eternal life was just that, eternal and infinite.

In her conversation with Philip at the diner, she found out he had an education. He had two college degrees, published a few papers on natural gas and oil drilling, and had taught at Tulsa University. He was now a consultant for energy firms and found himself becoming a greater expert on oil drilling. This work took him throughout the oil drilling States, including Alaska. His work and education intimidated her. However, she knew something had to change. She considered going back to school, to begin college and become an RN. They make good pay and she'd be working and helping needy, hurting people. She even considered physical therapy. A girlfriend of hers, Angela, made a great income from PT, and she loved her work. It would mean a four year commitment, but what else is she planning on doing the next four years, wallow in self-pity? Time was over for playing the victim, it was time to move on.

Her subsequent dates with Philip went well. He was not demanding of her in any form. He was fun and low key. This was the type of relationship she wanted. Yes, they held hands and kissed some, but no intense relationship was developing. They did challenge one another to positive thinking and enjoying the company of a person of the opposite sex.

When Philip went out of town on business, he'd call her and relate a few funny stories. She'd even go to his home and water the plants and check the mail. She also checked to make sure the place was not burglarized. Their friendship remained basically platonic. They apparently felt the need for this low-key companionship. He may have challenged her in word to fall in love again; yet he was not seemingly going that direction himself. They experienced one another at this conservative pace for several months. No love feelings were blossoming in their souls, and for now, that was fine.

One cannot force love; it either arrives like spring flowers or dissipates like snow to sunlight.

Things change; people grow and feel things in waves of awareness. As mentioned, Anne lived close to my country place. It was on one of my walks that I spotted her watering her garden's flowers. I stopped and began conversing with her. I had known that her husband was dead a year and that he had been a good officer. Always a sucker for a pretty face, attractive physique and long legs, I made sure to get close to her and look her over, top to toe. Don't discount the fact I was engaged to a gorgeous woman already, men are always looking, even when they deny it. Women too.

She stood there in her sweaty clothes; with her hair pulled back. I too was sweaty, and enjoying our conversation regardless of my appearance.

The fact was I liked Anne; respected her and her late husband, and appreciated her feminine charms.

Knowing and seeing Diana's beauty, made me realize how vulnerable Anne and Diana were in this world, and that men might seek out both women for marriage in my absence. I knew too well the impulsive nature of women, and of course, we men. These women were too precious to me to be taken for granted by myself or other men. Though I knew I'd be gone only a short four weeks, much could happen in that length of time They deserved nothing short of total respect and courtesy. Though our age was not one of chivalry, I wished it chivalrous. I wished to protect Diana and Anne from the harsh realities of male adult behavior, and wanted to be a renaissance English knight, with shield and sword defending their honor. It was a fantasy from my 6th grade thoughts of Susan, and a treasured fantasy and feeling it was for me at the time. Freud was not needed for me to recall my 6th grade feelings toward Sue Kingsley. My age twelve feelings were well understood within my heart and no emotional wall inhibited those feelings from being felt for the joy I received. There was no sadness to remember.

Anne and I stood outside an hour talking, she then invited me inside for de-caffeinated green tea and I accepted.

"You have a beautiful lawn and garden, Anne. It looks as if you really enjoy working the earth."

"Oh I do. A day that I'm not outside doing something like planting, pruning, weeding, or just watering the flowers, is a day I feel unsatisfied. My life draws life from the earth, or at least it seems that way," she said.

"Like Antaeus?" I asked.

"Who?"

"I'm referring to the Greek god who drew his strength from earth."

"Oh, that's me. Tell me more."

"Antaeus, son of Gaia, retained his strength intact as long as he remained in touch with earth. Earth was his mother."

"Then Gaia was earth?" she asked.

"Yes." I said.

"Is it Greek or Roman mythology?"

"Greek. Are you interested in mythology?" I asked.

"I think what I'm really interested in is learning. I married young, kept house, and slowly sank into a routine with a policeman as a husband. I lived in constant anxiety over the possibility of his dying in the line of duty, and darn it if it didn't happen, just like I feared it would."

"I'm sorry, Annie. I can only imagine your pain. Loss of a loved one would drive anyone nuts. If I lost Diana I'd be a mess, I'd . . . be lost."

She spoke, "That's exactly how I felt, and sometimes still do. I'm lost in a big world full of people and we all behave like strangers. People intentionally isolate themselves into islands of despair."

"Islands of despair, that's well said, and poetic."

She looked at me with a tired yet quizzical look. "You called me Annie."

"Yes, I suppose I did. Does it offend you?"

"No, but it reminds me of my parents. Mom and dad called me Annie; my sister and brothers too."

"Did Tony call you Annie?"

"No, he usually called me after my favorite flowers: Iris, Rose, Daisy, or Sunny. He liked variety. Sometimes he'd even call me babe or sis. He liked nicknames. His work was full of nicknames, like characters from Dick Tracy comics: Mole, Flattop, Fly Face, Prune Face, Lizard . . . the police love to describe their prisoners in such ways. I suppose it made a difficult job more bearable, less direct. It was easier to send Lizard to prison for twenty years than Harry Ballwin or a Joey Medina. Names, real ones, were more personal. Tony always said that the day he took every criminal personally, every suspect too, that's the day he needed to die, retire, or step down and work on his parent's wheat farm in western Kansas."

"He was a good man. I didn't know him well, but I liked talking with Tony. He acted genuine and down to earth," said I.

She laughed, "There's 'earth' again. I truly draw my life from earth, and friendships."

I laughed and smiled, and sipped more tea.

"Thanks for stopping by, she said, and visiting. I feel lonely out here when the sun goes down. My main companion is King Tut, my Retriever. And I notice our dogs enjoy one another."

"Do you think they'll have pups?" I inquired.

She laughed again, "No, King Tut was neutered. No need to worry. You're little Duchess is safe. I like that name, Duchess. It's regal and feminine; it's real pretty. Makes me think of my childhood when I imagined myself royalty and I married a Prince or Duke or King. And I always found fascination in Egyptian history, in eleventh grade, Mr. Steele taught us about the pharaohs. I never loved history more than that semester. I didn't realize I'd name my dog after a high school class experience; however, I did."

"Anne, you're a special lady. I feel happy to have you as my closest neighbor, even if it's a mile away."

"I have a confession Gordon."

"Go ahead."

She hesitated a moment, then said, "From my bedroom window I can see your house. At night when King and I feel lonely we sit on the bed and look out toward your house and take comfort in the lights shining out through your windows. It's a comforting feeling to know you're there. I think that you're probably reading, or better yet, I think your spending time with your fiancée, and that both of you are very happy in each other's arms. "At least someone is in love," I say to myself."

I sighed, "You have just given me a reason to always keep a light on. If you find comfort in it, I'll burn lights in two or three rooms."

"You're too kind, Gordon. One light is enough!"

"Yes, I'll burn at least one light for you. On that note allow me to depart. I'm tired and in need of a shower."

"Would you allow a young woman to drive you to your home? Why walk home in the pitch black of night?"

I was ready to decline, and then I said, "Yes, I'll take up your offer."

In minutes we were in her Escort going slowly through the night with two white 'arms' of light ahead of us, in other words, headlights, to see our way to my place. I thanked her and asked her to come over to dinner soon. I enjoyed this woman and wanted to be friends. When she pulled up beside my house, I grasped both her hands with mine and said, "Thank you." We understood one another at that moment. "How fortunate," I said to myself, "I know two women and they're sweet, beautiful and sensitive."

In the last few hours something new had been created within our hearts, now we were truly friends. How fortunate to be friends with two women, similar, yet different females.

I walked inside and found Duchess on the old couch of the enclosed back porch. Before entering the back porch I turned to wave goodbye to Annie. Whether she waved in return, I did not see. But her car backed up and was disappearing down the road. I felt good, good in the fact that I shared friendship and gave of myself. In return, the other party did too. Thinking such thoughts made me feel that Anne and Diana were royalty; that they both deserved castles, and servants, and court jesters to generate spontaneous laughter. In their laughter was their charm; in their charm, their mystery; in their mystery, their attraction. To me laughter was the most attractive feature of a woman. Without laughter, she could have the most fatal of charms and still disinterest me. Laughter was a mystic adhesive force, like gravity, the sun holding out its unseen hands to guide earth in its journey in orbit. Do not two people in love and friendship imitate the solar system? My thoughts were too deep. A shower was my need and I yielded to the warm spray of well water heated by my rooftop solar cells. Soap covered me and I was happy. Warm water erased the day's dust from my being, and in moments slept well. The kitchen light I left on, just in case a lonely and solitary figure in the distance needed comfort and a guiding light; for now I better understood a lighthouse keeper's vocation.

Chapter 10

Within a few days I faced the fact that Diana and I had a lot now to talk about. I called her at work late one afternoon; the reason I called so late was that I got lost in my work. Calling late was something we both disliked and I apologized immediately. Upon calling, her secretary came on first. "Hello, this is Gordon. May I speak with Diana, please?"

"Hello Gordon. Diana's been expecting a call all day. She just got out of a meeting so you're in luck. I'll put her on."

In a moment Diana was on the line. "Hello darling, long day for you?"

"Yes, sweetheart it has been a long day. I got caught up in my research and all of a sudden it was 4:45. I apologize for being tardy with calling."

"Thanks for saying you're sorry. Anyway, I've been busy all day and we took lunch in the conference room. It's been go-go-go all day since 8:30. I'm tired, frustrated, and ready to be kissed."

"Is that an order? I inquired.

"Yes, so what are we going to do, elope, go out for dinner, or stay inside and kiss passionately all night?"

"I like these ideas a great deal. However, how about coming out here and having Chinese carry out and watching a few movies?"

"What, no romance?"

"Of course darling, who cares if we watch the videos? I'd rather be snuggling with you."

"Don't kid me buster, you're a movie freak. Men would rather watch a movie than be romantic for an evening."

"Don't underestimate me. I love you too much. Besides, let's get romantic movies. How about "Casablanca" and "Gone with the Wind," and a couple of others? Would those satisfy you?"

"Sounds like a nice selection," she said enthusiastically.

"Let me drive into town, pick you up, get the food and bring all the goods back here for an evening of romance."

"Now you're talking like a future husband, not a selfish fiancé."

"Diana."

"What?"

"I love you."

"Thank you Gordon, I love you too."

"Darling, I'll return around seven thirty p.m. to pick you up. How does that sound?"

"Fine, I just need some time to shower and pretty up. Good bye, Gordon, I'll see you later."

"See you soon," I replied.

We hung up and I went to the refrigerator for a cold container of Ozarka water.

I had worked all day in the lab on my computer and Ross hadn't been by. That was unusual. I needed to call and discover what's going on with him. The fact that he was drunk last Sunday doesn't mean we're not on good terms. He's my best friend, next to Diana. No one other than Ross can supervise Trans-17 from Tulsa while I'm "out there." His not being around actually generated some fear, fear of failure, fear of losing a friend, and fear that my "Galaxy Game", a.k.a. "The out-of-town trip," would not happen.

Just then I heard a vehicle pull into the barn above the lab. "That must be Ross," I thought. In a few moments it was the man himself.

"Dr. Einstein, good to see you." said I.

"If it isn't Isaac Newton and his flying fig machine, how goes you?"

"Well professor, where have you been?"

"Overcoming my drinking binge and finally drying out."

"Ross, I said startled, I had no idea your drinking was getting out of hand."

"It's not, Isaac, I'm in control. It's a woman who's out of control. That burnt biscuit from Tahlequah told me to get lost."

"Why?"

"I was supposed to take her out and I forgot. I just plain forgot."

"Ross, that's a pretty serious offense."

"I suppose you, Gordon Paradise, a.k.a. Isaac 'The Fig' Newton never forgot a date?"

I hesitated, and then said nothing more. Actually I had come close to forgetting tonight's date. Who was I to lecture Ross?

"Ross, we all make mistakes. Did you call her and apologize?"

"Yes, I sent her roses, or was it orchids, or a six foot white pine tree? I can't remember. It's one of those things women adore; yet I never did hear her response to my gift."

"I'm sorry, I really am. I was hoping you would find the bride of your dreams in the gentle Indian woman from Cherokee County. Besides, she needs a man to love."

"By the way, I pray you didn't send a six foot white pine to plant. Joke?

"Oh, I suppose I could telephone her."

Like everyone, Ross detested being dumped. And yes, the six foot tree statement was his humble way of easing emotional pain; he believed anyone could relate to his silly humor amid distress.

I appreciated his humorous attempt to ease the pain, and recognize we men do not wish to be easily dismissed. Being 'dumped' makes relationships appear disposable, like cardboard orange juice containers; we, too, dislike being thrown to the trash bin. Women take such action personally; we men take it personally too.

Then I spoke friend-to-friend, "Ross, you were in the wrong and you know it."

"Hey pal, don't lecture me on etiquette, you're no Emily Post or Gloria Vanderbilt."

"Gloria's a perfume Ross."

He grimaced and felt out-of-touch between Gloria and Emily. He felt like replying,"What's the difference between a Vanderbilt and a Post?" Surely he could arrive at some clever retort to be spoken in a future conversation?

Yet his spoken words were, "I feel like a jerk, and prefer this Cherokee woman over other women. Something about her I really care about in a loving manner. Besides, she has a great little . . . . ah, let's see, oh yes, 'personality.' I don't want to think of her as an object. Besides she's cute and listens well, and nice to look at too."

"Wise guy, go call her if you want. Use my phone. I must pick up Diana and our dinner, in town. Yet we're coming back here for Chinese and videos. I'd invite you, but it's exclusively for two."

By the time I went inside my house to change clothes and wash my hands, Ross had already called his lady and things were better. He was smiling ear to ear when I saw him next.

"What's new Ross?"

"She told me to come over and take her out for pizza and a movie. She's forgiven me. Besides, her dad was placed in a Phoenix hospital Sunday, sudden-like, and she had no time to forgive me before now."

"Is her dad all right?"

"He's recovering and he's off booze. The doctor told him 'lay off the liquor from now on, or he'd be dead in a year.' I think the fear of The Great Spirit got through to the old Indian."

"Indians aren't the only alcoholics. There are plenty of Caucasians addicted to booze. Look at the Germans, the Irish, and Russian men in this country, and you'll see a fair amount of the same disease, alcoholism."

"True, but alcohol and the Indian were never compatible at all, never, nada,"

"I've never heard you say such a thing before, but I never read a study on Indians and alcohol. Yet I never sought one out either."

"Forget the studies, just look for a trail of tears in the line of destroyed Indian families." Ross replied.

We parted on that note and I drove into Tulsa. The expressway was busy as ever, everyone was heading home from a hard day's work. People were getting their groceries, videos, and liquor for the week. The latter is one item I rarely purchased, though Diana likes pina coladas and wine with meals. Yet she rarely gets a 'drink' at my place. Occasionally I purchased adult beverages, but preferred not to. I actually detested alcoholic drinks. They were to me a waste of money, similar to buying lottery tickets, both were a fantasy desired. This desire derived from scratch off cards to amber bottles, and both left a feeling of loss. The only "gain" was purely wishful thinking and a temporary illusion of happiness. Yet so many of us live our lives in the realm of illusion; inside each person who derives pleasure from gambling and drink, was a little voice saying, "Reality is too difficult. Give me illusions or give me death," thus the mind paraphrased the words of patriot, Patrick Henry.

Then I realized I was being too judgmental again, an old Paradise family habit. Why be so opposed to wine and lottery tickets? My feelings, developed in my formative years, were repressed; yet why? I may never know, or the reason will emerge suddenly as a submarine emerges from the ocean's depth. Feelings so often seemed like submarines, emerging without notice to the rest of the world. Truly, one day I would understand my opposition. Yet now, it was buried in my subconscious, an artifact from the my past; buried until an archeologist of the mind made it conscious,

I had called ahead to the 15th Street Wok and ordered take out for two. They were noted for their great oriental cuisine. This meal would be a real treat. Yet it would taste even more superb eating there at the restaurant, it always does. Takeout food soon absorbs the carton's flavor, or was it my imagination? Whatever the reason, to eat in their place of business was a delight. In fact I had brought my parents here to eat when they visited last. They both loved it. Yet dad's not keen on oriental foods. Having fought the Japanese in WW II, he never made a conscious effort to consume oriental food. Could it be related to the fact friends of his died and starved in Japanese concentration camps, and his interest in this food was, therefore, 'off limits' subconsciously? Why second guess, they both enjoyed the meal, but dad was visibly uncomfortable with oriental waiters and waitresses bouncing around.

Besides, Iwo Jima was never far from his mind. He earned a Silver Star in that battle on a sulphurous smelling island, and never told us, his children. Mom told her us two decades after the battle ended. Silence had finally been broken regarding his war record; however, to him the silence would always remain. For mom, the denial finally dissolved to one of confidential conversation with her adult children.

Driving into Diana's parking lot I cruised into the empty space in front of her condo. She had parked her cars as usual under the roof of undercover parking.

I hopped out and rang the bell. It took about three minutes for her to open the door. She was in her bathrobe with a huge white towel drying her hair.

"Come in darling, I just got out of the shower, Baby's running late. Is Papa Bear hungry or can he hold on a few minutes?"

With those words we embraced and kissed soft and sweetly. Then she turned a bit crazy as her robe opened up and kissed me harder, and embraced me like a vise. Her aroma was that of fragrant shampoo and cleansing bar.

"Gordon, you're driving me crazy, we must behave! What would mom and dad think?"

"I don't know, what would they think except that we're in love? Besides, we're adults, not their teenage children."

Her ability to tease me, then pull away at the most sensitive and emotionally climatic moment was becoming standard. It took my breath away as she then dashed across the room to her bath. I headed for the kitchen for a cold glass of purified water. We both drank purified water, never tap water. We both preferred 'reverse osmosis purified water.' Such were the small creature comforts of two educated people in their late thirties. Oh, did I ever mention that Diana was three years younger? At least she tells me so. I always take ages lightly until I see a birth certificate.

It was another half hour before the woman with the golden hair finished. Or was it closer to an hour? By then I had watched the local news and a rerun of M*A*S*H. Tonight Hawkeye was accused of theft. In fact I watched this program routinely; one of my few vices regarding the media of television. So yes, an hour had gone by, and my intoxication and hormonal response to her robe scene had started subsiding, with my internal thermometer reset to normal, acting as if I truly felt 'normal' around Diana, I did not, love consumed me as appetizer, entrée, and dessert all in one moment; she was, as Hemingway said of Paris, "A moveable feast."

Now, ready to depart, she wore a red turtleneck pullover and tight shell-white slacks. Her gorgeous mane had been combed to perfection. My hair never looked that nice. Mine was not in a halo light like hers. But I wasn't complaining. Her hair was a gift from God, as was her entire being, and I loved it all.

We soon were on the road to my place, for I had completed the video and meal pickup, prior to driving to her residence. I had brought along a special container, invented by Ross, to keep the food warm.

As we drove toward my rural residence, crossing the river heading west, she said, "This food smells wonderful, Gordon."

"It sure does. And it will be as warm as when I picked it up."

After eating and relaxing, two hours passed as we watched a movie to its conclusion; then suddenly she bolted upright. The abruptness of her move made me realize it was our time to talk; to listen.

The movie was turned off and she turned the television to a classical music channel, Chopin played in the background of the room's ambience; our meals, drinks, and entertainment completed for now.

"Gordon, I've got to tell you something, and it's quite serious."

"I have some serious things to tell you, too." replied I.

"Well, who goes first?" she asked.

Without hesitation I said, "Women first. You go ahead sweetheart."

"Gordon, I love you. Remember that fact above all else."

"Wonderful, I said with a smile, I accept that divine fact,"

"Here it goes," she was in her serious business mode now. before flying to Tulsa last week I was offered a job and accepted it within a day. It was a job I had interviewed for and wanted. It means a lot of extra work, but a bigger salary, company car, more perks than I imagined, and, she hesitated . . . the office is in Houston."

"Houston?" I droned.

"Yes, dear Gordon, my office would be in Houston."

"And naturally, your Tulsa office would also be utilized?" I asked.

"No sweets, just Houston. I'd be living in Texas."

With those words my feelings exploded. "What do you mean you'd be living in Texas? We're getting married. How in the heck are you going to live there, with me in Tulsa? Or did you lineup a job for me at a University or the Space Center? How can you already have accepted this position without running it by me?

I shook my head and felt angry. I also felt betrayed and left out, though I only realized those feelings later. Now I just felt angry and sad.

"Why live in Texas, why not Tulsa? I asked.

"Sweetheart, this position needed to be filled quickly. My supervisor accepted the European opening and I'm filling his shoes. He went to 'bat for me.' I couldn't say no, I just couldn't. I felt responsible to take over."

"What are we to do, live 500 miles apart and fake it? How are we going to share our lives if we rarely see one another?"

"I've thought it through. We could see each other every weekend at first, then go to an every other weekend pattern."

"Are we to live in an every other weekend pattern? We're talking about our marriage, not a prisoner pass program," I emphatically stated.

"Diana, what kind of talk is this from my future wife?"

"I'm angry, Gordon. Think about my career for once. You seem to forget that I work too. Why should my career be placed in limbo for your sake? Besides, you're independently working anyway. You could move to Houston and do what you're doing here, down there. Besides, I make more money and my employer gives me a great income, benefits, and a way up the success ladder. You're living on your uncle's inheritance and grant money. Why can't you be flexible? Houston's a great town. The weather is warm all year, and it has major universities. For heaven's sake, get a real job. I'm tired of your fantasy world of gadgets and machines that look like washers and dryers and microwaves."

"Diana, I ask your respect for my work. It's important."

"Important for what purpose?" then she backed down.

A moment lapsed; I continued speaking, "All right, your work is important. I love you and believe in you. However, I want a true married life, not a virtual one."

She replied in a low tone, "Love is the first thing to suffer in a bad marriage, just ask my divorced girlfriends."

"I don't need to talk with your friends. I need you to live in Tulsa with your husband."

"But Gordon, why couldn't you move there with me? What is keeping you here? Your parents don't live here, mine do. I have many relatives here, a sister in Broken Arrow, and a brother teaching in Stillwater. Looks like I'm making the sacrifice, not you."

She had a good point, why was I opposed to moving?

"Diana, your news hits me like a pitcher of cold water. How in the heck does a guy respond, if not with anger?"

"Acceptance would have been nicer, sympathy and understanding too," she said flatly.

"Sympathy?"

"I meant empathy. Don't confuse me with facts. Just think about it Gordon," she said turning to me and touching my arm. "This is our chance to succeed. Besides, Blithe Petroleum might use your inventions some day. I bet we could get you into research. Those gentlemen have it made, no regular hours, work at home if they like, and have a corporate PC of their choice. Then when I go overseas, you could travel with me and see all the sights, sharing time in Europe, South America, and the Caribbean, Would it not be heavenly to be together on my journeys overseas? Can you honestly tell me you wouldn't enjoy these adventures with your corporate wife?"

"Diana, slow down. I'm wearing out from all this talk of travel, and yes, it excites me immeasurable."

Then for a few moments, silence prevailed. Then we returned to eating the dessert purchased, but never touched until now. She complimented the meal, which always made me feel appreciated.

"You're welcome, anytime; only the best of everything for my Diana."

We winked at each other and embraced. We had both gone through the ringer of emotions and needed to quiet down. We polished off two liters of Perrier water, one apiece and consumed the fortune cookies too.

We kissed for awhile as the movie was set on rewind. As the rewind was completed, I immediately jumped up to set the next movie in place. Diana was displeased at my sudden jolt from our embrace.

"Gordon, must you be so compulsive, the movie can wait!" She sounded exasperated and I apologized and agreed with her, I was frequently impulsive and compulsive as well.

It was exasperating to her as it was to me. In one sense, these human flaws made us both victims to the unconscious realms of our minds. I did not enjoy being a victim, nor did I appreciate the thought of victimhood. Neither did Diana appreciate being victimized, especially by those who loved her. It seemed too easy to cry, "Victimized" in any situation. Doing so made me feel uncomfortable, and too vulnerable.

She leaned back into the couch. "All right, what's next?"

"I have *The Quiet Man;; Casablanca, Chariots of Fire; How to Marry a Millionaire; Now, Voyager; Harvey,* and *Little Caesar.*

"At least you've offered nice choices," and she laughed. "It's hard to stay angry with you. You're so cute in your own dysfunctional ways."

"I'll take that statement as a semi-compliment, nothing more and nothing less, now name your choice."

"How about, *'Gone with the Wind?'"

"It was checked out." I stated.

She laughed at my response; she knew well that movie had not been rented; yet had been discussed.

"Then put in Bogie's movie.

"Yes, the great film noir, here it goes."

Later we munched popcorn after an hour of watching this film. She enjoyed making popcorn in the microwave oven. And enjoyed real melted butter poured over the popped kernels, not margarine or synthetic "butter." Besides, her metabolism effortlessly consumed calories.

"It's late," I finally stated.

"Yes, I know. However, I'd prefer to lie next to you and forget the morrow. Besides, this ambience is too romantic, she said, except for your objection to moving to Houston; must you be so practical? Besides, men act romantic for only a short time during marriage."

"And how does Diana know all these things about men?"

"I have enough married girlfriends who keep me posted. They keep telling me that once a guy has been to the altar, romance starts to die faster than a speeding bullet. What was once a relationship that found the male species with his hands all over his fiancée, after marriage he heads to the couch, burps, reads the paper, watches television, while his beloved is washing dishes and cleaning bathrooms. His needs have been met with a hot meal, and now he must relax, thus taking his wife for granted."

"Diana, we won't let the fires die out, we're too much in love."

"Do you have any idea how many men feed that line to their future brides?"

"No, how many men feed that line to you women?"

"All of them, dear, all men speak that lie."

"My dad didn't lie. When he was home he helped dry the dishes and place clothes in the washing machine. Later he and mom would fold the clothes while watching "Perry Mason," or "The Ed Sullivan Show," Sunday night. They'd even watch silly comedy programs, "Hogan's Heroes," or, in the '70s, "The Walton's," a delightful remembrance of their youth. They made time to be together and get some minor housework completed as a team. But we are not like 'all of them.' You and I are unique creations of God. No one has ever lived or will ever live, that's the same as either one of us. God's on our side. He provided us, His creation, with love and marriage. Marriage is a sacrament in our church; it isn't a mere contract or legal action. Marriage is to be raised to a new level of social community between man and woman. God invented marriage as a gift, and as His gift, it becomes a holy gift," stated I.

"Have you been reading St Thomas Aquinas or St. Aqua fina? You're sounding very theological," she stated sarcastically.

"Mocking our Catholic heritage, now that's a new low for you."

"Well, she said, theological and logical were sounding too similar, and I am not logical when it comes to marriage. I'm rather passionate on the subject of married love and all that other stuff."

"All that other stuff, it sounds part joke and part exasperation. Am I right?" I asked.

"Just a little, I was joking when I said St. Aquafina. Yet I understood your point. Besides, I'm the one who attended Catholic schools, not you. So who's more informed?" she stated.

I just had to laugh, saying to myself, "She'll always get in the last word and I loved it, It was pure Diana, or was it pure woman? It mattered not. Diana was "pure" versus concentrate. She was not a second-class orange juice, but squeezed, no pun intended, by that educated mind she was born with and used well." The mere thought of my unspoken words made me smile, like dad's smile in his WW II pictures, or mom's smile when my siblings and I were babies. Such smiles are worth a million dollars to this golden heart of mine. Diana's heart was platinum, more precious and elegant than I had ever known. Yet perhaps platinum sounded too metallic. If her heart was not platinum, it was pure crystal diamond. Yes, that image of crystal pleased my imagination more than platinum.

"However, once married we're wide open to His blessing of enjoying the acts of married love."

She rolled her eyes, and then allowed me to change the subject to my upcoming goal and invention and discovery.

"Though it's late let me tell you what's on my mind, then I'll drive you home. I've invented something that will knock your socks off."

She responded in pure Diana-like fashion, "Why are you trying to knock my socks off?"

"It's just a phrase dear, just a phrase, probably from the 1940s."

"Well don't leave me barefoot on this chilly floor."

"What did I say that was misunderstood?" I asked.

"The sock reference," she stated bluntly.

"All right, let's start over. Gordon, she said, some days it seems everything you say is misunderstood by me, Is it the male mind versus the female mind? If so, I'll always win our arguments,"

I responded with, "Let compromise. I'm misunderstood about 90%; with the other 10% questionable. Correct?"

"Gordon, how gentlemanly of you, you're accepting the fact women are superior in matters of the heart . . . . and mind!"

"Yes dear, because I loved my mom very much. Without her, dad and my siblings would have been lost. I do accept the trend believing women superior to men in many ways, but not in all ways! To say so would ruin my self-esteem as a man. Let me add, in respect to my belief in a moral engagement, am I right? I believe so; that we're doing the right thing. God will bless our lives now and later because we're obeying His commandments."

She sighed. "Well, to be on God's side is good. I always went to Mass with mom and dad. I even wanted to be an altar girl, but they didn't allow them in the 60s when I was growing up."

Then she gave me time to speak, "All right now, what's this big invention you've come up with? Is it for the oil and gas business? Is it an improvement on the camera or a new type of medicine? Is it a motor that runs on natural gas? Or have you developed a foolproof cure for the rhinovirus?" At this pronouncement she burst out laughing. She made me laugh too.

"Diana, you're a joker. Jack Nicholson could take lessons from you."

"Well, that's nothing; Henry Kissinger could take 'seriousness' lessons from you, you Siberian tiger."

"Siberian tiger where'd that nickname come from?"

"My calendar you gave me last Christmas from World Wildlife Fund. Each month has pictures of animals, one is the Siberian tiger. He's the largest of the big cats."

"And I suppose he's a cool cat at that?"

"Real cool, baby, real cool!"

"You're fun when you're ornery. Will marriage be this much fun?"

"I hope so Gordon, I'm easily bored and I do not want to be bored in marriage."

"Were you bored in your work? I asked.

"A little, I needed a new challenge and it sounds like you do too. Yet go ahead and tell me what you've invented, before I fall asleep on your couch."

"Diana, for a few years Ross and I have been developing the means to time travel. There, I said it." Her eyes opened wide in disbelief, and before she was ready to speak I placed my index finger to her lips. "Let me finish. The idea has been with me since childhood. Yet my idea differs from the fiction of H. G. Wells. My travel is not time past or time future, but time present. Not time present here on earth, that doesn't interest me. What does interest me is the ability to travel in our galaxy, in what might be called a time warp. The phrase is not new. I'm not saying it is. However, the means to tap into the channel of time's warp, or more accurately, time's flow, like a river, had eluded humanity, until now. Diana, I and Ross have invented a process that allowed two hamsters to time travel and return later, safe-and-sound. Now the opportunity has arrived to place a human into the time channel and explore, for about four weeks, and return safely. Time channels have various cycles that move by us and touch earth. I'm calling the Cycles symbolically as A, B, C; all the way through the entire alphabet. We realized five cycles at present. These are consistent and on time, no pun intended."

"And who is this lucky person going to be, Ross?"

"No Diana, I'm the fortunate son."

She looked at me with shock. She had really expected me to say Ross.

"Yours truly, Gordon James Paradise, future bridegroom, scientist, dreamer, poet, 'Sir Isaac Newton,' son of my parents, I'm the one traveling."

"Gordon this idea is crazy, you can't leave. We're getting married. How could you possibly think I'd let you go off on this bizarre, untested trip to . . . . nowhere, for lack of a better word. No way Jose, are you leaving Diana Fleming, the woman of your life. You are not making me a widow before we get to the altar. Certainly God, your parents and everyone else who loves you would agree?"

"Diana, I understand your opposition, it's a wild concept. But so was taking a monoplane across the Atlantic, or a small space vehicle to the moon. Yes, danger is involved. However, I'm not going just anywhere, or 'nowhere' as you referred to it. Rather the computer programming takes living beings and lines them up with hospitable places. Diana, don't you see, I'd be exploring our Milky Way. I'd be the first human to travel beyond the solar system. Actually I'd be able to walk upon distant planets, if their environment's allow it. All that matters is a nitrogen-oxygen atmosphere. The rest will take care of itself."

"How about food, shelter, and warmth, how do you supply these essentials?"

"I have that mapped out. Don't worry. Food would be lean, but so what? I need to lose fifteen pounds anyway. I have high carbohydrate and protein bars I'd be taking along."

"How about water, milk and going to the restroom?"

"I'll be taking water with me. Since I'll be automatically placed in a safe living area for humans, water will be there for the taking. However, I'll take purifying tablets just in case. I also have a food and water tester created by Ross. This devise will allow quick assessment of the edible foods on another planet. Think of it Diana, another planet. What more could a scientist ask?"

"That answer's easy, a beautiful wife, a wonderful home, money in the bank, and good health. You'll have all those things as soon as we get through the ceremony."

"Diana, I understand your feelings. It is scary to consider the danger of this time travel. However now is the perfect time to depart. Cycle A is nearing and we weren't planning anything in the next month anyway.

"Fine," she said in a disgusted tone, may you and your blasted machines enjoy one another." She then exclaimed again, after a pause, "You're not making me a widow before we make it to the altar!"

She started to get up when I reached to pull her back down beside me. I held her close and went to kiss her, she turned her face away. That sense of rejection hurt me, but I didn't yield to anger. With God's grace, I responded with compassion. We had both been through a lot this evening and our conversations had been extremely draining. We both felt tired and looked the part.

"Shall I drive you home, its late." said I.

"Yes, please do. I'm exhausted," she said.

"Darling, said I, let me use the restroom and I'll be right back." In a few minutes I returned to find her fast asleep on the couch. It was an easy decision to leave her sleeping. I went to her hall closet and took out a spare blanket. I smiled and placed the blue blanket over her. She used a couch pillow for her head and was sound asleep. The couch, like mine on the back porch, had been previously owned by grandparents.

Cleaning up and beautifying after an early awakening, with a juice smoothie of blueberries and organic yogurt for breakfast, I drove her to her workplace.

"Let's continue our conversation tonight, all right? she asked.

I nodded yes and told her I'd pick her up around 5:30.

The day passed quickly for both of us. As I drove her home, again with a meal just picked up to consume at her condo, I asked her how her day went.

No response. However, she immediately picked up from last night's conversation as if the day had been mere illusion.

"Tell me," she said, "what you told me last night is a hoax and that you're not traveling to galactic playgrounds."

"Diana, I can no more tell you that than you can tell me that you haven't taken a job in Houston."

"For two people in love we sure know how to keep separate," she said in exasperation,

That phrase went through me like an arrow. It seemed too true.

"Diana, is there any possibility of compromise?"

"On whose part Gordon, mine?"

"No, both of us need to think on this matter."

She shook her head. "Gordon, I've already decided I'm working in Houston. I had hoped you'd move with me, or at least live a long distance-commuter marriage. Movie stars have such marriages. We're as good as they are, don't you think?"

"It's not a matter of being good enough; it's a matter of marital togetherness. I suppose moving to Houston might be a possibility for me, it just caught me off guard. I felt a truck hit had run me over, a Blithe Petroleum truck, with a woman driver. Yet having survived, I realized an attitude modification was in order, one to please the driver; naturally, the driver was you!"

"I was hoping to hear you say you'd move," she said smiling, and reached out to touch my hand.

Then she switched the conversation to me, an act I appreciated, and said so with a kiss, which she liked, as did I.

"When is your time zone going to be ready?"

"You mean Cycle A?"

"Yes, Cycle A."

"In a few days I'm departing."

"You're leaving so soon?" she fearfully stated

"Yes, too soon for you, I sense, but not for me. I'm ready."

"Pardon me while I have a coronary. It's pretty sudden timing and I don't like it one bit."

"Yes," I nodded.

"No, more than that, it's sudden for us as a couple. You keep forgetting that fact. When did you think about us getting back together? How do we communicate with one another in that thirty day span?"

"One month is the first answer, and the second answer is Ross will handle communication. Just rely on him, that's all I ask, thirty days and rely on Ross."

"No Gordon, I meant going with you in spirit, in worry, fear and emotionally being all tied up while you're out there in cosmic Disneyland."

"Cosmic Disneyland, that's choice."

"Stop it would you? I'm trying to get my feelings out here on the table and don't care for your wise remarks." said she.

"Go ahead," I said.

"I don't know what to feel but fear. I'd feel the same way if you had decided to shoot the rapids in the Grand Canyon or had taken up skydiving over Mexico. Can you honestly tell me that you're not afraid? Can you sit there and say that going to galactic planets way out there in the universe doesn't scare the Hades out of you?"

"Yes it does concern me," I stated bluntly

"Concern you? How safe Gordon for you to say it."

"All right, I'll restate it. I'm scared, I'm anxious. But I'm excited too. Columbus I'm sure felt the same way. So did Shepard and Glenn before they rode their Atlas rockets into our history books. So did Armstrong, Collins and Aldrin feel the same way, or so I'm surmising?"

"But you're not those people, she exclaimed. You're Gordon Paradise, not an astronaut or a navigator. So you get my point?"

"You're saying I'm not qualified?"

"You're not a geologist or an astronomer. And you're not a wilderness survivor-type, are you?"

"No dear, I am not. You bring up some good points."

"Yes, I sure do. What I'm saying is send someone qualified. Send someone safer . . . ."

I cut in to complete the sentence, "You mean someone you're not getting married to; someone who can take the risk for my experiment?"

"I guess I am saying that very thing. Someone who can take the risk other than you, would be my choice."

"Diana, don't you sense a parallel here between the job you've just accepted and the position I'm taking for myself?"

"No, I don't."

"Diana it's simple. We both chose a job that we believed in, and one we feel no one else can do as well."

She sighed heavily. "Come on, Gordon, others can do my job, or your job."

"But not as well as I can do it, Diana. I have the motivation, the 'feel' for the challenge ahead. Tell me that statement is not true?"

"Yes, I suppose it is true. I feel I'm best qualified, as well being motivated and excited for this Houston position. By the way, it's a heck of a lot safer than your job, and has better benefits." Diana spoke loudly.

"Diana, my benefits may assist humanity in some way. I might be introduced to new medicines that could help us here on earth."

"Or you might open the way for one big war with aliens and earthlings." she exclaimed.

"Don't be a pessimist, think positively. It's not like you to think negatively."

"No, but my fiancé hasn't been putting his life on the line in our conversations like he is now."

"Diana, let's talk more tomorrow. How about sandwiches outdoors at Woodard Park?

She accepted my picnic invitation and I drove her home as we listened to soft instrumental music on the radio; it relaxed us. Then we departed and waited tomorrow's time together.

The next day, with our meal prepared, we ate on the grounds of Woodward Park. We sat amid its trees and flowers, as we enjoyed our lunch in the shade of a sunny Tulsa Park. Such perfect days, truly these are the times we lived for and remember all our lives.

"I wonder what Ross is doing?" she asked.

"He's at the lab," I said.

"How do you know?"

"We passed him ten minutes ago, didn't you recognize his truck?"

"No, and you did I suppose? How could you be so observant when you're with me?"

"I make it my business to notice what's around me. If I don't, I'll miss something. A scientist is always on the lookout."

"Well, I'm on the lookout too, for a great looking guy with a keen intellect and a handle on life."

"You found him, Goldie, that's me."

"Goldie, you haven't called me that nickname in months."

"Do you still like it?"

"No, I still dislike it. It was my nickname with my first high school sweetheart."

"You hadn't told me before."

"It doesn't bring back pleasant memories."

"I'm sorry, what happened?"

She hesitated a few minutes, then proceeded to speak. "The young man was socially rude to me while at the drive-in theatre on Admiral Drive."

"Diana, I'm sorry, I had no idea."

"I took care of myself, but feared his intentions. My parents pressed charges and the boy was returned humiliated to Paris, and never graduated. At least that's what I heard."

"May I ask who he was and his name?"

"You may not."

"I respect your privacy."

She hesitated a moment, and then said, "He was a foreign exchange student."

"You just told me to mind my own business."

"I'm still not telling you his name, but he was French. Though a good student, his interests soon turned from mathematics and chemistry to human biology, and mistreating American teenage girls. Yet I admire the French and speak the language fluently. I admire their artists, their writers, and sculptors, like Rodin and Bayre. Do not Cezanne, Monet and Seurat thrill me? How can I hold a grudge against a nation for one person's actions? Besides, when my dad landed in Normandy in June '44, the French underground saved his life."

"It was a traumatic experience for you and I'm deeply saddened by his rudeness toward you." I seriously stated.

"This young 'gentleman' failed to use me, and wound up a discredit to AFS."

"Such was life in middle America in the 60s." said I.

"Life was hell in the 60s, Gordon; at least it seemed so to me."

"Because of one bad experience you've condemned the entire decade?"

She hesitated again, in complete silence, and then began to relate more of her story,

"Gordon, I was naive in high school, but very well built, and apparently a 'turn-on' for the boys in school. My popularity as a 'looker' got me access to a lot of guys my last two years of school. However, I was always hit on, though I never encouraged their advances. It seems like every guy had only 'one thing' on his mind when he went out with me. It made my early experiences with men unimpressive. In fact, I still feel angry with those guys. I wasn't taken seriously. I was a good student and a member of the French Club, band, and girls' basketball team. But the guys tried to use me as their little toy. Finally I gave up and refused offers. My last six months of school were lonely. My girl friends abandoned me, mom and dad were busy with their work, and I felt alone and used. I cried a lot, ate poorly, lost fifteen pounds in a month, and felt suicidal."

"Diana, I had no idea you had such difficult times as a teen. Did you seek help?"

"No, I did not; I tried to put on a happy face and must have succeeded. No one knew I was down in the dumps, depressed actually. It seemed every guy had misguided intentions when he went out with me socially. Why are young men, or men of any age, so rude to women?"

"Diana, I can explain their behavior. They're not gifted with a gentlemen's mind, let alone a gentlemen's judgment. A young man learns from his dad's example. If his dad is a cad, so will his son act the same."

"You're saying it's all learned by their dad's actions and attitudes? That sounds too easy, Gordon," she exclaimed.

"It's not easy at all. All action is based in the mind's hidden recesses. The unseen bubbles upwards into consciousness, and what was once hidden becomes conscious behavior, either good or bad is chosen."

"Gordon, you're driving me mad with your theology and psychology."

"It's due to my analytical nature, remember, we discussed personality's four modes, analytical, driver, amiable, and expressive? It derives from a book, one I can't recall by name, but it's certainly not my work. Some brilliant person listed these four personality modes and showed that each of us has two main aspects of personality, say driver-expressive; yet we are all variations of the four major traits."

"Then what am I dear man in this combination?"

"You're driver-expressive, with amiable and analytical qualities in smaller measurements. Instead of a gallon of analytical, maybe you're just a few quarts. Yet for driver-expressive, you're gallons of each. In this manner you behave as God made you, nothing more; nothing less."

"Driver? Yes, I'll accept that description. I'm driven to succeed. But expressive, does that denote I talk constantly? Be careful how you reply."

"Actually, in retrospect, you're equally expressive and driver,"

"So you're saying amiable is the least of my personality?

"No, you're very amiable. Yet in a business setting, you're driven and expressive, with Amiable being present, though less seen by others. In other words, you'd rather have power and expression, rather than being seen as amiable and analytical,"

"Gordon, don't analyze me. Analyze someone else, like yourself or Ross. Besides, when did you become a Psych major?"

"I wasn't. I read books and went to personality seminars, and, went through several years of counseling."

"Why, are you nuts?"

"Yes, nuts about you!"

"You should date a squirrel then, not me," she stated sarcastically.

"Darling, in our differences we compensate for each other. In your plusses you assist my negatives, and vice versa."

"So we're attracted to each other because we're so different?" she asked.

"We're not so different; yet we're not cut from the same pattern. That reason alone is enough to rejoice in our lives. Besides, let me ask what women would wear the same outfit or dress two days in a row?"

"None," she said.

"That's right. Our differences are suitable enough to showcase something new every day. Our personalities unite us. In no way do we diminish the other, we compliment each other as purple does to yellow. It's an artistic expression, so to speak.

"So you're saying we are just works of art, not people?"

"Absolutely not Miss Fleming, I would never say such a thing,"

She burst out laughing having put me through the blender, with sliced apples, peaches, plums, and orange juice. I was just a composite of fresh fruit reduced to a health drink.

She ceased laughing and paused for minutes with a most serious look on her face. I failed to understand the sudden change of heart. Then I realized she was still traumatized by what she had told me earlier about the

AFS student and his antics. I felt stunned and pained by her pain. Only after several minutes of silence did she say anything again.

"Gordon, I can't believe I told you all this junk. And that's what it is, self-pity junk."

"It is not junk. You're relating your feelings and that's always acceptable. I did not sense self-pity; in fact you relayed the whole story without much anger."

"I still feel anger, believe me, I do. But I'm afraid to let the anger out. In fact, this whole thing surfaced because I feel pretty mad at you right now for planning to leave me on some bizarre, weird trip among the stars. Come on, Paradise, who do you think you are? How can you sit there and say you plan to time travel? The whole idea is absurd, it has never been done, and you're saying you and Ross have made it possible?"

"Yes Diana, we have made it possible. Why God chose me over someone else I don't know. Why did Bell invent the phone, or Edison the light bulb? God chose them to accomplish His goal. Besides Diana, you're not the only angry party here today. You chose to accept a job five hundred miles away without consulting me."

"You didn't consult me either, Paradise."

When she was angry, really angry, she called me by my last name.

"I think we need to call a truce. It's been an emotional afternoon. We've been at each other since lunch. We haven't laughed much at all, that's unusual for us. We kid around and cut up a lot. We're a comedy club for two when we get on a roll." I said.

That last sentence made her smile and I immediately felt better.

We parted with an emotional kiss. Then spoke not as we drove, yet held hands. Sometimes silence acts as a healing medicine.

I retuned her to work just in time, we'd been gone two hours, and she disliked being late for anything, especially work. She would finish her day's work with renewed vigor, at least, that was the sense conveyed when we departed. Kisses do not lie, they always tell the truth, as do our eyes. I sensed only veracity in her kiss, and the look in her eyes; they each expressed subconscious confirmations.

We did not see each other for 17 hours. At that point I was either leaving immediately or postponing for several months. The shortest time cycle, for weeks, would not occur again for awhile. Diana called me first and it was probably best. We both needed space, no pun intended. Her words surprised me.

"Gordon, how's my man?"

"Hello dear, I'm fine, missing you though."

"I'm missing you too, you galactic Galahad."

"Now that's a new nickname."

"I just thought it up too. In fact, it actually came to me in a dream. Last night all I did was dream about you on a star, and I kept talking in my sleep to warn you of dangers. But you told me not to worry; yet my dream said over and over 'danger,' however, you ignored my plea."

"Diana, I'm sorry. It sounds like you were frightened with my travel plans?"

"Yes, but I've decided that decision-making based on dreams is pagan. You have my permission to time travel. All I ask is that after marriage you give up privileges on the timeshare in space and let others do it for you. Is it a deal?"

I accepted immediately. "Deal," said I.

We were pleased and happy. She made humorous remarks about time travel that had us both laughing. I made equally humorous remarks about Texas and Houston that made her laugh until she could barely breathe. The whole incident was a release of the pent-up tension from days before. She invited me over for a cookout, just the two of us. However, upon arriving, she had Ross present, his girlfriend; several of her friends, and Dr. Lanier and his wife.

We ate hot dogs, hamburgers, pop, beer, chips, potato salad from Rib Crib, and had a great time. Later, toward midnight, we toasted marshmallows over the fire. Such was the depth of our sophistication; such was the innocence of our lives. Ross was pretty tight by midnight but kept from answering or speaking in four letter words only. He started rambling about lasers and fat cells, and cities of the future. He always divulged his ideas when loosened by alcohol. After lasers he began saying that roads in the future would be able to melt snow and ice by means of electric cables placed within the asphalt. It caught my attention. Even when drunk he was a genius. Never take a genius as a fool. His or her words are years or decades ahead of many.

By midnight I realized this gathering was a sendoff for me. Though only a few knew I was leaving, my dense mind had not caught on to Diana's whole object of the evening. When all departed by 2 a.m., we kissed the rest of the night away. Then we went for breakfast at a pancake restaurant on 15th Street. Rarely did we venture below 21st Street, and I had no good reason to explain this territorial feeling; this limiting of myself to my own little world. And little it was to both of us; yet it felt comfortable.

Basically, humans act solely on feelings of comfort or pain. Both reasons defined human activity; it was a realization cherished. Why? Simple, self knowledge provides power. Then again, the power, when used, was it positive or negative in effect? Power does not always imply positive feelings or results.

"Gordon, I read recently that food is a substitute for emotional intimacy and commitment."

"Strange, I said, I read excessive talking was a substitute for emotional intimacy and commitment. Would you agree dear that maybe we're both right, at least a little? Yet I prefer basic descriptive phrases, like . . . ,"

She stopped me right in my word track. She was afraid I was going to use profanity, however, that only proved she truly didn't know me yet, at least not fully.

Diana looked intently at me as if reading my mind, then spoke an interesting and serious question. "Gordon, do men and women ever truly know one another?

Her intuition was on target. Then I thought a few moments before replying; then stated, "No dear, we can only partially know one another. It takes time to fully know a person, or at least 85 to 90% of our beloved."

"You analytical robot, putting numbers to whether a man and woman can know one another!" she spoke in a frustrating voice.

"Diana, if I'm a robot, I'm the nicest one you'll ever know."

No facial response whatsoever. Obviously my reply did not measure to her expectations. How true of communication between men and women, almost always a misunderstanding.

"Yes my dearest woman, I put numbers to everything, the nature of my work. Probabilities versus possibilities, that is life and I sincerely believe 95% to be quite accurate. Does that per cent bother you that much?"

"I was hoping to hear 99%. I already realize 100% is humanly impossible, even for those married 65 years, like my grandparents. My expectation was higher than your assessment, that's what generated my anger."

"Diana, do you realize what just occurred?"

"Yes, she said immediately, I feel we communicated our feelings without playing a guessing game. You spoke, and then I relayed my feelings, and backed up my feelings with the source, my grandparents, and my own expectation. We've just had an epiphany!"

Her excitement illuminated her face, already angelic in any light. So within minutes I refreshed my knowledge of women; the extremes of talking with women, sometimes you lose; sometimes you win.

"Yes my dear, we just had a communication breakthrough, not a breakdown. We just learned more of one another in the last few minutes, and we succeeded well, nearly 100%!"

She leaned over and hugged me and whispered in my ear, "You're not a robot; you're the kindest man I ever met. I love you Gordon Paradise. I can't imagine loving any other man." Her sincerity brought tears to my eyes.

"My dear Diana, we have just made emotional intimacy and commitment sweeter than it was just 30 minutes ago! We're talking without fighting or sarcasm. That's progress, pure human progress in our journey toward marriage, a better marriage."

We were immensely happy in our conversation and after awhile told her I had to depart and start packing. Now her eyes swelled with tears. I took out a clean kerchief and dabbed her eyes with a loving touch.

"Thank you dear, I was dreading this moment when I knew you were going to tell me you had to pack for your journey. Here I've just returned from world travel and unpacked, and you're leaving the planet and loading your mini suitcase. Life's ironic; would you agree with that premise?"

"Yes dear, it is ironic, and irony is a 'law' in the universe of human life. Animals don't comprehend irony, only we humans. I call irony, "Gordon's Law.""

"Oh, how convenient, naming a revelation after yourself. She then asked did Shakespeare have any kind words about life's irony."

"Yes, as I recall my lines in the play *Julius Caesar*, "Marcus Antonius: When that the poor have cried, Caesar hath wept; Ambition should be made of sterner stuff; Yet Brutus says he was ambitious, and Brutus is an honorable man.""

"Now remember, Brutus was part of the conspiracy to murder Caesar, hence, there exists the irony of the lines Marcus earlier speaks."

"My dear, what a memory you possess. You remembered your lines from a play in high school. Or was it college?"

"Both, actually, high school and college," I replied, with a dash of pride.

"I think I shall enjoy being married to such a brilliant man. A scientist, explorer, actor, poet, and an honest man, this describes you. Shall many women be as fortunate in love as I?"

"You're sounding Shakespearean, and I adore it!" Then Diana improvised saying, as if performing, "Shall we perform on yonder stage when my future husband doth arrive home from distant stars and galaxies?

Shall not our love be expanded by your journey, as to bring greater wisdom and love to our marriage chamber; our home? If indeed a castle is a home, then homes are made of stones; yet my heart doth not contain stone, just mere flesh and blood. Our stage then is alive, not dead with rock upon rock; life and love is people living for others, thus life becomes a constant well, never depleted of its refreshment; our lives exist as barriers to overcome, our smiles and open arms invite us, and open our mortal gates surrounding us unseen, except in our future lives. Yet if our lips and arms remain closed, no future exists; it's dead as stone upon stone."

"Diana, what great improvisation you own, and as natural as if William had written it four hundred years ago. I'm impressed!"

"You forgot I read all his plays and sonnets, and at such a tender age. Besides, corporate women need to improvise in their sales approach, and I just felt my creativity leap at your actual quotation of Shakespeare. It made it easier to improvise the Shakespearean English."

"No woman has your talent Diana, for you are truly one of a kind in this vast galaxy; who compares to you?"

She replied immediately and with laughter, "No one, simply no one!"

We held each other tight, and then I drove her home. She let me go, in more ways than one, and I drove off watching her in the rear view mirror, waving, I was Romeo to her Juliet; I refused to be the somber Hamlet to her as Ophelia.

Yet I knew too well the conclusion of, *"Romeo and Juliet."*

Ross was in the lab upon arrival. I started packing, then called him before commencing further.

"Dr. Stein, Newton here."

"Yes Newton, how goes it?"

"I just got in a few moments ago. Time to pack my things, as time is truly running out; by the way, how does it look for departure?"

"Fine, Gordon, looks excellent. The time cycle is smooth as an eggshell."

"That smooth?"

"Yes, tender too, just like mom's Thanksgiving meal, tender meat and smooth, creamy pumpkin pie."

"Are you sentimental today? That's certainly the first time you've described time cycles as tender. What's with these descriptive phrases? Writing your memoirs are you?"

He wasn't listening to me and went back to his computer. I hung up and mentally started "the packing" I had contemplated for years. I asked myself over and over, what would one take on a trip beyond earth? Though I had previously written a list, it felt incomplete. Then I asked myself, what food, clothes books, paper, and pens do I pack? What exactly does one man do on another planet not of this solar system? The thought still overwhelmed me, for I was actually going to land upon another sphere, not earth, not Mars; not the moon's hanging crescent in the morning sky. I was departing for a place never before seen by humans. To dwell on such thoughts was not productive. The mere fact of traveling to an unknown land was too powerful. I had to think of it as a normal trip, and not a milestone of human achievement. I had to reduce the size of my anxiety.

However, with anxiety reduced, I carefully followed my previously written list, and all was well. I would and could not allow temporary emotional fear control me. I had to control the beast of emotional uncertainty, or I would be opening myself to unconscious failure, and failure was not an option!

At that moment, I believed Freud to be totally accurate regarding the unconscious, how it hung suspended beneath the conscious self. It truly seemed as a proverbial iceberg image, with 90% submerged, unseen and unknown. Hence, the rational mind was truly connected to the irrational-unconscious mind, but it was too well hidden for the realization to be recognized. Indeed, human minds are composed of multiple dimensions, named by Freud as "id," "ego,", and finally, "super ego. For a moment I wondered if future psychologists and psychiatrists would name other mental dimensions unknown to us now. With science, anything is possible, but what of its probabilities?"

Chapter 11

My packing was complete and Ross was getting things ready for my departure.

"Gordon, it's close in time for you to leave; you better say goodbye to Diana and be done with it. You're leaving in the morning."

"He called me Gordon; rarely does he call me by my real name unless he's intensely serious. This travel thing is overwhelming Ross as well," I said to myself.

I called Diana and told her the time had arrived and I was to leave in the early hours of tomorrow. She started to cry. I did my best to comfort her. She expressed sadness and abandonment as her present feelings. I told her anxiety ran around inside of me like a caged tiger, ready to spring out any moment. Then I invited her to stay the night and witness my departure. She agreed.

Diana arrived after work and brought Olive Garden lasagna, jumbo salad and bread sticks as my departing repast. Ross and I were delighted. We both enjoyed pasta, as did Diana.

"Are you pleased with my dinner offerings?"

"You know I am, Diana. Thanks for being so thoughtful. We two were getting so involved in my leaving that taking care of dinner was not on our agenda."

"Absent-mined scientists at work," now that's a sign I need to have made and hung around your necks."

She was being sarcastically humorous despite her pain. That's all right; it's a way to express anger, not necessarily at me, but at the action taking place.

"Gordon, there's one change I want to relate to you," stated Ross.

"What's that, Ross?"

"When you're being translated, so to speak, into the time flow, you won't be plasma-like matter at all. You'll be encapsulated with an electromagnetic shell, and then placed into the time warp."

"Ross, I thought we had this matter clarified. Now you're telling me something entirely new. Where have I been that you didn't mention this matter to me earlier?"

"Gordon, wouldn't it be safer to be in a shell, like an egg, than to be transformed into an alternate energy state? Diana asked.

Ross answered, "Yes Diana, he would be safer, and that's how it's got to be done. Before I let you proceed, I'll read your mind and answered your question. You're wondering if the hamsters need to be retested with the 'shell mode' rather than the energy change mode. The answer is they're too similar to be concerned. Instead of the traveler changing, we change the space around the traveler. It's like being placed in a Gemini or Apollo spacecraft. It's protection. 'The shell,' as I call it, will be the cocoon of alternate energy. Then I slip the entire thing into the time flow, and then off you go into galactic darkness."

"I still feel scared to walk into an untried delivery system."

"I've run the numbers through the computer. Here, look for yourself. The data doesn't lie. It's still the same travel mode, just a variation."

"This variation won't kill me, will it?"

"Hey, I understand your fears, but I'd let myself go without hesitation. In fact, Gordon, you stay here and I'll take the risk. Besides, it's similar to a cab or bus, another one's always on the way. You can catch a later ride."

"I appreciate your confidence. Fortunately for you I have total trust in your judgment, or else I'd stop it for now."

"Gordon," Diana spoke up, "please be careful. Stop it for now and retest your equipment. It sounds dangerous."

Ross protested her lack of faith, and then proceeded to challenge Diana and me to review the computer information. If any data looked suspicious, then fine, halt the departure. Otherwise shush up and don't criticize his mathematics.

We all sat at the table and ate our meal. Afterwards we reviewed the data and I agreed all was fine. Diana felt better too.

"All right, we'll go," I said.

"Isn't that what Eisenhower said on D-Day? Besides, why are you speaking in plural? she asked.

"I do that frequently; I'm not sure why."

"Diana, did you hear me, really hear me? I said, "I'm going."

"Yes, I heard you, that's why I changed the subject to Eisenhower. It feels too hard to let you go. It's just too painful," she sighed, and tears came to her eyes.

I walked over and embraced her. We said nothing, just hugged. Ross continued to examine the data and said nothing.

"Have you finished packing?" she asked softly.

"Yes, I have."

"And there's no way that you'd let Ross go and you stay behind?"

"I'll let Ross go next time. This is my baby, my journey."

"Okay, I resign to let you leave. Just return as soon as possible," she said.

"That I shall do; when I return we shall marry."

She kissed me as those words left my lips.

Ross looked up and said, "Be ready to leave this evening, and not early morning. The time warp draws closer than originally indicated.

Diana did not cry but looked sad. Ross looked excited and I admit to feeling both sad and excited. My dream was coming true, and afterwards, marriage to my beautiful woman.

"What more could a man want?" I asked myself.

The hours drifted by like limbs in a clogged river, slowly. It was all relative. My wish to depart could barely be emotionally contained. My excitement was child-like, and thus I was once again a child in my heart; my thoughts.

As the time for departure approached, Ross had me recline in a chair between the Trans-17 equipment. From this chair an energy field would form its shell around me and transport me into the time warp.

Sitting in my chair, Ross began operating the instruments and a pale glow began to encircle me. As the moments passed, the glow intensified until it became fiery red and sparks like July 4th sparklers began to dance about me. As the fields of energy created the "shell," Ross explained to me, the visibility would diminish. I too concluded the same; however, his confirmation comforted me

The last thing I saw was Diana waving to me. The very next moment, sitting in this chair grounded by wires so as not to be electrocuted, I was transported out of my basement laboratory and into the time flow! I was there within my energy shell, moving toward the unknown; beamed into the darkness as a laser light into the night sky; transmitted by way of an outdoor satellite dish.

Ross and Diana held each other as they scurried upstairs to see an energy beam released into the star filled blackness.

Chapter 12

I was still conscious of who and what I was. I could not see earth below and the energy shell still glowed about me. Ross and I had discussed many times that the human or animal traveler might be rendered unconscious for all or part of the time. However, at present, this event had not occurred.

Further and further into space I traveled with the energy/time flow. My moment within time was happening with my dream unfolding, and I felt cheerful and at ease.

My intuition told me that time travel and light speed were not the same, that time travel within my shell, could surpass the speed of light, and thus, place me in much more distant locations that if I were merely traveling the speed of light. I had no conclusive proof; intuition is not proof. However, Ross and I had discussed this possibility, but knew not the probability. However, I believed my intuition to possess a veracity outside mathematical equations. In future journeys we would have to develop an spatial odometer to inform us of distances traveled, thus my intuitive theory would be proven correct or incorrect. However, never doubt the role of intuition, even in the spectrum of the sciences. Science did not make us less human, rather it enhanced our humanness. All aspects of knowledge enhance human understanding, or else we humans are made less perceptive than other mammals, and this I did not believe. We were the most perceptive of all mammals; however, always living in dignity with all mammals; all animals. We were the same, except we humans possessed a soul, though many humans argued this point. I refused to argue my faith; defend it yes, but arguing proved pointless. I've never witnessed an argument where the mind of either side of the discourse ever changed. Our pride; our egos, refused to conform with others we argued with, for indeed, if someone opposes us, they must be intellectually inferior. Though I knew such belief as untrue.

One might wonder about my air supply during this journey. It was provided for by the air trapped within the shell. Unique to Ross' revised travel mode, was the simple fact that the energy shell purified the CO_2 I expelled. I told you he thought of everything, even if I did not.

We also discovered the traveler's metabolism slowed. This event also occurred as one approached the speed of light. Have you ever read a book on Einstein's Relativity? At one point in the theory, Dr. Einstein stated that if two twins were separated, with one twin traveling near the speed of light, for fifty years. The twin in space, upon return, would have barely aged. Whereas the twin who remained behind on earth, would have become an elderly man or woman in time future.

Amazing, but true, though I say true, it's still theory; yet I truly believe this galactic journey will prove the theory, and thus become factual to physical science's reality. Yet my time away would not be fifty years, or fifty days. I would only be moments younger than prior to departure. It was not a cure for aging, though it could be in the future. For now it was an agent of travel, a ticketless ride.

Another question the curious might have is how and what did I pack and carry with me. How I packed is simple. I packed as little as I could in a backpack that may also be hand carried. These items were situated in my knapsack: two changes of clothes, pullover cap, a thin coat that has the ability to retain nearly all body heat (invented by Ross), a knife, a pistol with sufficient ammunition, food items (compacted protein/carbohydrate bars), water, water purifying tablets, notebook, pens, pain medicine, Imodium, tissue paper, a tent (one invented by Dr. Lanier that compacts to the size of a shoe box; yet when unfolded will hold two to three people, a few books (Holy Bible, Walden, Almanac), and a few photos of Diana and Duchess, a small camera, soil test kit, soil containers, anti-nausea capsules, Dolorphen #3, a prescription analgesic given to me by my Internist; a wrist watch, rope, compact telescope, compact microscope, and finally, my life meter. The life meter was designed by all three of us, with Lanier having most of the credit for this instrument I'm wearing. A patch the size of a half dollar was placed over my heart. It appeared as a nitroglycerin patch used by cardiac patients. However, a small antenna within it relayed my pulse, heartbeat, blood pressure, respiration rate, and temperature, to the folks back home. Here I'm floating in time, and not feeling my acceleration to a tremendous velocity. In this case, it proved similar to an airline flight.

Rarely was the plane's velocity actually felt, and my vital signs were being transmitted every thirty minutes, and hence, provided a sense of security.

The energy field remained a protective shell and it continued glowing like sparklers, and hummed like a vibrating reed. Far from being irritated by this sound, it lulled me to sleep. The sparkler effect amused me, or perhaps the acceleration finely placed me in a semiconscious state for what seemed like hours or days. My bodily functions slowed, no hunger came upon me, or a need to defecate or urinate. Yet this semi-consciousness gave way to total oblivion. My watch slowed to a near standstill, twenty-four hour periods on earth meant nothing here. I soon lost all consciousness of travel.

The next event was a rough landing accompanied with an abrupt awakening. Yes, I had finally been delivered upon land! I made it; excitement ran through me like fire and rushing water. My body rolled lengthwise, like a log, upon the surface of the new planet. When I stopped rolling I felt a bit dizzy and found it awkward to stand up. Yet I finally got my balance and looked about.

"What a hostile place," I said to myself. Then I looked up to the sky, a pale lemon yellow, and a color I've seen in some Van Gogh paintings. The land around me resembled the photos from Mars in 1976. Small stones scattered about with red soil stretched out in every direction. For a moment I entertained a belief I was on Mars, however I knew I was not. As previously mentioned, Trans-17 was designed to place the living traveler upon an earth-like surface. It sought a planet where air was similar to our earth's air. Without this control feature, the hamsters and I would be placed in hazardous environments. Though seemingly a lifeless place, I began to walk and soon noticed an outcrop of reddish hills before me and went directly toward them. Surely I would find something or someone of interest. Imagine "someone," what if I did come upon living beings? I was both elated and frightened, making me aware once again of the duality of human emotions.

The hills were large boulders, with cactus-like plants growing spontaneously; so yes, there was fauna on this planet. The rocks were red, like western Oklahoma rock, and sparsely situated grass grew amid the boulders. Sitting next to a rock I pulled out my water canteen and drank slowly. I also ate a food bar. These bars contained all the essential ingredients found in fruit, vegetables, protein, and carbohydrates, and powdered milk for dairy portion. Two such food bars daily provided me with enough nutrition to live on in good health. Both Ross and I had invented them, improving on protein bars already available.

Looking about I wondered where the sun for this place was hiding? Nowhere was it seen; yet I knew that a planet without sufficient solar light could not and would not sustain life.

Then I thought, "Perhaps life here doesn't need much light?"

My watch showed that only a few hours had passed since my departure. I knew it was incorrect. The date showed three days had passed, however, was it accurate? Unfortunately we had not devised a means to tell accurate time on this journey. Or perhaps the time could be transmitted by way of the message meter, something akin to a "beeper" that transmits and receives messages? This idea would prepare the next traveler with a greater sense of security. Or was Ross ahead of me with a device I was knowingly unaware? Such surprises are not his style, but possible!

I slept well the first night, being in a new place, a very new place! Regardless, I awoke feeling fine the first morning, and that feeling surprised me. The night had been cool but not cold. I did not set up my tent. I drank water and ate my food bar. Yes, a boring breakfast, but what do explorers expect, first class meals?

No real sun appeared in the sky, just the pale lemon color I had seen yesterday. I continued walking and within a few hours noticed more hills. These hills were grayish-red with streaks of purple, and the hills covered the entire horizon. Within a few hours I was walking upward among these hills, exploring the variety of plants, rocks, and soil they contained. I performed soil tests and discovered the similarity between earth and this planet, "the unknown place." I nearly named it "Camille" in reference to a young woman I knew in my late twenties. The desolation of this planet compared to her emotional bareness. If this place had been lush, full of life and a paradise like a Caribbean isle, 'Diana' would have been the name imposed upon it!

My exploration led to the discovery of caves. How I hoped to find cave art, pictographs from some living society who had passed this way. I found none; yet late in the afternoon, a few miles from my original climb, I came upon a cave dwelling apartment complex. Inside were bones, human in appearance, blackened circles where fires had burned, and pictographs on the wall. These markings appeared like calendars. I sat upon a rock inside this cave, the main cave, for I discovered other rooms. I reflected upon this place. Then I decided to look even more intently for other rooms and other caves where dwellers had lived. Searching these rooms was the most fun I'd had since leaving home. Inside each explorer is a child seeking something new, and loving every minute of the search. The child within was being recognized and treated to the ultimate fantasy, being beyond earth and seeking other life! I still felt overwhelmed and unbelieving that it was me, Gordon Paradise, on this trip, and not someone like Richard E. Byrd, Sir Edmund Hillary, Columbus or Magellan.

What seemed like a short time for me, soon found the day dissolving into night. The sky began appearing less opaque and I hoped to see the stars tonight. Did I say already that I missed the star show last eve? Well, I did miss seeing what this planet offered for its starry night display. The clouds of this place covered the night sky like a shroud. Tonight would be different. As darkness covered the planet, stars began to shine brilliantly above. Not thousands of stars like a clear night on earth, millions! Tonight the brightness became as intense as to appear as if the entire night were filled with full moons. Lunacy! Star-crazy wonderful, beautiful, frightening, majestic, fear inducing light! My excitement shivered with anxiety over such a powerful display. With such intense starlight overhead I accurately stated my galactic position to be within the spiral known as the Milky Way. On earth we are on the outer rim. Here it was entirely different. Only now did I realize how far from earth I really was, and felt lonely. However, a small antenna within my "life meter" was sending bio-readings to our lab in Tulsa County, with Ross and Diana knowing my existence confirmed, continued giving me a feeling of comfort. Peacefulness dwelled within; a prayer came to mind.

"Thank you Lord and Heavenly Father for my safe journey to this strange land; allow me to travel safely the entire time and may you bless this time. Allow me to witness your glory in my one man search for life beyond my home, planet earth."

I then read the opening paragraphs to Genesis, as the astronauts did on Christmas Eve, 1968. Afterwards I fell asleep beneath the glory of God's creation, with my knapsack as a pillow.

As morning dawned over the distant hills, I was startled awake by the sound of human crying! Fear raced through me like cold fire. On my feet in a moment, I grabbed my sack and cautiously walked amid the boulders and dirt piles at the base of these hills. Within a few minutes of following the lamenting sound, the sight of an elderly couple startled me. One lay on the ground prostate; the other, crying, kneeling beside him.

I came upon them quietly and startled the kneeler, an elderly woman. She shrieked and picked up a rock, ready to cast it my way in self-defense. I put up my hands and spoke softly, "I come peacefully. I wish only to help." Her reply was immediate and in English, or at least a language similar to English, as I understood her speech, surprisingly in its irony.

"Who are you? Are you a penal victim too?" she asked.

Confused at her knowledge of English I replied, "How do you know my language? I'm from Earth, light years away."

"Are you not Assidian?" she asked. I know nothing of . . . ."

"Assidian? No, I'm . . . ." She took to nursing her husband.

"Is he your . . . . ?

"Yes, we are married but he is dying."

"How long have you two been in this place?"

"Weeks, months, I don't know. We're exiles like you."

"Exiles?"

"Yes, from Assidia. Our ruler, Yannic, exiles all his enemies here. This is Xertran, penal colony #7. The rebel forces are trying to kill the other six of us survivors. Yet why am I telling you? My husband is dying, please help."

I knelt beside her and examined the elderly man. I felt his pulse, which was weak, and he appeared dehydrated. I placed my canteen to his lips. His wife wanted water too. I offered her a food bar as well, and she devoured it quickly. He consumed a few bites of nourishment, no more.

The food and water helped them both. He felt slightly better, and within a while she had more energy. She went on to tell me they had been exiled here with little food and water. I finally convinced her I was not Assidian, and for her to tell me what had happened. By this time, however, we found a cave and withdrew from the heat of the day. Inside the cave it felt cool; this coolness revived us all.

She spoke, "We were sent here as enemies of Yannic. We dared oppose his rule with others our age. He was in the process of killing off all the planet elders. He was obsessed with youth, the young are strong and can be easily manipulated. This is the craziness he believed. Actually the younger ones tried to assist us elders in disposing Yannic; many died. Others were sent to penal areas, like asteroids, and planets called Shiredome, Tammik, and this place, called Xertran. Xertran being one of the few left.

Yannic then destroyed the asteroids. Their decaying orbits brought them burning into the atmosphere, where they exploded to give him a visual thrill. He's wicked, that Yannic; cares only for himself. His goal is to satisfy his lust for women, power, and wealth."

As she spoke I heard an all too familiar story. It was the faces of tyrants projected on the screen of my mind, Mao, Stalin, Genghis Khan, and Napoleon. Even out here in the middle of our galaxy, history repeated itself. One thing did surprise me, her knowledge of my language. How can it be that we both speak a type of American English?

She quieted down and tended her husband who slept peacefully on the ground within this cave. As darkness descended she went outside and quickly gathered what appeared to be wood. She also found some round shaped things looking like grapefruit.

"Where did she find food?" I asked, seeing her begin to munch on this native fruit.

"Pardon me, dear friend, please have some wiggan, it's delicious!" I bit into this food and it tasted like bread and cheese!

She delighted in being able to provide something for me. We both ate wiggan and she had found some wiggan growing wild near the cave. She also began a fire and dozed off as both she and her spouse reclined next to the flames. Her means of starting this fire was from flint and granite, or what appeared to be these two rocks. I fell asleep; overhead the stars of Xertran glowed in their own fires.

The next morning I found her missing, probably searching for more wiggan. Whatever kept her happy was fine with me. I desired water to refill my canteen, and to wash. I however would wait for her return before venturing out.

Her husband's bulbous nose was laced with miniscule veins, and his hair was long and needed cutting,. He may have been a prizefighter in his day. He appeared muscular and built for heavy work. Yet his energy lapse made him appear rather pathetic. In his day he'd be helping others, I bet. Yet now he was at the will of others. She returned just as my hunger progressed with being awake. We greeted each other and she offered me more wiggan. I gladly accepted and leaned back against the cave while looking at her patting her husband's weary head. Her face was lined with wrinkles; yet her hands looked soft and delicate. Her gray hair was once neatly coiffed. Now it appeared chaotic. It doesn't take much duress to appear totally in disarray. Yet her devotional care gave her the angelic appearance of Mother Teresa.

Their clothes appeared well worn, dirty and of cotton-like fiber. Though their appearance seemed rough-hewn, their goodness and dignity radiated from their hands, their faces and eyes. Though his eyes were closed, I sensed peacefulness about him. They seemed like ideal grandparents, or folks who live down the road from you in the country and bring you eggs, corn-on-the-cob, and peaches from their orchard. Just thinking this made me homesick. I longed to see Diana and my home, especially when the morning light comes through the curtains and falls upon the carpet and walls, beaming through my collection of prisms causing sunlight to shimmer over entire rooms in rainbow colors.

I missed everyone. Just to see their faces and hear their voices would be pleasant again. Such is the life of the explorer.

After our repast I inquired as to a water supply she might know. She said to walk among the hills and look for the Keltac tree. Inside each tree is a water supply. My first question was, "What shape and appearance was this tree?"

Thereupon she found a twig and drew in the gritty sand of our cave, the shape of the tree. It looked like our cactus plants.

"Do you have any containers?" I asked.

"No, but beware of the Isis."

"What's an Isis?" I inquired.

"The Isis is an attacking lizard. Grabbing it by the tail renders it defenseless. Good meat for any meal."

Immediately I unsheathed my knife and went out to search for Keltac. Walking out of the cave I realized she had finally called me by name and that for some odd reason, I never had asked her name! Talk of social skills, I was unknowingly rude. I realized the years living years in the laboratory-science environment, and having little social integration outside the circle of Diana, Ross, and Lanier, caused my repeating adolescence social awkwardness.

The day's heat mounted. I sweated, I looked, I walked; I observed. My knife was in my right hand in case any lizards pounced upon me.

I walked and enjoyed myself, though thirsty and dirty. I needed a bath, but a shower was my preference. I approached a grove of trees and a outcrop of protruding rocks; hoping Keltac cacti would be growing among them. As I entered beneath the rocky formation, suddenly, a reptile two feet long fell upon me! Falling to the ground I struggled in a fight between man and reptile, but the antagonist clung tightly to me. I felt its teeth in the back of my neck. Never had an animal attacked me before with such ferocity. Yet an uncanny sense of déjà vu swept over my mind. While this thought flashed through my consciousness, I placed several calculated stabs into the beast. It screeched in horror!

"Good, I thought, I've injured it as it had me." Immediately I felt its claws loosen. Another stab and it fell off, however, not without another bite to my clavicle area. Blood dripped from my neck; yet I intended to kill my reptilian adversary. I sliced it head to toe, holding it upside down as suggested. As it died, I flung it upon a rock, and tore off my blood soaked shirt.

"Water, I need water!" I screamed in anger. Later I composed myself and prayed.

"Surely Lord, you are here with me, though I am far from home. Hear me my Savior, you who were scourged, know my pain. Please save me, Amen."

Within a moment an intuition, which was His immediate response to my plea, lead me through the rocky terrain until I came upon a pool of water. Delightful, this pool was fed by water trickling over rocks protruding from the very mountain our cave resided. I stripped and entered the water. It felt great and I washed my neck and shoulder. The lizard had bit deep. Did I need stitches? If I did I was not going to receive such medical attention, no physician here. Within a while the bleeding stopped, and I hung my washed items to dry. I also filled my canteen upstream and hoped for no more leaping Isis, not today or any day. As I filled my canteen I suddenly remembered that a German shepherd had bitten me as a child delivering a prescription to Mrs. Beckman. Sadly her dog was put to sleep. He had attacked his last victim. She bought another watchdog afterwards, and thereafter used another pharmacy. However, I began to feel unsteady and ill, while these thoughts sent ripples of memories, acting like waves upon a lake when a breeze blew.

Immediately I collapsed; the trauma had shocked me. I was unaware of anything for at least two hours, perhaps three.

When I came about, I drank enough water for two people and after resting, redressed myself and walked to the cave. Entering I saw the elderly woman smile. Then she realized I was bleeding and immediately assisted. As she examined my neck and shoulder I told her of the attack and my collapse. She motioned for me to recline next to her husband and rest. I soon fell asleep, again, overwhelmed by what had occurred just hours before. She placed an herbal poultice upon the wounds, one she intended for her husband. She also found a sewing kit among my garment bag, and sewed the largest gapping wound during my unconscious state, after the poultice had sat upon my wounds for hours.

When I awoke the next day I was silent for awhile, as she saw to the medical needs of her husband and me. It was then I asked her name; yet only after thanking her for her kindly assistance. She also told me of her surgical sewing, and I thanked her again, Her sewing my flesh together with thread and needle meant for cloth, had saved me from losing massive quantities of blood, thus saving my life.

"Augusta's my name; my husband's name is Hardius. I call him Hart."

She proceeded to tell me of their lives on Assidia and how Hart had been a builder for the rightful ruler, Octillion. His family ruled with peace and harmony for a century. Hart supervised Octillion's dreams, the construction of its museums, municipal buildings, and gardens for the last 40 years of Octillion's rule. However, a madman named Yannic led a small guerilla band, and killed Octillion, replacing Octillion's peaceful rule with tyranny. Regrettably the Assidians' did little to topple Yannic's rule. Only later did the Assidian "underground" attempt a failed coup; the survivors were exiled to penal colonies, such as this barren planet.

She continued, "There was a time when he populated the Assisdian moon with dissidents, and then exploded the moon for all to see below. It was a cruelty comparable to none other. Naturally Yannic denied responsibility and stated a meteor had exploded the spherical moon that hung overhead millions of years."

I sensed her sadness and despair and felt helpless to assist my elderly friends. I couldn't take them back to earth or transfer them to a safer planet. All I could do was assist them in the present moment. Besides, I too was ill.

She continued, "We are old people with no home or hope. Soon we will both die unless you know a means to keep us alive?"

I replied, "You've taken care of yourselves for this long, surely you can continue?"

"Yes, she said, we've survived. Yet we are weak and our time nearly gone. I ask you to bury us in the back of this cave and cover us with rocks to keep our corpses free from the Isis lizard. Will you do this for us if we're both deceased by the time you leave? The lizards are disgusting; they're scavengers of the desert. Isis lizards normally avoid caves; hence, our burial spot will be quite safe. However, why take a chance?"

Replying I asked, "Truly, you're not dying. There is enough food and water to survive for years. Please stay in the scriptural, 'land of the living.' I will assist in all manners to your lives here."

"You call this life, with this desert, this cave, and these threats of Isis lizards? You're young and do not understand. Besides, you're a new exile and have time on your side. Time has no use for us. Hartius is near death; I too am weaker than ever. And I fear your leaving us and abandoning us in our simple needs for survival."

"Augusta, I will stay here for you and Hart. I am a time traveler, no exile am I. Truly we must focus on survival. I shall remain with you, for we are friends and depend upon one another."

Replying she asked, "You will stay with us though we are not family?" She also asked the meaning of 'time traveler.'

I spoke and explained myself; then she reached for my arm and moistened it with her tears. I placed my arms around her to comfort us both. Yet she did not comprehend my explanation of time travel; besides, it meant nothing to Assidians'. And for the present time, it meant little to me. The meaning would return to me when circumstances improved.

Later I placed my hand on Hart's forehead to gauge temperature, his forehead was warming, and thus, not a good sign. I looked at all three of us from a position of imagining an outsider viewing us. We looked hopeless.

However, refusing the helpless feeling, I knelt and prayed, "Heavenly Father, we three, alone and hurting people, live by your grace. Please help us to survive and bear the burdens put forth upon us. Please protect us from death and injury. We commend ourselves to your care, for you are all we have, and in that knowledge, we have all your power and love we need to live, both now and eternally. I ask your blessings, in Our Lord's name, Amen."

With my prayer finished, I placed myself upon the ground and slept. Augusta and Hart were soon asleep too. The prayer lulled us to perfect peace.

Late the next morning I awoke, only to find Augusta placing her hand on Hart's forehead; then she felt his temple for a pulse; then felt his wrist for a pulse, none existed. He had died in his sleep.

"He is gone from us now," she said and looked at me and wept. I comforted her, embracing her in my arms. After an hour or two I told her I must gather some food and water for the day and that she needed time alone to assimilate the death of her husband.

Striking out I sought wiggin and water, two essentials for desert survival. I also thought it curious beyond words that Hart and Augusta were both Caucasians and spoke English. How was it happening? Had Ross' mechanism of locating similar cultures with similar languages really worked? Logic said yes, it worked well.

However, my neck hurt like hades and I prayed for God's protection. One Isis attack per lifetime was enough for any man or woman, within minutes of that prayer and thought, a five foot long lizard leapt from nearby boulders and lunged toward me. Its red eyes glared at me. Yet with knife in hand I hunched a bit and thrust the blade into the lizard's belly. The animal screamed in agony and I cut its belly from head to tail. Its purple blood dripped from my blade like paint from a paintbrush; its body fell to the ground.

In a moment I realized food. I now had meat for Augusta and me. As I dragged the lizard homeward I came upon a small pool of water. I filled my canteen and proceeded to the cave opening. Augusta was surprised by the carcass I dragged behind me and knew tonight's meal would be a good one. We soon prepared a fire and I sliced portions of lizard to be cooked to reptilian perfection. We ate well and I told her the story of the lizard's attack and his last moments of life. In his death was our survival. We drank water and we both mentioned the need to place Hart's body in the cave's depths, or the odor would be unbearable.

As another day awakened us, we placed Hart's corpse in the back of the cave and piled rocks all about him. We filled the open spaces between the rocks with sand. When completed, we were both exhausted from the strenuous work. Augusta barely said a word and fell asleep. I sat outside the cave for a few hours and entertained myself with the starry night before me. It was luminous and well beyond an Oklahoman night of star gazing.

The next morning I awoke and left Augusta to awaken at her chosen time. She did not awake. After a few more hours, I attempted to awaken her, and felt for a pulse. She too had died. The stress of Hart's death and burial, and the privations they both endured in exile, were too much. Now I prepared her burial, and placed her among the rocks and sand of Hart's grave. United in life; united in death; no longer exiles, they were in the Promised Land.

The next few days I continued to eat lizard and contemplate my future.

Near the cave opening, I came across a small box amid the rocky and deserted landscape, making a humming noise with flashing red lights. Apparently Ross had devised a means to communicate, through a radio transmission would have been preferred; however, we had not successfully completed the means of radio transmission due to the multiple frequencies of electronic wave patterns we had to deal with at this tremendous distance between us. However, he had devised, and quite successfully, a means to transport a boxed message to me utilizing my ionized trail as a pattern to follow me. Inside the box I found a texted note from Ross and Diana appearing as a pager-like device. Their message was a welcomed treat from home.

"Gordo, hopefully all is well. We are tracking you and your life functions.

Remember the patches I placed on you before departure? Your current status must be difficult. Readings show dehydration, and stress to the heart and lungs; yet, we are hopeful of keeping track of you with this device; please use it to relay messages to us here on earth. We sent it to you tracing your path. Your best friend, Ross."

Diana continued, "Dearest one, I miss you as a poet misses words, or an artist misses paint. I am just a woman and I miss you as a woman in love misses all she holds dear to her heart. Please return soon. Surely your trip has proven what you set forth to prove, time travel is possible.

Isn't it wonderful to receive this package from home? We retraced your journey and placed the box on the same course. Please my dearest, respond immediately, and tell us you've found our messages.

Tell me you love me, and that no place is better than earth. For here on earth, many love you, D."

I re-read their messages several times and began texting my return transmittal.

"Greetings Diana (my love), and Ross, I am well, and yes, I've just experienced intense challenges since arriving here.

I will enjoy being home in a few weeks. It's comforting to know you're monitoring my existence beyond earth. Thanks for sending this pager. I found it without a hitch.

Ross, your judgments regarding time travel continue to prove themselves. I'm pleased to be here, though I met two elderly friends, both exiles, who are now deceased.

I miss you both.

Diana, I live to love you, and appreciated your loving words.

Ross thanks for everything. It's time for me to move to the next location. Help me. Please relocate me to someplace new.

Keep the home fires burning, and I look forward to returning soon! Best Gordon."

I relayed my message without texting the truth; therefore, I reduced their fears, while feeling the agony of my recent reptilian attack. However, I could not generate anxiety to loved ones on earth. All my experiences could wait to be spoken until I arrived home, besides, what are a few weeks?

The next day I received a reply: "Gordo, great to hear from you. Get ready to rock-n-roll out of your present locale. I've sent new co-ordinates; Diana sends her love. Somewhere between the new co-ordinates and love, you can't expect more! We look forward to your quick return. Be prepared for media coverage of this event, we can't keep it quiet much longer . . . . you'll be famous! And I'll never run out of beer and you'll never leave Diana again. Prepare for departure, any day, any moment. Farewell R & D."

Not long afterwards, as the sun shone brightly in the desert before me, and my thirst had been quenched with local water, I felt a sudden weakness. Then a haze encircled me and I knew the warp was transforming my surroundings. The encircling energy wove a "oblong sphere" about me, and with a rapid motion, lifted me from my current position and I disappeared into a spatial darkness, one that placed me asleep for hours or days, I know not.

Oblivion was now my only companion.

Chapter 13

No communication was possible now. I was hurtling through time and space at unknown velocities. Within this electrically charged sphere I was in REM sleep dreaming of my hometown, Glen Iris, delivering prescriptions to the community. I dreamed of old neighbors and thoughts of high school. I remembered too those friends in college and high school who laughed and taunted me with my ideas of time travel, and here I was, accomplishing my life long dream. Those who laughed were at home watching television, drinking beer; living lives of "quiet desperation," with a whole host of modern maladies: obesity, anxiety, hypertension, depression, and chronic bronchitis. I was vindicated. Then at one point I dreamed of the lizard's attack, and how I responded the second time with deadly force. I dreamed too of Augusta and Hartius; my parents; and friends. Yet I dreamed mostly of Diana. Ross came to mind too. His brilliance had been instrumental, pun intended, in placing me in the time warp. Then too, the Lanier's came to mind, their belief in me when no one except Ross thought it possible to time travel. My memory of these dreams actually implied I was in a semi-conscious state of mind, for few dreams are remembered, unless awakened while they occur. Have not others realized the same about dreams? How few dreams are truly remembered, not many!

As these thoughts rambled in my mind, the energy sphere encircling me was dissipating and I found myself rolling upon a grassy field. I had landed again, a rough landing too, just like the first.

Standing, I surveyed my surroundings. It was a brilliant sunlit day, I noticed tall grass everywhere, growing upon undulating hills; clouds making their way casually across the sky in a whiteness similar to earth's clouds.

Then I realized, "This could be western New York or the tall grass prairie lands near Pawhuska."

It appeared earth-like in every way. However, it was neither New York nor Oklahoma.

Amid the grass I walked among its subtle colors of yellow, purple and red. Soon I came upon a grove of trees, a grove appearing as oaks with pine trees at the perimeter. Walking amid this forest appealed to me with its fragrance and coolness from the heat. As I walked, I walked quietly; there were few twigs to step upon or leaves to crunch. It appeared as a natural cathedral, trees like pillars, and cathedral arches of long branches stretching from one tree to another. My first thoughts were, "Ross did a good job placing me here, for I had tired quickly of the desolation of my previous landing, Xertran."

Indeed, this locale would inspire artists and composers. It inspired me to find such happiness in the distant landscapes of our galaxy. Looking up through the trees, the sunlight filtered by leaves projected random shadows upon the ground. The whole place reminded me of childhood days, living as deliberate as the sun, with no other purpose but to enjoy the moment. The day's agenda echoed simplicity. It's leisure pace appealed to me.

Yet my joy of the moment ended, as I suddenly fell into a large pit, surely a trap for an animal.

It was cleverly disguised and indistinguishable from the rest of the ground. Now I was the entrapped animal, for I knew a human intelligence had created this pit. The pit was deep, more than thrice my height. I dug holes into the sides of the carved pit and attempted my ascent. I thrust my fingers into the soil and attempted to climb in this fashion. The soil prevented gripping action. Progress proved minimal at best, and my attempts found me faltering and falling. Yes, gravity was present here on another planet. Newton was not forgotten in this corner of the galaxy, as the soil was clay-like and very slippery. Sadly, I was incapable of overcoming gravity's grip.

After awhile I rested and ate a snack and had some water, all the time analyzing how I was to escape this dungeon. Then I looked up and saw three youthful faces glaring at me from above. I surprised them as much as they surprised me. They appeared to be around seventeen or eighteen years of age, with dirty countenances, and all held bows and arrows. I was captured by a "Stone Age" clan of disheveled pagans. They grunted to one another as they discussed their captured game. In a few minutes they lowered a handmade rope and motioned me to tie it around my waist.

Doing so, they pulled me upward. Yet my beeper fell from my traveler's bag onto the ground below. I yelled at them to lower me back to retrieve my item; yet they ignored my pleas. Now I faced my captors, youthful misfits, little else described them verbally. As soon as they noticed my knife, they snapped it from my belt and I was motioned to place my hands above my head. I felt I should have taken them on, when several other "Lord of the Flies" characters appeared with lances, ready to kill me if I attempted escape. Now I knew how it felt to be a prisoner of war, or at least, a prisoner. We walked several hours amid the trees and vines. I noticed only small mammals running about, no Isis lizard here to combat. A few times I felt as if a Hobbit might appear from behind the forest tree stumps, or amid the many tree trunks of the forest. Yet nothing in my imagination equaled being held captive by youthful tyrants.

Their communication was brief and guttural. They all appeared in need of a bath and haircut. Yet what they thought of me I knew not. Their clothing was contemporary caveman, all fur and leather; no cloth, no cotton, no linen. Soon we entered their camp where more youths were performing chores and serving as lookouts from atop tall trees.

"Where were the adults?" I wondered to myself; would I ever recover my beeper, my mode of transportation back to earth? Could I find my way back to the pit even if I tried tomorrow, using the freshest of memory's recall? No affirmative answers; questions like storm clouds hung over me. My trip home was to occur in two weeks, and I didn't need high school age 'students' ruin my return trip, let alone the rest of my time travel experiences. Just as I was about to scream, "Freedom," much like William Wallace's rumored last word while being tortured by Edward I of England, my entourage stopped in front of a wooden hut amid softwood trees. It appeared 'Thoreauvian,' in its innocence and sylvan beauty; thus it appealed to me to greatly. For such an abode was my childhood, and present fantasy.

"Truly, I thought to myself, so far my time travel has been devoted to caves populated by humans. Would I ever see a normal house or place of business?"

Waiting a short time in front of this pastoral domain, a young woman dressed in leather and carrying a spear appeared before me. In a flash the spear was pointed at my throat.

She said in broken English, "Who are you and why are you in our woods? Did Tragon send you as a spy? Are you part of a deceptive rear attack upon our people?"

Responding I said, "I do not know Tragon. I'm from earth, a planet on the far reaches of the galaxy, and a mere time traveler. My name is Gordon Paradise and you might conclude from my attire that I am not part of any army or a spy."

Silent for a few minutes, she circled me and observed my clothes head to foot. She noticed my shoes and my coat. She felt it with her fingers and stared into my face.

"You speak our language while wearing strange attire," she said bluntly.

"Yes, that's true. I said I'm from earth."

"Earth? I know not earth," she said forcefully.

"Now that you know my name, may I ask yours? Also, may I ask where I am within the galaxy?"

"My name is Zena, daughter of Senator Phillrey; I know nothing of a galaxy.

I am leader of this group and we find your presence troubling. We are considering killing you here and leaving you as a reminder for Tragon's army that intruders die quickly, no mercy."

"May I call you Zena?"

No response.

"Listen Zena, I'm from a distant planet and ask your help to permit my departure home. There is no need of killing me. Yet my knowledge might prove temporarily useful in your cause. I suspect a war or conflict with this Tragon?"

"You're right, you might prove useful. If not, you die on Zollerin."

I responded, "So this planet is called Zollerin?"

"If you are lying to me or intrude upon our mission, you will wish never to have seen Zollerin, or have met us. We intend on killing Tragon. He's a tyrant and tyrants must die. All who assist tyrants must die too. As for your language, you speak similar to us; yet sound more similar to another Zollerin tribe, one thought extinct. If I trust you, it will last until you misuse my trust. Then you will die with a spear thrown into your chest while tied to a tree. No mercy for tyrants. Mercy is for the weak."

I owned a few bruises from my rough landing upon Zollerin, and to my surprise Zena motioned two females to attend my wounds. They placed salve upon my sores and had me drink an elixir tasting of berries and peaches. Evening became night, and sleep followed its natural pattern. I did not notice the stars above me, for I was too tired to gaze upwards, as I was tied at my wrists and ankles.

Zena appeared before me at daybreak, looking for allies, not adversaries.

She spoke softly, and then affirmatively, "If indeed you are not Tragon's spy, and are truly from a distant land, then perhaps we can use you for our purpose of defeating Tragon? Here is some food, called quamm."

It appeared as bread with a sunflower seed-like taste. She gave me water and freed me. Yet she kept two guards with me and motioned to the group to break camp.

I was grateful she did not threaten me. I was also grateful for the nourishment provided for the day ahead; as it soon appeared I was to be part of an expedition.

Not everyone in camp seemed to be preparing for a trip. Yet some were busy packing, gathering people and things. With so many young people gathering, it appeared as a "Children's Crusade." Yet I wasn't about to make comment. They were adolescence in manners; however they were all equipped with weapons, and possessed the skill to use them offensively and defensively as mature warriors. I did not question their integrity as hunters and warriors; yet I did question their motives and ambitions.

Within a few hours I was being led into the forest with two guards beside me and Zena leading the expedition. The woods smelled fresh, clean and piney. The sunlight filtered through the pine trees like a giant colander. Below my feet the mat of pine needles felt soft to walk upon. Along the way I listened to their conversation about me. In this banter of youths I overheard that the young man who entered Zena's hut last night did not come out alive.

"Was she a moralist who killed her intruders, or a human 'black widow spider' who killed male companions?"

My curiosity was piqued. Who is this woman of the woods? Who is her father, Phillrey? Was there hope for my return and the safety of my life? I needed to return and retrieve my 'beeper,' such action would increase the probability of both a safe return and my life, as if they were separated in my present reality!

Surely her father, someone my parents' age, would be reasonable. I needed to assure myself that hope was doubtless; my ability to return home, feasible.

Our expedition consisted of 60 to 75 people, looking somewhat like a Cro-Magnon hunting party, as they carried spears, bows and arrows, and shields. So actually they did live in the Iron and Bronze stage of technological development.

We eventually walked to a clearing and I noticed the sloping land. Then I saw a narrow and beautiful river emerge from amid the forest.

"Were we to travel by water? Would we be on a float trip?" Within a short time my questions were answered. As we walked upon grass, I saw a forward party dragging rafts previously hidden from view. They were small built crafts, and appeared sturdy despite their diminutive appearance. I was motioned to join Zena on board her boat. In moments we were set into the smooth current alongside other boats and drifting downstream. Each craft had oarsmen and oarswomen with long poles. At the back of each craft a young woman steered it with skill. Apparently Zena gave opportunity to both young men and women.

She might like earth, as well as teaching men a few things about a woman's strength. Yet she might detest earth and the twentieth century obsession for fashion, facials, makeup, pantyhose, designer jeans, petite and lacy lingerie, deodorant and dresses, and the whole gambit of female attire and attitude. Her life was so simple compared to Diana's, or other women in America. Not only was Zena from another realm time-wise, she was of another millennium.

Our view was magnificent as we entered a canyon. Between us were smooth limestone-like cliffs, white as clamshells or chalk; thus composed of calcite. This scenery impressed me for its beauty. I enjoyed this watery excursion and felt hopeful for my situation. As I began to feel comfortable and complacent, lying on my back along the edge of this boat, we were suddenly thrown into white water! Water surged angrily about us, rock-like teeth jutted up from the rushing current. The cliffs hid the sun and we seemed to be living within a canyon of death. I hurried to my feet and clung to some rope in the center of the craft. Others were too. Zena however acted calm in this tempest. She held tight as she gripped the wooden keel. This wooden shaft was prodding our craft to stay on course and prevent collision with rocks. As we bobbed up and down upon the white water, Zena nearly fell. She then motioned to be secured with rope as she maintained her position. She looked with disgust at the younger ones on board who were terrified of drowning, as she hung on in courage and grace under fire. One youth tied her and he was nearly thrown over into the raging waters. Spray soaked us to the bone and the water was cold, chilling us all. Zena was an honorable heroine; yet I feared for her life and saw her tumble. I lunged forward to grab her waist in my attempt to secure her life, only to have one of my guards crack my back with his staff, as if I was attempting to leave the craft!

"I'm trying to save her," I screamed. Too late though, she was in the water. I freed myself of the restraints and jumped into the river, its water felt iced cold. The boat rushed past me as I groped about in freezing water for Zena. One guard followed me into the water, only to have a raft hit him, making him unconscious; sinking to the river's bottom, for the items he wore prevented buoyancy.

Struggling in my approach, I noticed another craft heading right toward us on a collision course for our heads! I lunged deep into the river, grabbing Zena's limp body. I bubbled upwards to the surface as the craft passed by. A rope was soon suspended amid the water before me, as it hung from the side of another craft. A pair of hands hung overboard too. Between those hands and the rope, we were on board another boat. It was a miracle. I panted for breath, and then saw Zena beside me. Immediately I proceeded to give mouth-to-mouth resuscitation. This procedure was difficult enough for someone like me, who had not administered it in years. Now in raging water, upon this small raft, I was trying to save the life of an adversary.

"Love your neighbor as yourself," Jesus said. Zena was just that, a cosmic neighbor, not a galactic adversary. She spared my life a few hours earlier, now I was attempting to save hers. The hands that pulled us within the boat tried to pull me away from Zena's mouth. He perhaps thought I was offending the dead, indeed, her companions thought her dead. I refused to accept Zena's demise. I still attempted my lifesaving work and felt a faint breath from her nostrils. Again I placed my mouth to her mouth; again a rude hit across my back. I ignored the pain and intrusion. Then a cough, Zena was coughing! Water ejected from her nose and mouth. Her eyes opened and stared right through me with a piercing surprise. It was me who was saving her! She did not smile but gripped the rope I clung to as I held her to my side, and I liked it; she did not, but gave no fight. Her fight was with death, not me. She nearly drowned and my lifesaving attempt had saved someone I had just met. Little did she know her life was saved by a twentieth century medical procedure called CPR. Yet her goal was downstream. Our lives had met and merged on this planet, however, was my effort appreciated? Surely I would find out later. But now we clung tight and eventually found smooth water, smooth as the river first appeared this morning. It seemed as if the river had a personality going from calmness to rage to calm again. I've seen it in people and it's scary as hades. We made it; we survived; yet one warrior youth had not been saved.

We came ashore to rest and dry off. Everyone set foot on the sandy bank and stripped their garments off to dry. I was self-conscious; yet did the same. I couldn't help but gaze at the young women who felt no shame in their nudity. Everyone rested and behaved with genuine concern. Some couples huddled together and encircled a fire quickly made for warmth and cooking. Provisions were drawn out from leather bags and we ate a brief repast. Zena came to my side and we talked. I provided my coat to offer warmth, she accepted; then smiled. It had been safely kept in my unsinkable travel bag.

"Thank you," was all she said.

Then only later, did she speak again, asking. "Why did you save me on the river? I'll never understand; now I owe you my life, if not my heart. I will not forget this moment. Never has anyone risked themselves for me, except my own father."

I responded, "Zena, I already owed you my life. You spared me. It was my turn to offer you Christian charity and love."

She laughed, which hurt my feelings. "Your life was not mine to spare. It is always the role of the Zollerin Elders to decide. I played my role to manipulate and scare you."

"You had me convinced that you held authority."

"Authority," she said, "may be passed to me upon her Father's demise, never before."

Then she asked, "What was a Christian?"

"It's a way of life. One who follows God's Son, and His Son's teachings, as set out in Holy Scripture. Have you not heard of the Holy Trinity? Have you not heard of Jesus of Nazareth, Son of God?" asked I.

She looked at me and shook her head no.

"Do you have a god here on Zollerin; whom do you worship?"

"We worship the sky, the stars, the sun and our two moons. Otherwise, worshiping humans is not our way."

"Don't get me wrong. My God is more than human. But I can't explain it all now. Yet I'd like to in the future, and tell you of His love."

She nodded her approval, "Yes, I'll listen. Your God must be one of love if you would risk your life for me. It is not our way here on Zollerin. We would not attempt such action. However, we do not oppose it in another."

It didn't make sense to me and I had no interest in debating this woman. We sat in silence before the fire and soon darkness enveloped us; by then our clothes were dry. A few mocked my garments but I did not envy their clothing. We continued to huddle about the fire and kept warm as a chilly night approached. A meal was prepared and we enjoyed some fresh meat that a few hunters had killed before dusk. Even a few fish were caught and some enjoyed baked fish, head and all.

In the 'back' of my mind I wondered, "Would a Zollerin someday make it to earth and roam about? I wondered if Diana would have fun showing Zena about Tulsa, shopping at Utica Square or Woodland Hills Mall.

What would lunch at the Polo Grill do for Zena? How about dinner at The Chalkboard, The French Hen, or Michael Fusco's? Would rock 'n roll interest Zena? Would ballet at the Performing Arts Center intrigue her? Would she enjoy "*Star Trek*" and "*The Brady Bunch*" reruns? Would cable television fascinate or bore the woman of the woods? How about the western art at the Gilcrease Museum or the paintings at Philbrook? Do they have fine art here on Zollerin? Would they care for our advances in transportation? Would Zena drive a Porsche or ride a horse? Would men dance with her at Saigon Sally's and take her to concerts at the Brady Theater or PAC? What would she think of the play "*Cats?*"

I'm seeking answers to a million questions. I'm overly analytical as to be a nuisance to myself. Yet I was challenged by these prospects of social interaction between earthlings and her people. This was my last thought. I lay on my back only to find her do the same. I looked up into the star saturated sky only to have Zena place her hand on my arm. It was a sweet gesture. What would Diana think? I thought no more; therefore only enjoyed the moment, as nothing else mattered. For all I knew I would never see earth again. I fell asleep with a sad heart.

Morning came too quickly for me. I felt drained and exhausted. Yet the boating party began another day on the river. I then prayed for today's rafting to be calm and easy going.

I asked Zena if this second day would be uneventful, and she nodded, yes. She then stated, "This second day is easy and takes us to my father's hideout."

I wondered from whom he was hiding?

Her words were true; our trip was easy and fun. The river was a friend and a joy to be upon. Some fished and others hung to ropes and were being pulled behind the fleet while clinging to logs. It looked enjoyable; yet I had all the water action the previous day. I rested on my side and watched the landscape drift by like a dream world; soon I was lulled asleep.

Zena again took the rudder, though today not much work was required. It seemed as if all craft were on autopilot and headed to port. Nothing seemed important but to enjoy the green and full trees hugging the riverside for water. Brown and golden spotted sand shimmered beneath the water. This water was clear, and the pebbly bottom easily seen as if it were only inches from the surface. I saw fish dart about the current and rejoiced in life. My heart renewed its hope.

Zena smiled at me when I chose to look her way, which was often. I enjoyed her presence, her face, her physique of womanly charm. Did I feel guilty for admiring another woman? Yes, I did feel guilty. Yet what was she feeling? For the moment, perhaps trust, that was enough for any friendship.

By early afternoon we were nearing her father's camp. We weighed anchor, which were rocks tied to vines, a simplicity to behold. We jumped off; greeted by more teens toting spears and swords, and another bunch assisting our arrival. Unloading procedures began and Zena grabbed my arm and headed into an area 200 feet from the river. It was her father's outdoor table, upon which we found an array of food. Within a moment her father, Senator Phillrey, appeared from the woods where he had been contemplating the war's next action plan.

Father and daughter embraced, hugged and spoke words of affection. Zena proceeded to introduce me.

"Father, we have a guest, Gordon Paradise, who dropped in unexpectedly at Hilltop a few days ago. At first I thought him a spy from Tragon; however, he saved my life as I was thrown into the river. We were in the canyon's white water and he risked his life to save me from drowning. Later, as I returned from the 'sleeping death,' he had brought me back from its darkness. No one from Castlethorn would act as he did."

Her father extended his arms to embrace me. I extended my right arm, earth-style.

"You must be from earth, he said. Here on Zollerin we extend both arms. You earthlings never caught onto the ways we gave you."

I was stunned. "You know earth?"

"Yes, we gave you a start. We helped the Greeks and Romans."

I was incredulous. "How, I asked, could you have been on earth?"

"Apparently you have found the Xenos lines. We have not used them in centuries. We were a highly developed order; however, a horrible war arrested our development. We have yet to recover. Apparently earth has access to Xenos, the time wave."

"No one on earth had used these Xenos lines you speak of until I discovered them, Senator. At least I believe myself to be the first."

"Let me say welcome. You are the first who has made it to Zollerin," said Senator Phillrey

"How, Senator, did you have access to the time warp, as you call it, the Xenos lines, and be living in the Bronze Age?"

"Our great war set us back centuries in development. Our culture was ruined and we lived in a dark age. We lost track of earth and other outposts after our war began. We helped establish the language of Greece and later, the Romans. We did have much contact with Angle land and their language. Oh yes, that was at the end of your Dark Ages. Ours came as earth was renewing its interest in learning. So we had influenced the language you now speak. It was an actual outgrowth from our language. We set it in action on your earth. Otherwise you and I would be unable to communicate in the same tongue."

"It all makes sense to me now, but how about Assidia? How do they know our language too?"

"Understand that the time warp, as you call it, goes in a pattern from earth to other habitable planets. In the path lie Assidia and others. Apparently you had set your travel to locate livable planets and places, you arrived here next. To leave here would put you in line with Malamar, and Deltos. Yet we have not had contact, trade or exchange with these places in centuries. Our life is like your Bronze Age, you are correct. Apparently we are lagging behind your scientific prowess. Our days are basic; life and death are struggles for most. I am proud of little earth for finally discovering the Xenos lines. I have never visited earth; yet I know the brief history of your planet. Few books survived the horrible destruction of centuries ago. Otherwise I would have no knowledge of earth, Xenos lines, or any old history."

"Xenos, does that mean stranger?"

"Yes, Mr. Paradise, the 'stranger lines,' loosely translated. It seems as if strangers emerge from them, like you, though you or I remain strangers for a short time. You, a captive, saving Zena, amaze all. Thank you. For a reward you will have access to the Great Book of Zollerin. It relates more about Xenos travel, as I recall. This text will help you perfect travel. Yet it will serve us not for years to come. You are welcome to learn our knowledge. Perhaps earth would be so kind to teach us the lost arts and sciences that now exist as shadows over my people?"

"Allow me, Senator, to ask some more questions. Yet let me say thank you for your kind offer of knowledge and access to the Zollerin Book.

And sir, not to be impertinent, I ask however, why are your people hiding out, and who is Tragon?"

The Senator shook his head in disgust.

"I hesitate to share our problems. Guests are not meant to shoulder pain, however, he continued, let it be said that Tragon has enslaved many of our leaders and adults, parents to these children who surround me. Tragon, a former Senator in our capitol of Zollene, became power hungry and maniacal. He planned to rule Zollerin with absolute control. He now has many enslaved in Castlethorn, his residence. It is located not far from here, set at the base of Glacier Ridge. He protects himself with a mountain behind him and a desert in the frontal position. We are planning to tunnel beneath the desert area to Castlethorn. It may not succeed, but we are pursuing the work. Our project maintains morale. Our youth are digging in shifts, day and night. They're dedicated in freeing their parents."

I shook my head in admiration. "Would the teenagers of earth be so dedicated?" I thought to myself.

The Senator continued, "There are two concerns while digging this tunnel, Mr. Paradise, first, a cave-in; secondly, the Colmec lizard, whose sting can place one in 'frozen' death for years. The person hangs on with an inability to talk or move, to see or feel. The victim sleeps, that's all.

Yes, two major concerns, and the youths are doing an excellent job. My own Zena digs, and also guards in a special vigil against the lizard. Everyone takes turns digging, and watching for the death lizard."

"Is it like the Isis Lizard?"

"No, not really. The Colmec is small, yet its venom places one in a coma. The Isis has teeth that will tear a grown man to shreds. The Isis reaches lengths of two men, or women for that matter. We are not as tall as earthlings appear to be, judging from you."

"I'm taller than the average men of earth. Most are five inches shorter than I. An inch being half the length of my thumb," and I held up and wiggled my thumb for all to witness.

"Well, Mr. Paradise, a man's stature is more than his height. Here on Zollerin, so much more is asked of us!"

I felt reprimanded, though I realized Senator Phillrey had a lot on his mind. Here I was discussing height, and his people were attempting survival.

I strolled around looking at the camp and wondering how far away Castlethorn was located. I also saw Zena practicing with her sword and drew near this action.

She was battling a young man nearly twice her bulk and she was doing well. She defended herself and was on the attack! She lunged forward and nicked her opponent. Twirling around she sought to disarm him, unsuccessfully. He whacked her sword from her hand. Then she dived under his legs and pulled his leather waist garment down over his legs. He stumbled and let fly his weapon. Zena pounced on his weapon with alacrity. She also retrieved her sword and now held two swords, both pointed at her opponent's throat. She had won her practice bout and I applauded. She looked embarrassed by my applause; however, she smiled and nodded in recognition of my gesture.

As she walked away I quickly paced myself to be beside her.

She looked at me as if I was intruding. "Something wrong Zena?" I asked.

"I am soon to guard against the Colmec lizard. Care to join me? That is, if you do work, I wouldn't know except for your swimming in the river." I agreed to her request and in our time together, guarding for lizards, we began to know one another. She was more mature than I realized, and wiser than I thought. At first she seemed a foolish young woman, now I sensed an intelligence and cunning I had not perceived earlier.

For further amusement I later viewed the war games of other youths, and watched others fish by the river. It all looked like earth, though I was far away and feeling lonely. Previously, I was always too busy to feel lonely, and now to feel this way, surprised me. I'm fulfilling my life long dream of time travel, so why feel lonely? This was a trying time, to an extent; yet really nothing more than an excursion with newly found friends. Some say that people "grow" in times of trial. I felt not growth, but emptiness.

Perhaps at another time I'd look back and sense a difference in myself, a new maturity as opposed to selfishness, and perhaps selfishness had previously dominated my personae? Yet I didn't know for sure. Life moves on at varied paces, and I wondered what I really hoped to accomplish here on Zollerin? Then I realized I had no need to accomplish anything, than return home safely.

I lived on a different planet far within the galaxy; I lived where no other human had lived. I bluntly said to myself, "Enjoy the moment and dispel loneliness. Cease your whining, it's unbecoming!"

Then another wave of doubt overtook me. Did I take the attitude of discovery, or inflated ego, or perhaps a mixture of both? Was I able to say my journey had been productive? Was I better for it? Were my contacts better off? Surely my elderly friends from Assidia had benefited? I suppose I needed to be grateful for where I was and that I was in the hands of decent, caring people. What if this maniac Tragon found me instead of Zena and Phillrey? I'd be in prison or killed.

Then I also realized I needed to regain access to my "beeper," or I'd be here indefinitely without access to home base. I knew that Ross and Diana were worried about my "disappearance." I'd be upset too if they were missing in the cold recesses of space, especially with a maiden voyage of devices as new as Trans-17. Sometimes I think it was pure ego that drove me out here into the center of the galaxy. What sane guy would leave the green hills of earth for unknown landscapes, and wasn't I being too analytical, as usual?"

"Yes, I said to myself, You're analytical nature generates too many questions; too many self doubts. Dismiss them or emotionally thrash myself; which one would I choose? I decided to dismiss my anxiety and live bravely in the moment; now change your thoughts and enjoy life more fully!"

I decided to approach the Senator and ask for retrieval of my beeper. I needed it like I needed water and air. It was my lifebelt in this maelstrom of galactic goop.

Searching about I inquired to the old gentleman's whereabouts. I soon found myself outside his tent. Having announced my presence, an escort led me inside to a majestic table covered with books, charts, and drawings of Castlethorn. On the floor were scattered swords and shining, mirror-like shields. Candles burned brightly on his table and he sat up at my approach.

"Mr. Paradise, please comfort yourself."

I found some cushions to sit upon. I immediately told the Senator of my lost item within the pit, two days journey away.

"I will have our people find it. We keep active contact between our outposts and here. Yet I've been so preoccupied. Please do not think we are ignoring you. Perhaps you have found amusements with which to pass your time before returning to earth? Allow my dear Zena to show you around our beloved woods, and display our tunnel to Castlethorn."

"Thank you Senator for everything you've offered to me. Yes, I would enjoy Zena's time in showing me around, and your tunnel fascinates me. I've always liked underground caves and caverns. A day or so ago you mentioned your books. I must see them. You have much to teach me, and perhaps there is information I can have relayed to you upon my return to earth? In fact, perhaps you and Zena would join me for a brief visit? I'd enjoy showing you Oklahoma."

"A visit to your home planet would be delightful, Mr. Paradise. Yet my priority is to free our people from Tragon and have him disposed. Doing so may cost many lives. My mind is searching strategies to minimize death, for both my people and his. War is brutal, disgusting and criminal. Yet when the mad seek power, the sane resort to mad tactics, would you agree? Evil is not undone easily. If it were, then good and evil would not be so different. Rather they appear as two sides of the same coin. As it is, survival is brutally difficult. When we fought ourselves, we approached extinction of our race. Our engineering and scientific progress nearly disappeared. That, Mr. Paradise, is a shock; that progress may so easily regress to mere survival after decades of hope and centuries of order, is incomprehensible. War both divides and destroys us inside out. To think our great culture is lost except to a few books; they're guarded under penalty of death. The storehouses of knowledge came at a price, and by price we protect them. All men and women over age fifteen do such duty. Without mandatory duty, we'd make exceptions and grow apart as a culture. We need always to be one, one people, one culture; one future. Tragon interrupted our progress toward regaining the great culture we once owned. For that reason, and the blatant acts of terrorism, his life angers me. Such anger frightens me, but I discover within myself the ability to hate and kill and plunder as he has done. What progress is that? If we use Tragon's tactics to destroy him, do we become one with him? Do we lose our sanity by using insane warring means to destroy another? Any answers, Mr. Paradise?"

"Senator, we on earth debate the same question. This was especially true in our great world wars. Yet we knew, or perhaps guessed in our ignorance, that our harsh war tactics against enemies were temporary. Once the war was won, the brutality ended. Warriors and dictators like Tragon maintain no restraint in these matters. Their hate is unending. A decent society puts war away as soon as possible and resorts to laws and human kindness at enemy's surrender. Such was General Grant's compassion toward the rebel forces in April 1865; such was the rebuilding of Japan and Europe after our World War II. Sanity can easily be restored, if we know that upon victory, a moral regime returns unquestioned. Like a butterfly emerging from its chrysalis, the rules change when the event concludes. Then we confront peace from a mountaintop of new hope; new expectation. At least this action is pursued by my native nation, the United States. Otherwise, the good dissolves into its own evil and becomes the object of self-hatred and destruction. Am I helping you process your thoughts in any way, or am I babbling?"

"Yes Mr. Paradise, you are helping me 'process,' as you call it, my thoughts. I appreciate your interest in my conversation. It is difficult to discuss ideas with these younger warriors. Their intellectual development has been stunted by war and wanting. They are not interested in ideas. Indeed, I would welcome a visit to earth for the intellectual banter alone. Zena is great company to me, however, as you've noticed, her mind is on war, not philosophy. I do try to discuss ideas with her, however, she bores easily. She's a doer not a thinker."

"With all due respect, given time, I know the native intelligence possessed by your daughter would bloom to abstract thought and debate. I believe her to be keen in mind and body," I said respectfully.

"Perhaps with proper educational opportunity, she would indeed bloom as a rose in the desert?" the Senator replied.

We both nodded to one another at his spoken sentiment, and then I departed for the riverbank. I felt drowsy and lay beneath a wide oak-type tree to seek sleep. As afternoon gave way to dusk and dusk to evening, my sleep was rudely awakened. I found myself entangled by a fishnet and was soon hanging from an oak's limb. Anger surged through me. Then I saw who was behind this action and began laughing. Yet Zena did not see me laugh. I yelled out for immediate release and she and her gang left me hanging overnight in this net. Uncomfortable was an understatement for this overnight entanglement.

By morning Zena herself cut me down. Then the thought flashed before me. She tied me to reciprocate the humiliation she felt toward my saving her life in the river. It was pure pride, and I now understood Zollerin thought one level greater than yesterday.

Yet I yelled out to her, "We're even now Zena; you can back off your pranks." She looked at me whimsically and smiled. Saying nothing more, she pointed her finger, thus I followed her into the cave beneath Castlethorn.

I followed her to the underground site and was impressed by the work being performed. A neatly carved tunnel was being formed from sand, rock, dirt removal, and hardship. Only the Colmec lizard living in underground cavities this time of year had attacked a few workers.

We walked through to the lead digging area and I congratulated all the shift workers. I told Zena of my pride in her companions' work, and success would be forthcoming in freeing their parents. How surprised the parents would be to have a tunnel opening "pop up" in the middle of their confinement, and set them free from the enemy. We would rejoice on that day! It felt Biblical to be part of this endeavor. Soon I asked to work beside the lead diggers. Zena joined this shift and we dug together for several hours. My back ached, but I felt positive and happy, especially after taking the pain medication I had brought with me, for it eliminated the ache, and thus eased my mind, and my back. However, the work too was satisfying,

Zena and the others joked with me about being from a different planet; a "foreigner," or "alien" are the words I told them to use. They kept mispronouncing the words, saying instead, 'forner,' or, 'alleen.' I shrugged and kept digging. Yet I was not *Atlas Shrugged (or better yet, Shrugging)*, to use the name of Ayn Rand's masterpiece of Capitalism, as a pun.

This digging took me back to my youth when I would shovel snow off the sidewalks in Glen Iris, our sidewalks and dad's pharmacy. Snow shoveling is hard work, so is tunnel digging. I felt like an East German trying to escape Berlin. Yet that thought was of earth, my work was here on Zollerin. I wondered what Ross and Diana were doing, were they giving me up for lost? And when would Phillrey's people find my beeper?

After a long shift digging, we all broke and gave our tools to the next group. Phillrey stated their tunnel was two-thirds completed. The next third would be the most difficult and labor-intensive work; the most time consuming.

As we left the tunnel, lit with animal fat candles and surprisingly bright, we found our way to a hot meal and cold drink. We all talked of the tunnel and how we would all attack Castlethorn, and how great it would be to free the imprisoned parents.

Now time for dinner, a few of the younger ones starting throwing bones at one another, as they ravenously ate the meat clean off the bones. Zena got in the fight too and they started throwing wooden cups of water at one another. It became a food fight. Such childishness irritated me, for I was not raised in Glen Iris to be a fool. To be a gentleman, like my dad, was to possess and utilize good manners. He proved himself by example.

However, Zena leaped on a big warrior and mashed his face into a bowl of animal fat. Fortunately she didn't light the goo on his face. Yet she wasn't malicious in her fun, just mischievous. The guy beneath her grabbed her simultaneously. She slapped him hard and freed herself. No one touched her and got away with it. Then with a burst of incredible strength, she put this man on her back, and led him to the river, then rolled him into the water like a huge log!

I admired her gumption and strength. She proved unique in her barbarian, yet charming ways. Or was I just infatuated with her? Yes, I admit it, I was infatuated.

My infatuation was a guilty pleasure. Yet guilty pleasures become emotionally painful to those sensitive to right and wrong. How could I love Diana and be infatuated with a teenager from the Bronze Age? Again I sensed an unconscious psychological drama being played out in my feelings.

I soon realized I wanted to be the teenager again. It wasn't unconscious at all; in fact, the entire situation became quite conscious to me once this realization bubbled upward into my mind's eye and heart. The mind and heart are one; yet we humans pretend them to be separate. There is no separation between mind and heart unless we willingly deny, or refuse to see, the interaction of the two entities as one. In their interaction is their synergy. Was I right or was I wrong? Probably neither, I was merely sensing my youthful shyness, and hence my inability to speak and relate one-on-one with teenage women. Yet now I was doing just what I only dreamed of as a teenager. I did not yet realize if I was sinful or innocent in my thoughts, feelings, and actions. However, I sensed guilt, which was not surprising.

Therefore, I said to myself, I was acting out the repressed feelings of my youth, decades after the fact. The broken circle of emotion had been made whole; indeed I felt a wholeness speaking to her,

The gang applauded her triumph and the victim swam to shore and disrobed. He hung his garment on a tree and then began to chase Zena into the woods. Others followed in the chase. I stayed behind and swam for a while in the river. Others joined me and a few had canoe races. Some others practiced archery, and a few were young couples in love, lazily being together on anchored rafts.

I was on shore when, after a few hours, the renegades returned from their merry chase and found Zena captured. This time she was tossed into the river. She looked irate and delighted at the same time. Upon returning to shore she stripped off a few of her wet garments and tossed them at me.

She returned to the water while I yelled out, "Do I look like a laundry service to you?"

She waved at me from the river's shoreline; then dove headfirst into the river only to pop up again at the opposite bank. I stood up to see where she would reappear, fearing a potential drowning. Yet she was fine, my concern unwarranted. She waved from the other bank, and then proceeded to climb a fiber rope dangling from a tree. I certainly would not want to climb that rope as she had just done. Yet she climbed with ease and got atop the supporting limb. From atop this branch she flung herself out into the air and screeched in delight the entire way into the river.

I sat down and shook my head, "What a character." I kept saying to myself, and, "What an actress." After performing this trick a few times she swam to a raft tied to a dock and sunbathed a few hours. I departed and thought of home.

Later Zena and I sat together speaking. Then I realized an aspect of their culture I found vulgar. Only later I realized her people possessed an innocence like Adam and Eve knew prior to their eating the forbidden fruit.

There was no shame in their lack of clothing. It bothered me, but had no ill meaning to them; no impurity of heart or spirit was intended. They were child-like; it was such a simple realization that took me many days to comprehend. No need for guilt or shame. Her people lived their own version of Eden. In one sense, their culture was more European than American. My Puritan-based heritage was not their heritage. Their immodesty, as I first saw it, literally, was not immodesty to them, rather it was their culture. They were living their lives as they had for thousands of years.

Then a shrill, terrorizing scream reverberated throughout camp. "Cave in! Cave in! She grabbed my arm and her clothes, and in moments, we two, and a whole crowd, had gathered at the tunnel. The rescue teams had all arrived in minutes; ready to save their fellow tunnelers.

Senator Phillrey stood before us and proceeded to speak, "Two have died in a tunnel cave-in. I ask for volunteers to enter, dig, and retrieve our brothers and sisters."

Zena volunteered immediately, as did other young women, and the bigger, stronger men. I volunteered too, without hesitation.

With tools in our hands, we entered the tunnel and walked to the dusty, dirty choking mess before us. We began digging, and buckets of our work were hauled away. We worked for hours and were making progress. We found the body of one dead. Zena and I volunteered to drag him to the opening. As we were slowly making our way to the fresh air, a Colmec lizard sprang up before us and bit me on the shoulder. Zena tore it off me as it opened a gaping wound in the process. She drew her knife and sliced the lizard head to tail. She looked at me as if I were about to die. My last conscious moments were of her trying to stop the bleeding, and holding me in her arms.

Chapter 14

Six months passed. Nothing was heard from me. Ross and Diana had no idea what had happened; they feared for my life and were angry, scared, and mournful. Ross was in the lab and the phone rang.

"Ross, it's . . ."

"Oh, hello Diana how's life today?"

"Ross, have you heard anything?"

"No, I'm not receiving his life readings at all."

"Please Ross, find out what happened. I am so angry with you and him I could scream."

"Hold it Diana, you're losing control."

"You're right, I'm losing control. My fiancé is lost somewhere in the middle of the galaxy and his best friend is doing nothing. Heck with you Ross. Just let me go after him with your Trans-17 and I'll return him home."

"Diana, I know what you're feeling and it's as natural as pecan pie at Thanksgiving. I just can't get up and dive headfirst into Trans-17, let alone allow you. You or I may never find him, or he might be ready to come back at any moment."

"Don't give this girl a bunch of excuses. I've had enough of you and Gordon. I want him back or I'll go public with this trip and force you to relinquish control."

"No Diana, you can't do that, it's too dangerous. Publicity would be lunacy."

"No, you're totally nuts and obnoxiously lunar."

"Lunar?"

"I give up." she said in exasperation.

"Diana, let me drive over and take you to dinner, it's Saturday night."

"I really don't want to see you."

"All right, eat with your eyes closed"

She gave a muffled laugh, hesitated, and said, "All right, drop over in an hour."

His truck pulled up into the parking lot and he realized he didn't know her condo's number. He leaned out the window and started yelling "Diana," then honking the horn. Two residents yelled back, "Quiet down there," and then a third voice proved to be her voice. She waved from the balcony and he parked.

As he entered her condo, she said, "You dumb thing, how could you be so rude? Don't the reservations teach you any manners?" He knew from her voice that she was teasing him. He knew that Diana loved American Indians, and was kind to all. Yet he knew she was deadly serious about Gordon's whereabouts. This impromptu date surprised him.

Yet he sarcastically replied, "You whites never told us the rules; yet complained when we broke them. Besides, the land this condo sits on is our ancestors' land, now get off white woman or this Indian will spank squaw with canoe paddle."

She was placing earrings on and giving him "the look." "I've seen you stare at me when Gordon and I go out for the evening. I sense your jealousy, am I right?" she asked.

She was right, he was envious of Paradise. Yet he played along, "Well I've seen you stare at me a few times, white rich lady. I also say you're jealous of the Tahlequah woman I'm dating. However, her name escapes me temporarily. It must be Caucasian-induced stress."

Diana rebutted, "You can't even remember her name?

Isn't that rather pathetic when it comes to manners and social graces? A woman's feelings are as delicate as violets, and as easily bruised as day lilies."

She got him on that point, and he had no excuses. Ross felt pained. Then he realized he had never forgotten a woman's name when he was with her socially; rather, this memory lapse was a temporary thing, easily explained by stress. And the stress was Diana—induced; her constant harping on finding Gordon.

Then she came up to him and asked to have her zipper drawn up. "Be nice and zip up my dress"

"You're wearing a dress? What's with that outfit? We're going to Knotty Pine Barbeque, not the Polo Grill!"

"So you think I can't wear cowgirl clothes?

"Gordon said you rarely dress as a cowgirl." He laughed so hard, Diana pushed him onto the divan, hitting his head against the living room wall in the process.

Yet he could see her run down the hall with her bedroom door open, and saw a dress fly through the air. Apparently she agreed with his statement. Her agreement surprised him. He wasn't used to her agreeing with much of what he said or did.

In ten minutes she came out looking like a rodeo gal, hat included, with a massive, ornate belt buckle, the design composed of bison and oil derricks; it was pure Oklahoman. She also wore a red blouse, tight across the chest, and wore expensive blue jeans. Her boots too were expensive, however, as most men, he knew little of women's clothing, or its cost, other than being notorious for being expensive.

"Well what a change you made! You look great, as if you were trying to make an impression on an innocent country boy."

"Oh hush up and take me to dinner. I'm hungry, so make it fast."

"I get your point." he emphatically replied.

They drove about 15 minutes and pulled into the Knotty Pine's parking lot. Both walked in and sat at a table near a window, just in case he needed to stare out, an impulsive habit when thinking. Yet he'd rather stare and think of Diana, heck with Paradise! He, Ross, was ready to steal Gordon's fiancée if he didn't return soon!

They ordered, and then talked about Gordon. Drinks came and they drank Dr Pepper and Coca-Cola from chilled glasses, per their request.

"Glass is best, isn't it Ross?"

"You bet, for beer, Coke, or Dr Pepper. Speaking of beer, waitress, I'll also take a Bud Light, please, and make it fast!"

"Are iced glasses good for R.C. Cola and Pepsi?

"Yes, why do you ask?

"Curiosity."

"Diana, forget soft drinks, do you want any beer?"

"No, I rarely drink beer."

"I thought you drank adult beverages?

"Yes, wine, rarely beer. Besides, I'm just a teenager at heart, not an adult."

With that said, they had their own private laugh, because it made no sense, but kept their laughter toned down as not to disturb the other customers.

"Oh Diana, I just feel crazy tonight. Plus I feel all tight inside," Ross stated.

"Then take an enema if you feel tight. Maybe it will free up your imagination, and thus provide ideas on how to get my fiancé, and your best friend, returned home."

"Funny Diana, very funny. You just hurt my feelings. I suppose you white rich girls think Indians are cold and without feelings. We're red blooded people with . . ."

"And red-skinned too!" Now she laughed and slapped her thigh.

"Are you angry tonight? he asked.

"Yes, how did you know?"

"Indian intuition. Or perhaps it was the racist statement regarding my skin color?"

"Is your intuition always perceptive, or only when you're juiced up with beer? Besides, the comment on your skin color was rather innocuous, don't you think? Haven't you called me 'white' women a few times? And did I say it offended me?

He didn't respond to the retort, rather he simply stated, "You're right; I've been drinking all day. So, will you be the designated driver?

"Agreed, now let me make your request crystal clear. You want to drink and have me drive?" she asked sadly.

"Yes, exactly. I appreciate your tolerance in allowing me to pursue my favorite hobby."

"Your favorite hobby will kill you, or someone else." speaking with her judgmental voice.

He responded not to her words.

Their dinner was placed before them and it smelled wonderful.

"This barbeque tastes delicious."

"What a way to change the subject, Ross."

"Can't a man enjoy a beer and barbeque without some woman giving him a hard time?"

"Ross, I'll change the subject for you. When are you bringing Gordon home?"

"I don't know Diana. I can't do much. His beeper is apparently 'dead.' Any messages I've sent have not been answered. What would you have me do, chase after him to the center of the galaxy?"

"At least you'd be trying something worthwhile. This waiting is killing me. I can't concentrate at work; can't sleep well at night. I feel overwhelmed and angry. Plus you know I'm prepared to follow his tracks and find him. I made that offer already."

"I know, but I am not allowing it. So stop thinking about it and get some sleep. Besides, I know a cure for your insomnia."

"So do I, she said, warm milk and Ambien."

A cold, hurt stare stopped his wise remark before he finished. "Really Diana, all we can do is wait. If it goes on another six months, we will have to face the strong possibility that he's deceased"

Hearing these words she starting crying and left the table. Ross paid the bill and took the leftovers with him. He held the beer in the other hand and hobbled outdoors.

Diana leaned up against his truck sobbing. He reached out to her then spilled some beer on her.

"You clumsy . . ." She wiped the beer off her jeans.

At least let me offer you a clean kerchief to dry your eyes."

Diana took the cloth and wiped her eyes dry. Mascara blackened the cloth. They both got in the truck and drove off. She had forgotten her promise to be the designated driver.

"Any place specific you wish to be driven to tonight?"

"Just drive me anywhere. Drive and talk to me, that's all I ask."

"What do you want me say? Besides, I thought you were going to drive?"

"Tell me that Gordon's alive and he'll be back soon."

"Okay, Gordon's fine and will return any day now."

"Liar!"

"Diana, you asked me to say something positive and I did."

As she was speaking, Ross turned a hard right into a darkened pharmacy parking lot, and stopped. He was switching drivers so as to not be 'pulled over' and ticketed for DUI.

"Your heart wasn't in it." While saying that, she was forced too hard against the door and the door handle let loose, and she was on the ground, flat on her back; having forgotten to buckle her seatbelt. She felt pain radiating from her tailbone; the medical term for tailbone eluded her for now. Pain erases memory. She felt foolish and angry; she knew it was against the law not to wear seatbelts.

He reached out to pull her up. As he was drawing her up into the cab, a police car pulled up behind them. The policeman got out of his car with a long handled flashlight, saying, "Be careful you two. Don't do anything to break the law."

"Right officer," stated Ross and he ran his hand through his long black hair. He then turned to Diana saying, "Where did we leave off?"

"Forget it Ross, take me home, now, pronto!" They drove in silence as stars hung like candles in the night sky.

Arriving at her condo he walked her to the door.

"I always liked you Diana. I was jealous of Gordon. I've never come close to marriage and I'm afraid that I may never get married and live a regular life."

"Well listen to you, true confessions. I thought all Indians were a laconic race. You surprise me."

"And I thought all blondes were dumb and . . ."

"Don't say anything more. This chickie isn't dumb."

"Chickie?" he asked.

"That was my nickname in high school. For some reason you remind me of high school. Why, I don't know."

"How does that strike you?" he asked.

"Well, let me think. Oh yes, I had an Indian ask me to the senior prom and I turned him down."

"Why did you break his heart?" he asked.

"Daddy didn't want me dating Indians, Blacks or Asians."

"Sounds like a real racist," Ross said flatly.

"Daddy a racist, impossible!" she exclaimed.

"Well, wasn't he?" Ross inquired.

"What's your definition?" she asked.

He paused a few moments, ignoring her question for a few moments for him to gather his thoughts, stating these words:

"My head is fine, my heart lonely; my passions mixed as as a restaurant salad. Ross then continued, since Gordon is gone, perhaps dead, and I wanted to make my romantic intentions known. I feel I'm the better man for you, and think of you often."

And for the definition to racism, I withdraw my foolish question. I know better. My past experiences with you have already answered that question, and I know you too well to accuse you of injustice or rudeness."

"Well Ross, I had no idea of your feelings, especially after stating your dating adventures with the Tahlequah woman.

Besides, I still love Gordon; therefore your intentions make no impact on my heart. You seem to be going after two different women at the same time, and I don't respect that action. Yes, you're 'mixed up' right now, and its obvious anyone would be with the pressure you're under. Yet let me remind you, we are close friends, that's all. Yet let me also say, your drinking makes me sad, so even if I were a free agent, so to speak, for your romantic intentions, I would still oppose your intentions."

"Diana, I'm hurt by your rapid rejection," said he, stunned.

"Ross I'm sorry to hurt you, however, your feelings don't seem overly sincere. My intuition feels they're just words, nothing more."

"Diana, do you realize until several generations ago, the Plains Indians slept on bison hides, and we Seneca lived in long houses?

"Bison hides, that must have been aromatic for a tipi, she replied, and long houses, how long were they?"

"I'm sure it was malodorous in the Plains Indian tipi, though I doubt any complained. Now that's my first answer; as to your second question, the lengths of long houses were about 50 to 100 feet; on occasion, 150 feet maximum. We lived on what we called the "three sisters," corn, beans, and squash. We fished in the spring and hunted in the fall. When a male Seneca married, he moved into the woman's longhouse. The Seneca united with four other New York State tribes in 1570. Then as The American Revolution progressed, General Sullivan was ordered to burn Seneca villages and their fields. Hence, my ancestors lost their homes and food supply, in a punitive action still recalled. In fact, my ancestral home was just 5 miles from Gordon's hometown, though his hometown had not yet been founded. Quite a coincidence, wouldn't you say?"

"Why this sudden lecture on your culture; are you changing the subject? A few moments ago I hurt you're feelings and now you're providing encyclopedic knowledge of your ancestors, please tell me why? she asked.

"Psychologically I had to abandon my emotional pain and resort to something entirely different, conversation-wise.

It was self preservation. Do you agree, Diana?"

"Yes, until proven otherwise, I agree. I'll drive you home. However, first, I'm going to drive you to my place, and change out of these rodeo clothes," she stated bluntly.

Then she drove Ross' vehicle to her condo and invited him in, emphatically stating she'd be departing within ten minutes.

Once at her place, Ross asked for iced water, not beer.

"Yes, help yourself. I'm going to change." Diana said.

He headed to the refrigerator and found some Corona. Though asking for water was an innocent ploy to appease Diana, he hoped to find beer. He drank one-and-a-half bottles before she returned showing up in designer blue jeans and a Bishop Kelley sweatshirt; sockless in her Reeboks.

"I'm ready, let's go." Then she immediately noticed the two Corona bottles.

"Ross, you asked for cold water and now I see you've consumed the Corona that wasn't mine to give, nor would I give it to you if it had been mine. A friend left it here last weekend after a girl-only pizza party. Now you owe her two Corona beers and you owe me an apology for your deception."

"Diana don't you trust me?"

"Not right now," she said in an angry tone. She then walked out the door, headed to the SUV.

Ross did not follow her. He quickly polished off the rest of the Corona and fell asleep, face down on her divan.

When she returned to her door to see where he was, and that he had quickly fallen asleep on her divan, made her furious. Immediately she phoned Ross' brother, incensed at Ross' misbehavior, she yelled into the phone for Willard to take his brother home.

Within twenty minutes Willard arrived, hauling off his brother in Willard's blue and silver Ford F-150, and took off like a rocket. Willard, sometimes called Will by close friends, loved this truck, and loved his brilliant, but drunken brother. Alcoholism, what a curse it holds over people, smart people, and the not-so-smart! Will lived in shame regarding his brother, but knew no way to get Ross freed of his beer addiction.

Diana, now freed of Ross and Will, took an hour long bath, listening to Beethoven piano sonatas, with seven scented candles placed throughout the bathroom, de-stressing from the humiliating situation.

She slept well afterwards; yet only after preparing to view one of her favorite movies, *"Laura."* However, she fell asleep before much of the Dana Andrews and Gene Tierney movie had played.

Diana attended church and ate breakfast at IHOP on Memorial. She then went home and started reading. She read for hours then fell asleep in her bedroom, which also served routinely as her reading room.

She awakened to classical guitar music emanating from her living room. Cautiously tiptoeing to the front room, she carried her baseball bat Gordon had given her for protection a year ago. Creeping alongside the wall to the living room, she peered around the corner and saw Ross with his feet up on the coffee table and thumbing a copy of *National Geographic.*

What the—are you doing in here? How did you get inside? I thought I just got rid of you. I am so angry with you Ross; I'm ready to knock your head off! I had your brother take you home hours ago."

"Hold on Diana. I'm unarmed and innocent. So put your baseball bat down before you hit me. I returned 30 minutes ago and walked inside."

"Don't be a smart a—, you nearly scared me to death."

"Well, then make sure your door is locked. Unlocked doors allow all kinds of riff-raff to enter in-and-out."

"It was locked. I double check each night."

Ross then confessed, "I found these keys at Gordon's home. I owed you an apology, besides, Will brought me by so I could drive my SUV home, since we live so close to one another I thought I'd stop in."

She gripped her baseball bat and swung, hitting Ross' shoulder, intentionally missing his head.

"Now get out Ross, and fast. Don't you ever use Gordon's keys to my home again. If you do, the police will escort you downtown, and that's a promise."

"I know when I'm not wanted, however, I'm here with news about Gordon, but if you want me to leave. I'll just . . ."

"Okay, tell me, and then get out."

"Next week I'm planning on following his ionized galactic trail and find out where Gordon has himself seated, then bring him on home."

"What brought this missionary zeal on? And why had you not acted on this thought earlier, as in five months ago?"

"My drinking. I haven't thought clearly in the months Gordo's been gone, but I just realized, once again, I could retrace Gordon's travels by his ionized track. I had thought of it weeks ago; yet it seemed to float just beneath my conscious mind. Now the idea is firmly set in my conscious brain. It came to me in a daydream, just prior to the telephone call from his parents. Apparently they have another relative who wants to give Gordo cash from an estate. Seems like some Aunt died and has a sizeable fortune to disperse. I told Mrs. Paradise that Gordon was out of town, and unable to attend. She asked if you would attend the will reading, since you two are engaged. She didn't have your phone number, so I promised to deliver the message in person."

She stared at him and his utter disregard for her privacy.

Also, here's a six pack of Corona for your friend."

"So I'm supposed to get up and leave for upstate New York on a moment's notice? she asked.

"Diana, when's the last time you took any vacation?"

"Several months ago, Gordon and I flew to Arizona and looked over some land. And yes, we kept our trip secret, for reasons I don't recall."

"Were you two buying land out there as a marital investment or marital retreat?"

"If you're so preoccupied with marrying, start dating and get a wife, one who will worship you and fulfill every fantasy, bison skins and all. In fact, build a longhouse for all I care, and live off the land like your glorious ancestors. Pretend you're living out the pages of *Dances with Wolves*. Do something, but stop trying to put the make on me. I'm engaged. Besides, get out of my home. You came in unannounced and I'm really ticked. I came close to hitting you again a moment ago."

"Diana, I'm sorry for my bad behavior, it makes me realize I need to change, or to quote Lincoln, ' . . . All over this broad land will yet swell the chorus of Union, when again touched, as surely they will be, by the better angels of our nature."

She had no idea what Lincoln's first inaugural speech had to do with the present moment, and responded with silence.

However, Lincoln's phrase, "better angels," may have had something to do with her sense of tranquility. In telling Ross to cease his rude behavior and speech, she had expressed her feelings, and thus, had released the pent up frustration.

Expressing feelings was new to her; she never dared express her feelings in her formative years. It just wasn't done in her family; perhaps in no family she knew. Why was it taboo in her youth to say what she felt? Why did generations of American families 'frozen' in letting others know their feelings? It made no sense. And to paraphrase a title of a Jane Austen book, there was no "sense" in this lack of "sensibility;" feelings were hidden, and parents and society gave no reason.

Little did she know Ross was an amateur authority on both Lincoln and Red Jacket, Ross' ancestor. He had read their speeches and memorized a few of them, in parts, or as whole speeches. It was a hobby Ross never spoke of for reasons unknown. There again, the secretive side of human behavior and misbehavior prevailed.

"Oh, before I leave and seek my 'better angels' of behavior Diana, I have something for you. Here's the phone number to his parent's home. I'll leave it on the table. Mrs. Paradise will fill in the details. I do remember her saying she'd pay for your ticket to fly into Buffalo. There a relative will pick you up and drive you to Glen Iris. Mrs. Paradise has a big home and plenty of rooms. She's anxious to see you. Well, that's all for now. I am departing before you call the SWAT team."

"Please knock next time. Don't just walk in. A friend of mine was assaulted by someone who walked into her apartment unannounced. It happened to be a guy she hadn't seen in a year, but still had the key to her place. That bum is in prison now."

"All right, all right, I've been warned. Now have a safe trip to Buffalo and call me if you want a ride to the airport. Yet please do not take five suitcases on this trip, it's only a few days away from home. Gordon's warned me of your suitcase obsession."

She threw the club at him and he deflected it with his left arm. From there he walked off and drove away. Diana locked her door and called a locksmith immediately, asking him to install another deadbolt tomorrow, late in the day when she could be home to open her door for him. It being Sunday, the answering service took her message.

It was late, about 10 p.m. and she needed to get purchase milk and wheat bread for breakfast. She wore jeans, a short sleeved shirt and slip-on shoes; droving to the nearest Quik Trip. She filled up with gasoline too, and then went inside to pay. Suddenly an urge hit and she went to the restroom. The cleanliness surprised her. Yet she wasn't here to inspect. As she finished, getting up to leave, she opened the door only to see a scared young kid with a pistol holding up the cashier. Surprised by the incident before her, she quickly grabbed a mop next to the bathroom door and snuck up behind the robber. In a second she thrust the mop into the back of his head, and so startled the kid, he fired the gun and placed a bullet in the ceiling. The cashier grabbed the gun and Diana hit the kid again. The getaway car outside drove off in a panic, just as the robber raced outside to obtain his ride. In minutes the police arrived and the kid gave up. Diana was so shook up that she leaned against the soft drink cooler and nearly fainted. The police entered and got her statement and the cashier's statement. The cashier thanked Diana and gave her the milk and bread free; it was "on him."

The thought kept racing through her mind, "I could have been shot in an empty Quik Trip. What is life coming to; can't people shop for groceries without taking their lives in their hands?"

"Lady, mind if I drive you home?" asked the cashier, "I just called the manager and he's coming to relieve me."

"No, I think I'll call a girlfriend and ask her to drive me home, as I'm quite shaken by this near fatal incident. Thanks anyway. It was rough on you, too. Now you can go home and tell your wife and kids what happened."

"I'm not married, and that's why I was hoping I could take you out for a late night snack. We've just come pretty close to dying together as anyone I've known."

Just then a police officer came up to her and stated that he had seen her before and couldn't place her. Then he remembered. "Oh yeah, last weekend you fell out of the truck that Indian was driving. I nearly gave him a ticket for illegal parking." With that he laughed and departed.

The cashier felt despondent, "So, you've got a guy you're seeing?"

"Well actually, the man I'm engaged to is out of town, and the Indian is a close friend. I'm sorry to disappoint you. I'm sure another woman will gladly take up with you in the near future. You're a gentleman, and women like gentlemen."

He nodded and smiled, at least she acknowledged him as a man, not a boy.

Diana called Trudy, a Blithe Petroleum secretarial friend, and asked for a ride. Trudy was still up watching television while her husband snored in the background.

"Trudy, I'm sorry to be calling so late. I need a ride home after stopping a robbery in a convenience store."

"You did what in a store?"

"I stopped a robbery; the nighttime assistant and I nearly got shot while we unarmed a teenage robber."

"Diana, your life is exciting. I'm here in bed with Gene, just listening to him as he's asleep against me, smiling, and perhaps dreaming of the good times we've had over the years."

"It sounds good to me Trudy, sorry to inhibit your love life, but I'm scared and shook up. I want a ride home."

"You're not hurting my love life. I'm waiting for something to happen in this movie I'm watching."

By now Diana was feeling better, but proceeded to say, "I was offered a ride by the night manager, but turned him down."

"Why didn't you accept his offer?"

"Trudy, I'm engaged. It would be inappropriate of me to accept rides from strangers."

Trudy wasn't listening closely, for she was quite drowsy, however, she stated, "Now my husband is in deep sleep. That means I could have a party in the living room and he'd not hear a thing. Besides Diana, I'm too sleepy to drive right now."

"Trudy, I thought marriage was so terrific all the time. There's love, companionship, and unceasing closeness."

"Oh it is for awhile, and then the newness wears off."

"On second thought, Diana said, I'll drive myself home. Just talking to you has been therapeutic. I feel better now. For the last few minutes I was too frightened to drive. Besides, as you just said, you're too drowsy. It could be fatal for you to drive over here. I just needed someone to talk, really, I'm fine now."

The next morning arrived too quickly. Diana was still scared and ate breakfast in slow motion. Her fear was giving her a queasy stomach and she was unable to drink her juice.

The phone rang and it was only 8:15.

"Hello."

"Diana, mom and I congratulate you on your police duty."

"Daddy, hello; how did you know about last night?"

"Connections with Tulsa's Chief of Police. He called just a few minutes ago and told mother and me of your heroic action."

"Daddy, I'm so scared. I was nearly shot last night."

"Then take the day off. Your boss will understand. Take a personal day or vacation time."

"Well that's a good idea. In fact, it reminds me that I have to take off and fly to New York in a few days."

"Why dear, what's happening back there?"

"Gordon's parents want me to attend a will reading. He's out of town and needs coverage."

"Where is that man of yours anyway? We haven't seen him in months. I thought you two were marrying?"

"Well that's on hold for now. He's out of town and needs help. I'll be in Glen Iris, New York in a few days. Here's the number: (585) 555-1951, Mr. and Mrs. Paradise. I can't remember their first names. He runs a pharmacy though, Paradise Drug and Fountain, something like that."

"Well dear, good talking to you. We haven't seen you in awhile and were wondering about you. You keep too busy. You need to visit home more often, or at least call. Bless you daughter, we aren't going to be around forever. Besides, you need to get married so your mother and I can brag about our grandchildren. Old folks need grandchildren to brag on and spoil."

"Oh daddy, you're being silly again. You have plenty of time to enjoy grandkids. Actually, aren't you and mom too young to be grandparents?"

Then mom got on an extra line. "Now dear, you be careful about going out late at night. You nearly got shot last night. We talked to the Chief and he scared us to death with the details. You were blessed. Thank God you're safe and sound. You have got to be careful."

"Yes mother, I'm listening. I'll be more careful." To herself Diana said, "Thanks for the lecture." They hung up and Diana called work. Her boss approved her day off. Then she asked if Trudy could stay off too. As a favor to Diana, yes, Trudy could have off too with pay. Diana quickly dialed Trudy's home.

"Hello."

"Trudy, good news. You're off today with pay. I asked David and he gave us off for good behavior."

"He must be in a good mood. He must have had a good weekend at home. Besides, I was running late and now I have a perfect excuse to stay home with the children, a rarity these past few years.

"Well, Eugene left a few hours ago. I've got the children to take care of today; not the neighbor's daycare center."

"Tomorrow ask Gene to give you some hugs and kisses before he leaves!"

"Fat chance. Once he's ready to leave, nothing will stop him. He's such a workaholic."

"Not even for love?"

"Love? Are you kidding? That was before marriage. You're talking married with kids now."

"Then you hug and kiss him, and tell him you love him when he returns home tonight."

"Oh, one more thing, I'm flying to New York in a few days. I've got to call David back and get more time off."

"Diana, how can you take off time now? It's been years since you've vacationed."

"Now don't get sarcastic. This woman needs a break."

"Well at least you're going someplace interesting. Going to take in a play or two? Eat at Tavern on the Green, or the Russian Tea Room, for me."

"No Trudy, upstate New York, not the city."

"Oh, how boring."

"I'm going to a will reading for Gordon. He's out of town and needs me to be there. I'm going to stay with his parents and that may be enjoyable, besides, I've never met them! I hope to see Niagara Falls with Gordon's family."

Then Trudy asked if I was seeing anyone new since Gordon had all but disappeared.

"No, I'm not seeing anyone nor do I want to. I'm engaged, though Gordon's been gone quite awhile. Trudy, my dear friend, let's get off this subject. I need to get some more sleep, and then call Gordon's family. I've got to get this trip planned. "Trudy, get off the phone and make plans to have fun tonight. You sound in dire need of his loving attention."

"Yes, all right, I'll plan a romantic evening and rent the kids out to the neighbors. Bye."

"Bye, have fun." Click.

"That Trudy can be an airhead sometimes," Diana said to herself. Then again, Trudy can be the most delightful of friends. She reminds me of Teri Garr, who's so delightful!

Diana recalled David and obtained permission for two weeks off. There wasn't much going on anyway. He'd cover for her if necessary, and ironically the Houston job could wait a few weeks. David liked her a lot and had her over once in awhile to dine with his family. His wife, Hester, enjoyed Diana's company.

Afterwards, Diana was ready to enter the sleep zone, and then remembered that New York time was an hour ahead. If it's 9:15 now, it's 10:15 in Glen Iris.

She dialed the number for the Paradise residence. No answer. She called information and obtained the pharmacy number. Dialing the number she absentmindedly started humming.

The call was answered, "Hello, Paradise Pharmacy."

"Good morning Mr. Paradise, this is Diana _____."

"Good morning Diana, is this a refill or new prescription?"

"Refill? No Mr. Paradise, I'm Gordon's fiancée calling from Tulsa."

"Please forgive me Diana. What a memory I have. Too many years counting pills is my only excuse! Actually, pills should be stated 'tablets' or 'capsules.' Pills sound illegal. By the way, how are you dear?"

"I'm well and ready to fly into Buffalo," she said eagerly.

"Good. Fly into Buffalo and Gordon's cousin will pick you up. He lives in Buffalo. His name is Mitch Paradise. He's my brother's son. Mitch will drive you to Glen Iris safely. Mother will wire you the money for your tickets tomorrow. I mean of course, your future mother-in-law. While on that subject, you are to call us by our first names, and you must fill us in on that prodigal son of ours. We haven't heard from him in six months, and I'm ready to disown him for emotional abandonment!"

"I will fill you and mom in, though she had forgotten Gordon's parents first names. I'll do my best to keep him alive in the family."

Her thoughts shifted back to Gordon. With her words spoken to Gordon's dad, she felt a keen sense of irony. Gordon might possibly be dead. In fact, part of her recent behavior, or rather misbehavior, stemmed from the anxiety regarding his life. If he were dead, then she felt dead too. If he was alive, then she felt alive. She knew this thought pattern resembled a thing called 'co-dependency,' but she wasn't sure what she could do about it.

Well, things will improve when Ross goes after Gordon. That is, if he was telling the truth. Then she realized that Gordon had trusted his life to Ross and that things had to work out. The thought of Gordon's demise made her ill. She would lose her mind if he was dead. She would prefer to have died with him, or at least have died before he did. His reason for leaving Tulsa seemed nebulous, at best, childish; yet a man does what he feels is necessary.

Yet how did she put up with him over this 'galaxy game' he played? It angered her; she knew she'd let him get away with too much. Once returned, he's either selling his information to the highest bidder, or getting a regular teaching job at a university. No more nonsense of 'waltzing' through the cosmos.

The next day she awoke to a telephone call. Barely awake she said, "Hello, what do you want?"

"Good morning, it is I, your favorite Seneca Indian."

"Oh, hi Ross, what are you doing sober this early? And speaking grammatically correct too, you must really be sober."

"I'll ignore that remark and tell you the good news. I received a patent yesterday on my laser therapy for adipose tissue reduction, and I'm close to getting a patent on my solar powered automobile. What do you think of me now? Don't you realize that in three to five years I'll be swimming in money? I could buy you any house in Tulsa you wanted, with maids and servants at your beckon call. We could take a world honeymoon and see the sights from Stonehenge to the Great Wall; from the Hawaiian beaches to the Sahara Desert. We would dine in Paris and eat pasta in Florence. We would listen to Mozart in Prague and see the Hermitage Museum in Russia. We would . . . ."

"Hold on Chief Red Jacket, get your priorities straight. First, we are not a couple. I'm your best friend's fiancée and you are going to enter the time 'thing' and bring him back from his galactic adventure. I am, as you can tell from my tone of voice, fed up with your romantic overtures in our conversations, and demand that you cease and desist now. Otherwise, I will call my lawyer and slap you with a restraining order. So cool your passions with a bucket of ice."

"Diana, I thought I knew you better, surely you can't fault a man for being enthralled with a beautiful woman? A woman who may or may not be engaged anymore; truly you have got to keep an open mind. You need to consider other romantic options. Besides, what has he done to you except leave you at the time of engagement? What kind of man is my best friend? Besides, you've got competition from Anne, his housekeeper."

"Housekeeper? I thought you got your sister-in-law, or hired a domestic, to keep up his place while he was gone?"

"I didn't need to hire out this work for Gordon. The neighbor woman has been pretty devoted to his place since he left. Besides, it keeps her mind off her husband, the cop."

"What do you mean by that statement?"

"Her husband died in the line of duty, and this extra work keeps her mind occupied, and gives her extra cash. She's not financially endowed as you are Miss Fleming."

"Forget all the details Ross. Just tell lady domestic to stay out of his house and I'll talk to her when I return from New York. I'm leaving Wednesday. Gordon and I will be getting some inheritance money, so we'll be just fine. Besides, I pull down a hundred grand myself. Not bad for a dumb blonde, wouldn't you say?"

"Diana, any guy who would call you a dumb blonde is nuts, and probably blind and deaf too. You are absolutely a fine woman, mind, body and soul."

"Ross, I told you, no more comments. I mean it. My lawyer is going to write you a nasty letter if you don't stop your suggestive talk."

"This is one Indian who's heard the drums from your camp. I'll close my mouth and wish you a happy and safe trip to Paradise Drug and Fountain."

"Thanks and goodbye, see you when I get back, she replied.

She hesitated a few moments, then stated, "Ross, please forgive my temper tantrum. I'm not having any lawyer send you a letter. I'm angry over this whole event he took upon himself, and the fact that so much time has passed since we've heard from him. Now I have to meet his family and lie about Gordon's true location, one we don't even know."

"Thank you Diana, I accept your apology. By the way, do you need a ride to the airport?"

"No thank you; yet allow me to say congratulations on your patents. I'm proud of you. Now go and bring Gordon back, then we'll have a reunion when he returns."

The following day she received the Western Union wire and had the money for her ticket. Buying a ticket at the last minute cost his parents plenty, but they would all be getting an inheritance. This would be the second inheritance for his family, whereas her family had never inherited money; yet had inherited a delightful 1964 Mustang from her uncle Robert, when he passed away suddenly in 1975. Her brother, Jay, kept the Mustang in an old barn and had driven it only 3400 miles. Yet it wasn't only for Jay's pleasure, her mom and dad let Diana drive it in high school too.

Now it's kept once again in a barn space in Bixby, by family who grew various vegetables in that rich Bixby soil, and kept the car covered with a huge waterproof tarp, with wooden planks under each tire, and hidden in a stall from burglars.

The flight to Buffalo was smooth, for she disliked turbulent flights. Departing from the plane she immediately noticed a man who looked a bit like Gordon holding a sign saying "Diana Fleming." She stuck out her arm and shook hands with Cousin Mitch.

"Nice to meet you Diana. I've heard good things about you."

"It's nice of you to pick me up and drive me to Glen Iris. I look forward to meeting the whole clan." she said.

"The whole clan and nothing but the clan, so help me Senator Byrd, a former Klan member! By the way, speaking of Washington, D.C., when thinking of our Supreme Court Justices, just remember Rowan and Martin's television program's funniest line, "Here come da' judge, here come da' judge," he said laughingly, repeating himself several times, reprising the humor of "Laugh In."

Diana said to herself, "This guy's a little flaky and we've just met. This is not a fortuitous moment."

"Well Mitch, what do you do?"

"Why Miss Fleming, I'm your escort, though I drive a Continental. And my sign is Taurus and my favorite Presidents are Lincoln and Ford. Do you get it Miss Fleming?"

She rolled her eyes and hesitantly entered the front seat with this pseudo-comedian.

"I think you're rather beautiful Miss Fleming. Even your legs are shaved. Some women don't shave their legs or their armpits. Oh how vulgar, I mean arm cavity. Pit is so vulgar."

"Thanks for the compliment. At least I think it was a compliment. Perhaps a bit left handed?"

"Really Diana, don't knock us lefties. We aren't sinister at all, though we're occasionally gauche."

"Touché Mitchell."

"Oh my, touché to you Rhonda Fleming* for being so observant; by the way, I adore your sense of humor."

"You're a punster, aren't you Mitchell?"

"Only mother calls me Mitchell," he stated.

"What does your wife call you?" she asked.

"Oh, a host of things, for example: 'crazy, or witty; yet John Greenleaf was Whittier!"

"Nixon's Whittier too, Mitchell." Two can play this silly game, she said to herself.

"Touché again Miss Fleming 1951, born to charm, beauty, money and drive; yes, you're truly a 20th century woman."

"What's with 1951?"

"Your birth year, of course."

"You're wrong. 1955 was my birth year, not '51."

"So I was off four years, sue me! Or saw me, or see me off to Nederland or Disney World."

Diana was ready to strangle this lunatic cousin; yet attempted to carry on conversation.

"Were you born here in Buffalo" she asked.

"I don't know, I was an adopted child. Yet, indeed, I'm the good humor man. Good, so good am I. Oh, speaking of ice cream, lets stop and get a scoop or two of our favorite flavors. How does that sound? Besides, I feel my blood sugar level dropping."

"Are you diabetic Mitch?"

"No, just craving sweets, my dear woman, and future cousin."

"Sweets will make you obese and give you acne," Diana stated.

---

*   Rhonda Fleming: born 1923—Actress and singer, still very much a live (April 2010). She co-starred with Ronald Reagan, Robert Mitchum, and Charleton Heston.

"Oh I just love acne. I always shop at their stores."

"Don't you mean Acme, Mitchell?" she inquired,

"Acne, Acme, what's the difference between the two entities, my dearest woman? Besides, you forget, only Mother calls me Mitchell. And mother you're not. Not even my biological one. Unless you say, 'please,' then I'll let you call me Mitchell. Maybe my middle name too."

"Oh definitely, I wish to know your middle name. I'd enjoy knowing it." She was attempting to appease him with rational conversation.

"Well dear, guess my middle name?" he asked.

"James?"

"No."

"John?"

"No."

"Thomas?"

"I doubt it!"

"Daniel?"

"No."

"Abraham?"

"No, but close. It's a Presidential name."

Diana asked in sequence, "Jefferson, Lincoln, Garfield, Theodore, Franklin, Truman, or how about George, are any of these names correctly your middle name?"

"None are correct, now do you give up? Besides, this means you pay for the ice cream."

"What is your middle name then?" she asked in exasperation.

"McKinley."

"McKinley, why McKinley?"

"Mitchell McKinley Paradise. As you know, McKinley was shot and killed in Buffalo in 1901. My great-great grandfather witnessed the shooting; hence, I was named for an assassinated President. Amazing story is it not?"

"Yes, it is," she said with sincere agreement.

"Enough with my middle name, it's a fact and now let's forget it. Let's get a scoop of delicious ice cream at the next drive-in we pass."

"Maybe we should hold off on ice cream, it's too messy with a cone. Besides, I'm losing interest."

"Interest? Oh where were we before we spoke of banking? Oh yes, ice cream cones. I love cones, or any geometric shape. It's all so mathematical."

"Ice cream cones are mathematical?" she asked quizzically.

"Ice is nice, warm is better. Better is butter, butter pecan is my favorite, or as my urologist says, 'pee-can.'"

"Mitch, you're driving me crazy."

"You're right. I am driving. How observant."

"Let's be quiet for awhile." said she softly.

"You're no fun. You're just like my wife, actually, ex-wife. She tired of my humor."

"I'm getting tired too Mitch. Please stop at this ice cream store just coming up."

"What, no cones for my dear lady? Oh that's right, cones are fattening. And yes, you do need to lose some weight. Besides, I'll wait until Glen Iris and eat ice cream at my uncle's pharmacy and fountain."

Diana rubbed her temples and screamed out, "Shush up you moron! You are going to hush and drive me quietly to Glen Iris. If not I will take a bus! Comprende?"

"Are you Hispanic? Your Spanish is divine!"

"No, I'm not Hispanic. I'm Dutch-German and half Irish. So please be quiet now. Or at least talk normal, if you're capable of such dialogue. Tell me about your life and marriage. But no puns, no joker-isms. Just speak plain ordinary American-English. All right Mitch, do you consent?"

"I may never talk to you again. You can't take a joke and you're not able to follow puns with much enthusiasm. Really Miss Flemish, you ought to reconsider marrying my cousin. He's a punster too. We're so much alike. We used to have so much fun as children."

"Now there's a nice subject, childhood. Tell me about it."

"Would you like to see Niagara Falls now, or on the return trip to the airport?"

"Niagara Falls? I asked about childhood. How did you change the subject so quickly?"

"Childhood equals the Falls, Miss Flemish."

"Miss Fleming, not Flemish."

"Have it your way witch."

"Don't call me names. We just met an hour ago and I don't deserve this verbal garbage. Drop me off in the next big town, and I'll take the bus."

"Why Miss Fleming, I could never drop you off at a bus stop. There are weirdoes at such places. You'd be unsafe. I promised Auntie that you'd arrive safe and sound as a newborn baby to the doorsteps of the Paradise mansion."

"Mansion?"

"We call it 'the Mansion.'"

"Mitch, did you have a rough childhood?"

"I'll never tell. My lips are sealed. Good families never air dirty laundry. That's what we say. Yes ma'am, we never air our dirty lingerie in front of guests. We have our pride, our ego, and our fortune. We in the Paradise clan would rather die than hang dirty socks and long johns in our front yard for all to laugh at. Yes, we have pride. We're purebreds."

"I thought I asked you to quiet down."

"At least give me the courtesy to respond Miss Flame."

"Fleming, not Flame."

"Really Diana, you're something else. Have you ever considered group therapy? Or even in-patient therapy for your hang-ups?"

"What hang-ups Mitch?" By now she was quite irritated.

"Why your poor attitude and blatant hostility are both obvious to me. You have not only made rude overtones, or rather blatant passes at me, a vulnerable, newly divorced man, you have also yelled at me and told me to shut up, a phrase I find offensive. Besides, mother used that phrase on me for two decades, and then I moved out of her house and went to college. Then I attended law school."

"I never said 'shut up.' Then she changed the conversation totally around.

You're an attorney?" she inquired.

"Yes, University of Buffalo, Class of '84. The year Reagan was re-elected."

"Yes, I remember the year Mitch. I'm surprised that you're an attorney. What kind are you?"

"Simply the best, Miss Fleming, simply the best, that is what I am, the best attorney since former President Millard Fillmore practiced here near Buffalo many years ago."

For the next hour he was silent. Yet she was ready to talk law! She wanted to ask him some legal points regarding business. Yet this "nut" was quiet now and she enjoyed the quiet. She said to herself, "He needs to be written up in the psych journals. He's as loony as a lake in Canada!" She had never met a more obnoxious person. All this occurred so soon after Ross' verbal harassment. She doesn't deserve this mistreatment. She deserves wealth, beauty and fame, not this craziness.

In her innermost thoughts she asked herself, "Is life ever fair? Could Gordon really be dead? Could his best friend really be putting "the 'make' on her six months after his departure? Was the rest of the Paradise family this crazy? Was the Paradise clan composed of bizarre people who talk like Mitch, or decide like Gordon to traverse to distant lands? If life got any weirder she was going to go throw a Class A-1 fit, just like the one she gave as a child when she didn't get the pony for her tenth birthday.

They pulled up in front of the Paradise home, a rather modest 'mansion,' just like Gordon told her.

"Nice, but not a Frank Lloyd Wright design," she said to herself.

"Miss Fleming, did you know that Frank Lloyd Wright was never wrong?"

She was startled. How did he know she had just thought of Frank Lloyd Wright?

He smiled at her in a forced way.

"No way," she said to herself, "is this guy telepathic. If he is, I'm in trouble."

"Please Miss Flame; don't trouble yourself with the luggage. I'll have a cousin place it in your room, a room close to mine. My back won't allow me to carry heavy items. My hernia won't either. We must wait for my younger cousin."

"Not necessary cousin Mitch, I'm quite capable of carrying these things."

"Well I brought you this far. Now I must go to the pharmacy and get a vanilla hot fudge sundae with crushed walnuts and whipped cream. They make the best on earth at Paradise Drug and Fountain."

"Bring one home for me, please."

"I'm rather shy of cash, I have just enough for myself."

"Oh here, take a few dollars."

"Miss Flemish, contain yourself. People will think you're offering money for illicit reasons."

"Really Mitch, in your imagination."

Diana was dropped off and met Mrs. Paradise.

"Call me Nancy," she said shaking hands with Diana. Gordon's sisters were there too, along with their husbands and children. The sisters were a bit jealous of Diana's beauty. Diana felt awkward being with Gordon's family without him, and when the conversation centered on his absence, would she tell the truth or lie? How could his family believe that Gordon was in the galaxy somewhere? She barely believed it herself!

"Well Diana, please tell us, where is my prodigal son?"

"Nancy, your wonderful son is on a secret mission for . . . NASA."

"NASA? What is he doing for them?

The sisters leaned forward with a quizzical look.

"Yes, NASA has Gordon on a secret space mission. He's in orbit, and after landing from the space shuttle, he'll be placed inside an underground cavern for nearly six months. Scientists wanted someone who would live in space, then live inside the earth. They wanted to study the effects of contrast, outer versus inner space. He volunteered."

They were incredulous. "Why didn't he tell us? Surely he could have phoned us?"

"Gordon's absent-minded at best. His science and wild ideas blind him to family and friends. He barely told me."

"That's our brother, selfish brat. Intelligent, adventuresome, bookish, forgetful, and insensitive, however, we haven't heard of any space shuttle liftoffs recently."

"The liftoff was secretive. The public was not to know. NASA has its secret side."

What a bald-faced lie she was telling! Why was it necessary to con them? She felt that the truth was too much for them to hold intact. Besides, gossip could ruin Trans-17.

The mystery was "solved" in their thoughts, at least for now, in the Paradise family. Yet they all laughed and played cards that afternoon and drank lemonade in the back porch. Mitchell joined in too, though he was unusually quiet now and quit early. He returned to his room and slept.

Diana enjoyed her lemonade, and then took a walk with the sisters and their children after the card game ended, They took Diana to the town park and played on the swings and slide. It was a gorgeous fall day in New York State. Walking about, Gordon's sisters showed Diana their old high school, the stores of their hometown, the houses of old family friends, the county museum, and their elementary school. Most of all, the sisters excitedly shared the town's main attraction, an old stone watering trough for horses in the days prior to automobiles. It was called the "Bear Fountain," still with water but no bubbling fountain existed. Instead, on a masonry cylinder, a carved cub bear held onto a stone pole with a light atop its pole. It was a magnificently rounded stone trough, as mentioned, for horses to drink from in days long gone, and now served as a traffic light and guide, as cars were forced to drive around its dynamic presence, amid the center of Main Street. It was a well known Glen Iris landmark, and in days past, all walking children passed by the Bear fountain daily to-and-from school. Now, decades later, the elementary, junior high, and high school were situated on the north end of town. Few, if any students walked to school now. Walking had been replaced by the newer generation by cars, SUV's, and busses. However, busses had always played an important role in transporting those students living on farms in the school district. That part remained true today. It was to the town's children, that walking had been relegated to near extinction, due to the location of the school buildings.

However, the village's true fame resided in the village's State College, a part of the State University of New York system. And a proud college it was, with new and old buildings sitting beside one another in harmony. One knew the old buildings for the extensive ivy covering their exteriors, all green, for little brick was noticeable with nearly a century of ivy growth.

Thus college students were a huge part of the heritage and commerce of the village, and the Paradise Pharmacy was an excellent place for male and female students to socialize between classes or on weekends. It was also known as the location to several marriage proposals, so romance and business united under the same roof.

When young couples married and told Mr. Paradise of their marriage proposal occurring in his store, he instantly gave the young couple a free milkshake or double scooped ice cream cone. It was a joy for Walter Paradise to be part of another's life, a moment that made the life of two people one of great happiness. Love never ages, for each generation renews its pleasure, and the village had been incorporated for over 175 years! Love is indeed, eternal, even in a small village.

The pharmacy building had been constructed after the Civil War, and served at one time as a meeting place for veterans. Later it was a grocery store, then finally, at the turn of the 20th century, made into a pharmacy. Dad bought it a few years after World War II ended.

Upon their way home, they stopped at dad's store. The young woman behind the counter scooped vanilla ice cream cones for all, "On the house," dad insisted, while he filled more prescriptions. Diana still craved ice cream and ordered another double scoop, butter pecan in a cup, and it tasted great. The sisters drank a tall glass of water and gave the children gum to chew. They were amazed at Diana's ice cream craving; how could she remain thin and consume so much ice cream?

Diana looked about the store and felt the urge to shop. She noticed that Perm Shampoo was on sale, Revlon makeup too. Look at all those Hallmark cards! This store was a shopper's paradise. She needed a few personal items too. She bought toothpaste and a new brush for now. She also picked up a copy of *Young Corporate Women* to read later, and sugar free candy. This was a day of carefree living.

Walking outside to return home, the warmth of the day contrasted with the air conditioning of the drug store. Yet everyone was happy and commented on their enjoyment of Diana's visit to Glen Iris.

"I love old stores," Diana said.

"Yes, we do too. That place is our dad's. He lives there. Dad wouldn't know what to do if that store wasn't open. He's married to it; Mom is just his second wife!" they laughed.

"Dad would love it if we took over. Then he could retire and he and mom could travel as they said they'd always do. Maybe we should buy the old place Sis; wouldn't it be great to raise the kids where we grew up?"

Upon their return home Diana excused herself and decided to relax and shower. She went to shower, though once through with her shower, she realized she had forgotten her robe. She placed the biggest towel available over her torso and dashed through the upstairs hall to her room. While quickly attempting to get to her room for a robe, she strangely wondered if she'd have an appetite for dinner, having eaten such a large amount of ice cream this afternoon; perhaps her fears were the cause of this sugar craving. At least, that's her conclusion. Besides, when's the last time she ate ice cream? She rarely ate it at home.

Just then Mitch came out and caught sight of her uncovered backside.

"This incident is interesting, a nymph floating through yonder hall for her lover. This will be a delicious trip after all. To think I was bored with Diana. Now she's showed me her better side, dare I ask for more?"

In reply Diana slammed her door and yelled "Shush!" Once downstairs, Aunt Nancy had a few words with her nephew.

"Mitchell, you leave Diana alone. Don't drive the girl crazy. I regret you were the one picking her up at the airport. You probably bombarded her with your version of humor."

"Auntie Bear, hold your reins tight. Your nephew was the perfect gentleman for that woman. Besides, she's the one that can't be trusted. She gave me money for immoral purposes."

"Now don't lie to me. I'll slap your face even if you are a thirty seven year old attorney."

"Oh Auntie, spank me, I do wish it now. But only in front of my kissing cousins."

"Mitch, I do hope you get little from this will tomorrow. Afterwards you could admit yourself to Buffalo's psych ward." his Aunt replied harshly.

"Nana dear, I was hoping for a lot. I desire early retirement and the purchase of Uncle's pharmacy."

Nancy heard her nephew's words and was stunned, "Mitchell buying the pharmacy?" The mere thought was nauseating!

"Why Aunt Nana Bear, to own the pharmacy would keep me in drugs, get it? Besides, your daughters intoxicate me. If only first cousins could marry, I'd be happy."

Nancy shook her head, as Mitch went to the garage to look for a bicycle to ride. Once outside, ready to ride one of his cousin's bicycles, he decided to throw a small stone at Diana's window. The curtain was drawn and he tossed a pebble, then another. Soon Diana peered from between the curtains. He proceeded to yell, "I challenge you to a bicycle race."

Diana opened the window and said she was not interested.

"How about a game of tennis after dinner?"

"No." she said.

"How about competing in arm wrestling?"

"No."

"How about checkers or chess, do you play or partake in these games? I'm a chess wizard, the best at UB, or St. Bonaventure's, or any western New York University, even SUNY Geneseo, SUNY Fredonia, and SUNY Brockport. SUNY, SUNY, SUNY, never sunny, but SUNY, an acronym for the State University of New York, clever, is it nor? However, in New York City, it's CUNY. I've played chess all over western New York, and how appropriate, I so enjoy a good western—John Wayne, Gabby Hayes, Roy Rogers, and Oklahoma's Tom Mix and Will Rogers. I am a westerner at heart, though some say I'm heartless, but they who call me names are jealous of my many chess awards, ribbons, and decorations. If I receive anymore decorations, I'll become a 24/7/365 Christmas tree. Can you imagine me as a tree? Oh my, a tree is truly free. A family tree and free as a bird, but don't build a nest in my branches. Yet to branch out is my way of being social, a social rooster of sorts, and one who crows each morning, and whose love life is full of great looking chicks. Aren't I a dream date, as humorous; so brilliant and funny as to be 'punny,' though never puny."

"Punny? That's not a word, so shush up Mitch," Diana stated, irritated at Mitch's absurd requests.

"You're no fun. Besides, if I want to invent a new word, I will, plus I'm an attorney and know my rights, and my wrongs!

He laughed raucously, and then bicycled down the tree lined street. Yet he rode not on the side facing traffic, but in the middle of the road.

Mitch lived and spoke strangely. However, he was no 'stranger' to Buffalo's psychiatrists, psychologists, and therapists, they knew him well.

Diana departed her boudoir and walked gingerly to the kitchen below. A secret stairwell led right to this kitchen. This old residence was both mystical and novel. Her childhood home did not possess the charm or elegance of this 1875 residence.

Nancy was preparing dinner and Diana volunteered to assist.

"I see you found our secret stairwell. Gordon used it often and sometimes surprised his father and me. He enjoyed caves and old stairwells, and was fond of crawling beneath this old home as if he were burrowing; yet it was his curiosity. And like all the children, he never gave us trouble. Besides, his mind was always focused on the positive aspects of life, not the hurtful things. All my children were respectful. Well, I find myself bragging, forgive an elderly mother."

"Nancy, there's no shame in being proud of your children, I want that same feeling someday."

Nancy smiled and said softly, "You will dear, you will. Yet to change the subject entirely I dislike putting guests to work, but I would appreciate your help. Both girls are napping with the kids. Yet if you wish, please set the table, and then peel the potatoes. Thank you."

"Sure Nancy, whatever I can do to help."

"Diana, one thing though, was Mitchell behaving himself on your drive from the airport?"

"He was attempting to be funny."

"Was he?"

"No, Nancy, he was rather obnoxious."

"I was afraid of that possibility. I'm sorry dear that someone sane didn't pick you up. Mitchell is right out of the 'Addams Family.' He's bizarre."

"Do you know the reason for his behavior?" Diana inquired.

"No, not really, nothing that makes sense. Maybe he was born strange. He's a handful. Especially when he's committed to mental institutions, and that's a sad chapter to mention to you or anyone."

"What? How?"

"Oh dear, Mitch is our family secret. He's been in-and-out of Buffalo Psych wards for years. He's a bit loony at times. He's either overactive, or withdrawn. Often he's as irritating as biting into a peach pit."

"A real nut case I dare say!" Diana giggled, but felt Nancy's shame.

"Enough of Mitchell, tell me about you and your family," Nancy asked.

As they worked in the kitchen, Diana gave a brief Fleming family history, and then proceeded to tell 'mom' how great Gordon was to her, flaws and all.

"We mothers crave to hear good things about our children. Yet I'm repeating myself."

"That's fine Nancy, go ahead."

"Gordon was a fine child, loved books, worked hard, dreamy at times, sometimes lost in thought, and absent minded to the point of concern. He was a good in school. Yet his father had no time for any of the children. Mr. Paradise, I mean Walter, works all the time. He'll die filling a prescription for some old customer who owes him $300. He's so generous with others, but ignored the children, though unintentionally. Probably if he'd spent time with his children, someone would buy the store and keep it in the family. Daddy is so proud of his place. All our children were born there. I waited until the last minute helping him, and turned the backroom into a birthing center."

"Nancy, you've put up with a lot. You're a good lady." They smiled at each other, and then Nancy added, "The birthing center's back room was hardly sterile. Imagine, a mother giving birth to four babies in the backroom of a pharmacy; not a hospital's maternity ward. It's rather bizarre, but now it makes this backroom so special. It has memories so precious, and I'm as sentimental as my dear mother. Yes, this backroom was the first room my infant children breathed their first air. It's a personal museum for me and Walter. Yes, a museum full of memories; a museum no one else except the children appreciates. If we sell this old building, the new owners would not know, or care to know. what happened in their back storage room. To others it's merely a room, with no purpose except to store inventory. However, four infants were once part of its inventory! And what beautiful babies they were. Now I'm bragging again, pardon me."

Diana replied, "You made this storeroom a special place. And your grandchildren will treasure this room, for indeed, it is a treasure, a Paradise-family heirloom. In that sense, no price tag could be placed on its personal significance."

"Diana, you're going to make a great addition to this family. This time will be special for us all, the time we spent alone with Diana. If Gordon were here he'd take most, or all your free time. This way we get time alone to learn about Diana. What a pleasure it will be to have you as my daughter-in-law."

They hugged, Diana and Nancy, and a few tears fell to the floor, a reminder of the power of human sentiment.

Soon all the chores were done and the meal served. Even Mr. Paradise made it home in time to eat!

Mitchell returned home and sat quietly next to Diana. Yet a few times Diana felt as if someone were playing with her feet.

Mitch never looked up and ate the meatloaf, mashed potatoes, and salad, as if it were his last meal.

Diana enjoyed the talk and hoped that the two sisters would mention their mutual fantasy of buying their dad's store. Diana loved happy endings. Also, the dinner conversation bantered over tomorrow's will reading.

"Were they to be rich by this time tomorrow? Is it greed or curiosity?" the sisters asked everyone at the table.

The family bantered back and forth on this subject, and then changed their talk to children, movies seen, and the weather, and how beautiful the evening skies have been.

Diana wanted to speak about Gordon's galactic journey; yet knew this was not the time or place. It would have to wait a day or two before she told them the truth, or would she refrain?

Morning came and they went to the lawyer's office. It was an old building, red bricks streaked with white. The windows were old too, the glass showing prismatic signs of aging. The attorney came to the large table and all gathered here in the legal library of Luce, Hollenbeck, Heinzman, and Becherer.

Everyone gathered about the gorgeous wooden table, long enough for a Thanksgiving dinner party of twenty-five, generated excitement. Does money not stir emotions? Indeed the whole Paradise clan was gathered and wide awake.

As the will was read, Mr. Paradise received $75,000, and each of his children given $25,000. Gordon was also given Aunt Wendy's two canaries. Mrs. Paradise was to receive custody of Oliver Twist and Copperfield, the two cats; However, Mitch received the mansion and enough stock to maintain the gardens, two maids and one butler! Everyone was stunned. He smiled triumphantly and said in a low voice, "I was truly loved."

Diana, though, was not jealous, rather she was well pleased, as $25,000 was a great addition to their future together as husband and wife. If placed in the best stocks, they'd have a grand retirement fund in thirty years. Some pharmaceutical stock or even Wal-Mart went through her mind. Perhaps Microsoft and Exxon-Mobil would be worthy investments? And don't forget her employer's stock, Blithe Petroleum.

Other relatives were given smaller amounts. Walter's family made out well. Yet the sisters were angry and jealous that crazy Mitchell was given the Weston estate in Buffalo. Aunt Wendy Weston must have been on medication side affects to come up with her rationale. Yet the will reading was not over. It actually went on to read that since Mitchell was mentally unstable, making a living was difficult for him; that his role in the real world was lessened by what Doctors called manic depression, and that she, Wendy Weston, age 87 at the time of the will revision, was of sound mind and judgment. Besides, Mitchell was to open his doors to those in mental wards who sought a halfway residence in order to readapt to the outside world. If he did not open his doors to those needy people, the attorneys were to turn over the whole estate to the City of Buffalo as a psych half-way house. Three months were given to execute her wishes for the estate. Along with offering residence to mentally unstable patients, therapy was to be provided, as well as job training. Funds were set aside for the purpose of training and educating the mentally ill outcasts of society. Besides, she went on to explain in the will, that Mitchell was the illegitimate son of her granddaughter, Deborah Lea, therefore a responsibility existed that the family never knew. All were aghast! Cousin Deborah had an illegitimate son? Mitchell was thought to have been the child of another cousin, Lucille. Lucy raised Mitch as her own child. The events surrounding Mitch's birth were obscured by time, thirty-seven years. Life exists as the strangest of all things. Yet it was God's will and His will be done. As the family felt a wave of shock pulse through their minds, Mitchell leaned forward and wept.

When all felt reposed, they went out to eat at the finest dining establishment in Glen Iris, "Greco's." This Greek family offered filet mignon out of this world. "Filet for everyone," exclaimed Walter. They devoured a luncheon fit for Cleopatra and Antony; then drove to the pharmacy for ice cream. Mitch was silent during lunch and barely spoke. Diana went up to him and hugged him. He once again wept, using Diana's shoulder and hugging her closely.

However, his ice cream fell on the floor as he and Diana hugged, and the stock boy cleaned it up quickly, tossing it onto the backdoor's sidewalk for two stray dogs to devour. Mitchell just stared out the window from the seat of one of the pharmacy's row of dining booths, saying nothing.

"What is Gordon going to do with two birds?" asked the sisters.

"I have no idea. At present he has just one pet, a corgi named Duchess," Diana replied.

The sisters volunteered to take the bird's home with them. Their kids would adore having Aunt Wendy's canaries.

Mitch's face lit up as he said, "Send them to the Canary Islands." Everyone laughed and patted him on the back.

Out of the blue Diana stated, "It's been quite a day for the family. Is everyone happy with their inheritances?"

"Well of course we are! Now we can invest the money for our children's college funds."

"I like your attitude," Diana stated.

"How about you and Gordon, going on a year long honeymoon, wouldn't that be romantic?"

"I doubt it, not Gordon. He's a homebody. If we have two weeks for a vacation-honeymoon, we'll be blessed. We've spoken of vacationing in the Cayman Islands."

"Cayman Islands? We wouldn't dare take our husbands there, to a place where so much competition is literally hanging out."

"Competition, what do you mean?"

"Diana, are you really that naive? You're a gorgeous blonde; we're not. You can go to the Islands and look like a travel brochure's photograph. We're just two ordinary women from western New York."

"Come on you two, you don't do yourselves justice."

"Justice isn't the word, beauty is." they said in unison.

Diana felt on the spot and changed the subject. Soon they were all talking about ice cream flavors, and the difference in taste between Coke, Pepsi and RC Cola. Diana tried to uphold the flavor and delight of Dr Pepper brand soft drink; yet to these New Yorkers, it tasted terrible, something akin to prune juice, and how wrong they were too! It was a unique blend of twenty three flavors, among them raspberry, almond, and twenty one others. At one time she remembered hearing The Dr Pepper Company, was the world's largest buyer of raspberries. However, present company cared not, and that was their loss. And yes, Diana knew that soft drinks offered no nutritional value, but neither does music.

Walter returned behind the counter, and the rest of the family drove home. Mitchell, once home, went bike riding. Everyone else went to their rooms for a nap. Diana requested a fan to drown out the sounds of neighbors mowing lawns. She slept well.

A few hours of rest did her well; she was slowly awakening when she heard the phone ring in Mrs. Paradise's room. Then a scream followed!

Grabbing a robe, Diana raced into the hall where Gordon's sisters had immediately gathered.

"Mother, what happened?" everyone asked nervously.

"Your father experienced a heart attack at the store."

A wave of disbelief and heartache went through them like an electric current. In moments they were all in the car headed to the hospital in the next county. Glen Iris had no hospital. 911 had been called from the store and Walt was driven to Rochester's Strong Memorial Hospital. Diana prayed, and everyone else appeared lost in thought. What would happen if Mr. Paradise died now? Over and over in her mind, Diana kept saying to herself, "Gordon, where are you, where are you, where are you? Your dad may die!"

As the ambulance delivered Mr. Walter Paradise, father of four, grandfather of five, to Strong Memorial, each family member recalled his devotion as a father, a devoted husband, community landmark, diligent pharmacist and one time member of the school board. He also had given four years as mayor of this community overlooking the Genesee River. His life hung in question and Diana only wished that Mr. Paradise could be admitted to St. Francis in Tulsa. She knew not Strong Memorial's excellent reputation.

They all stumbled into the hospital's waiting room and Nancy was encircled by her children. All felt lost and prayed for their dad. Nancy prayed too, with soft words spoken to God from this waiting room that felt as barren as a stable.

There in the waiting room Diana sat numb for hours. She recalled the trivial things, as in Gordon's comments about his dad, and the fact that the five grandchildren had been assigned to a neighbor's house immediately prior to the adults' departure.

Diana asked Gordon's sisters if the two of them should not return home and pick up the children? All agreed it was a good idea, Diana would drive. Nancy stayed overnight at the hospital, an option not permitted in the 50s or 60s, as she remembered those times,

Diana drove while the sisters cried, and Diana attempted to comfort them, but to no avail. What comfort abides in such circumstances? None.

"Life is hard, so very hard," one sister said.

"And life is unfair," the other sister stated, with tears in her eyes.

"Yes, but tell me something about life that's fair? "Diana asked in a whisper.

No replies, just two sobbing sisters releasing their grief.

Chapter 15

Several days after my dad's heart attack, an event unknown to me, I began my ascent from the venom induced coma of the lizard. In the meantime the tunnel was being fortified and I was over watched by various caretakers. Though skin and bone, I was glad to be alive.

I opened my eyes and slowly focused on the faces around me. One was Zena and her father. They smiled at my reawakening. I lifted my hand to their grasp. Both touched me and I whispered, "Thank you for being here for me. I feel as if I've been asleep for a decade."

Zena spoke, "Please rest. You've been away a long time, an earth year according to my father."

I was shocked. Then I asked for help to get on my feet. She helped me, as did the Senator.

I felt wobbly on my feet, like a newborn calf. The Senator stated I needed food. I was helped over to the camp's canteen area and found a meal in progress. My noontime repast was soon before me. I ate slowly. Everything tasted wonderful; cold water a delight.

Days passed and my energy increased; stamina too. I was able to walk without assistance and slept a lot. Yet I awoke at a regular time, a predictable dawn, so to speak. Real living felt good. In fact, it felt wonderful to "feel" again. Life is not lived in sleep; only in the conscious passing of time does one sense time's existence. Yet without sleep, life cannot and will not survive. Again, one of life's ironies ruled life in unexpected ways.

"However, nearly twelve months of sleep?" it felt awkward to think such a thing.

My walks increased and I watched the tunnel in its final stage of completion. A lot had happened in the year I slept away. The attack on

Castlethorn neared. Now my fear increased for the safety and success of our attack. Seeing that I've been gone this long from earth, surely Ross and Diana thought me dead or, at best, lost forever. My ability to reach them was minimal, though I asked the Senator if my "beeper" had been retrieved. He stated, "No, it had not been found." Therefore my ability to reach home was non-existent. I felt hopeless.

Weeks passed and my strength grew ten-fold, I told the Senator I must return to the site of my capture, up river, and locate my beeper. Without it, I would be a castaway for my entire life here on an alien planet. Zena did not care to hear the word alien. Yet she understood my sadness in being forced to stay away from home. She offered to help me return up river once the parents had been freed from Castlethorn and the enemy conquered.

I asked Zena if the plans to overwhelm the enemy had been developed. She stated that once the tunnel freed the parents, it would be destroyed, and then all would flee into the woods. If the enemies followed, guerilla warfare would ensue.

"It was a plan, she admitted, yet not much of one."

Certainly, I could assist. With Zena at my side I viewed Castlethorn from a safe distance. Behind its immense and grotesque structure, a mountain range rose above it as a dark reminder to the evil Tragon. Fortunately, the entire digging operation was amazingly secretive to the point that Tragon knew not the effort to free his prisoners.

The furtive nature of Phillrey's efforts protected his people from constant battles and skirmishes with a sophisticated army. The old Senator was wise not to engage Tragon's forces face-to-face. There was no need to invite slaughter. Besides, he wished to protect all his clan from brutal warfare. He'd rather retreat once the parents were freed, than stand and fight against a well armed enemy. Tragon would one day fall from power anyway; it's a natural law. All tyrants die; falling before providential justice.

"Zena, look at that huge snow mass above Castlethorn."

"Yes, I see it. What of it?" she inquired.

"Would it be possible to 'encourage' the snow to slide into the castle, thus destroying it?

"Perhaps, but how?" she asked again.

I remembered the shiny and mirror-like surfaces of their shields.

"Perhaps, I said, the shields could focus the sun's light upon the mountain's snow and ice and bring them both thundering into Castlethorn?"

She looked at me with a puzzled expression, and then smiled. She understood my idea and ran to get the Senator. As I stood there viewing the scene, I envisioned hundreds of us focusing our shields upon the snowy mountainside. In time the snow would loosen and avalanching into Tragon's holdout. Perhaps the momentum would be so enormous that the fort's walls would collapse? I didn't know. Yet the plan had a flaw. We would be exposing our presence. Yet, during the day no frontal attack could take place, for if Tragon's troops confronted us, our people could literally blind them with the mirror-shields. In other words, we could focus part of our shields to the enemy and blatantly utilize solar power. The intensity of focused light would render a daylight assault impossible. Is a rear attack possible, I asked myself? At that moment Zena and her Father were at my side.

"Mr. Paradise, what is your plan? Surely a man who has had so much rest must be ready to see things more clearly," the Senator mused.

"I pray that is true, sir, I replied. My plan is simply one basic action. We utilize all our shields to focus a light beam on the mountain of snow and ice. Once melted, with the heat of concentrated energy, an avalanche will occur, rendering the enemy immobile. I see one of two things occurring. One, the snow mass will demolish their castle, and, secondly, if the avalanche does not crush their building, Tragon would be so preoccupied with tons of ice in his midst; we'd be long gone before he could attack us. We'd then have plenty of time for escape. My one concern is the amount of daylight available, though daylight is certainly more prevalent than a month ago."

"Your idea is excellent! I marvel at your ingenuity, Mr. Paradise."

Zena looked excited as I spoke. Her father's response was one of approval. Apparently she felt proud of my idea, just from the way she looked at me.

The Senator smiled as he replied, "As for length of days, have you not noticed that the nights are shortening to the point that daylight lasts twenty-plus hours?"

"Actually, I had noticed the longer days; summer draws near," I said.

"Yes," said Zena, night lasts only three to four hours. We approach Suntide, our longest day, in two weeks. We could keep the vigil of our shields aimed at the mountain for about 20 hours of daylight. Night passes quickly during Suntide."

My retort was quick, "Yet we open ourselves to nocturnal raids."

Once again Zena responded before the Senator could react, "Tragon is afraid of the night. He never attacks except in daylight."

My first impression was nonsense, no one is that superstitious. Yet did not the entire German Army in WWII refrain from an attack across the

English Channel due to Hitler's fear of water? Literally, he failed to conquer England due to hydrophobia, bizarre; yet a probable theory.

"You're saying then, Zena, that in two weeks we can align our troops to focus their shields into the daylight and point it toward the mountain?" Then a jolt from the unconscious ripped through my mind. "As the day progresses, so does the sun's movement, how to maintain focused energy on the mountain?"

As it went through my mind I asked the question out loud, then the Senator responded, "Place half of the shields on poles and the other half into the hands of our youth, who will move them accordingly to the sun's movement. Thereupon we maintain the heat's intensity in a line across the elevated snow mass. Surely in days an avalanche would occur."

I later discovered that certain words I used, like avalanche, were new to them. Yet they understood regardless of that fact.

We prepared to overtake Castlethorn as the days lengthened and the hundreds of mirror-surfaced shields were gathered. Dozens of young Zollerins gathered poles and made ready to place half of the shields upon them. Each pole being six to eight feet long, sturdy and placed secretly into the ground, this was the action undertaken. Tragon's forces once in a while scouted about during the day, but we'd all hide in the tunnel, now nearly complete. The Senator wanted no confrontation with enemy troops, while we prepared our solar attack, though we could easily blind them. As for our poles, they went unnoticed. The youths hung what looked like mistletoe from the poles, knowing that Tragon's warriors were fearful of the evergreen plant. Why? It was never explained. Superstition rarely made sense. Did mine? Did others'? Though a scientist, some superstition crept into my thinking; though Christian by choice, superstition sadly still existed within me. Yet it had greatly subsided over the years.

The tunnel diggers were now going deeper and delicately beneath the stones of Castlethorn. Excellent progress was made and the subterranean cave was widened and deepened. Now the youths must dig to the exact area where their parents' were interned, however, they had no firm knowledge of their parents' location.

Discussing the dilemma, Senator Phillrey concluded that he and three young warriors were to surrender themselves. Once inside, they would send messages to the digging party by thumping wooden clubs upon the ground. Zena thought her father's suggestion brave, but dangerous. Brave in that he would offer himself hostage in order to free others. Dangerous because of the avalanche planned. It was a complex issue, and tears ran down Zena's face as she bid farewell to her father and three warriors. Three of the most ingenious and strongest young men were chosen. They were all to communicate to the digging team with pounding noises, or else the entire plan would be subject to failure. Failure on this scale would destroy their society. They knew it, but spoke not of failure's cost.

If only my beeper, now called the "Z line" or simply "Z" was with me. I renamed the device as I pondered the Greek word Zoë, meaning "life". What better term to describe the beeper connection to Trans-17, my key to life. With Trans-17 I'd be able to transport myself inside Castlethorn and eliminate the need to place Phillrey and the three at risk. Yet would I not be at risk once inside? These were unspoken thoughts.

Yet the matter of truth was that my "Z" was not with me and that the Senator and three young warriors were in the woods ready to be seen and captured by Tragon's patrol. Today would change Zollerin history, and I prayed these four would not be tortured.

On the afternoon of his decision, the Senator set out and was captured along with his warriors. They were immediately taken to Tragon, appearing greasy and sweaty. His massive frame loomed before the petite and distinguished looking Phillrey. Tragon's beard was waxy and unkempt; his teeth stained; his eyes flaming like red embers on fire with rage. Long hair hung over his shoulders, like a lion's mane. Yet he looked not like a lion, but a wooly mammoth.

"Why are you here at Castlethorn, Senator? Did you think to free your people?" Then he laughed loudly and belligerently. His guards laughed as he laughed, snarled when he did, and were frozen with fear at his raging madness.

Tragon, a long lance at his side, grabbed it only to point and stab toward Phillrey. The Senator didn't move as Tragon hoped. He, the Senator, stood his ground and secretly impressed his enemy with confidence.

After harassing the group of four, Tragon went to practice spear throwing. He thought of using the Senator as his target, but not today, he said to himself, another day. As for now, something like arthritis angered his knees and shoulders, and tossing spears helped at times, or so he superstitiously thought.

As the four were led away to the dungeon in dark recesses of Castlethorn, they all strained their eyes to gather every detail to the layout of this morbid abode. The guards opened the rough-hewn door and the "majestic four" were rudely tossed inside. Once inside the prisoners rejoiced at seeing their leader, though fear surged seeing him captured. Dusting themselves off, the four made the rounds to greet everyone. All were ushered into a circle and Phillrey explained his plan. Soon afterward clumps of burnt logs were found and the pounding began. Fortunately the spear throwing contest was in full gear and the noise and excitement of Tragon's game blocked out the noise of thud-thud-thud-beat-beat-thud-clump-clump-thud-beat-.

Upon hearing the dull sounds filtered through the ground, the diggers became fanatical and made tremendous progress toward the exact spot of acoustical vibrations.

Tragon's games ceased, but another background noise took over to cover the sound coming from the prisoners' constant thudding upon the ground. Tragon created a huge grinding process for soft sandstone to be pulverized for road construction. He planned on creating roads from his Castlethorn to other locations on Zollerin, all roads in a five pointed shape, star-like in appearance, as they departed Castlethorn. He wasn't sure how to make roads; yet he wanted to crush rock to prepare for the final concept when his engineers concluded their design and scheme of execution. With all this slave labor available, he'd be insane not to build roads. No one could stop him, certainly not the band of ragged youths Phillrey left behind! As to the road's destinations, did it make much difference? His desire was to expand his conquest and feel himself stretch forth his control, as if the roads were mere extensions of his arms and legs.

Tragon's grinding continued night and day. Yet night was nearly absent from these summer days on Zollerin. Daylight nearly dominated the entire time spectrum. And as the grinders churned, everyone in prison took turns thumping logs upon the ground. Within days a shock of surprise raced through the entire camp of prisoners. Dirt was beginning to be indented beneath them as the tunnelers were now directly below. Gratefully the guards were high above them and rarely checked on the prisoners below. Freedom! Hearts were joyous; yet cautious. Suspicion must not be generated. Yet as the day darkened for a few hours, the tunnel diggers completed their task, and they opened a cavity directly into the camp's prison. How glad Phillrey and his people were at this moment. Soon freedom for the imprisoned would be bestowed. Now sheets of old fabric were placed over the hole and covered with straw and dirt. Doing so made it appear benign as the prison floor. Beneath the fabric, diggers widened the escape hatch and prepared for the exodus to commence.

As the sun began to rise into the pale green Zollerin sky, a row of bright objects shone forth from the distance beyond Castlethorn's gate. Startled enemy troops gathered along the sides of the wall, and Tragon himself stood angry and half mad at the spectacle of light. Within a few hours a row of intense light was focused overhead and onto the mountain side of icy snow. This scene made no sense to Tragon. He decided to attack the source of the beamed energy, however, his warriors found themselves blinded. As the advance progressed, Zena and her companions focused certain shields directly into the enemy's army. Blinded and burnt they retreated, screaming. Tragon was baffled. How does one conquer an enemy using blinding light? Then he realized that the short night was his only answer. His attack would wait until night. He'd destroy these invaders. He'd be embarrassed to learn that Phillrey's teenage warriors were stalling his attack. Yet Tragon feared night, as already mentioned.

Night came and the gang under Zena's command disappeared into the tunnel. Even the poles hung with mistletoe were missing. Tragon's raiders found nothing and retreated. At sunrise the troops were again assembled and focusing sunlight to the snow mass miles away above Castlethorn. Tragon puzzled at this occurrence. Why was his enemy beaming light at the mountain? Nothing came to mind. Not even his advisors knew what was in store for them. They curiously viewed the line of light as it streamed for miles through the air and shown like a brilliant horizontal line across the white snow.

Attack was fruitless. Patience must be his ally. Tragon rubbed his beard with one hand; then the other. He pondered the situation for hours, then in a rage, drank wine and ate fresh roasted meat torn directly off the rotating spit. His bare hands were commonly used for such crude dining behavior. He had one rule for eating, his pleasure!

Then satisfied, Tragon waddled to his outward post and stared once again at the spectacle. His imagination dulled and saturated with wine, he grunted and watched as if in a trance. He dozed off once in awhile in an upright position, leaning on a long wooden weapon, while his guards protected him from falling by leaning their Master against the massive stones of their military abode.

Yet beneath Tragon's Castlethorn, the digging party prepared to launch a mass exit of the captives. Their freedom sounded its own song in the cracking noises emanating from the snow mass. The focused beams formed a long line across the frozen surface of this mountain; the ice loosened its grip, and then moaned, preparing for an avalanche. Only a few keen-eared warriors of Castlethorn heard the sound. When they did hear the moan of the mountain's ice, they thought little of it. To them, nature was always making noise: thunder, waterfalls, wind, and swaying trees. Why should the mountain seem different? However, all day the sunrays hit the mountain, Tragon was dumbfounded as to ascertain why.

As the Zollerin sun moved slowly over the green sphere of sky, the teenage warriors kept the light focused on the mountainside. Their aimed shields kept them vigilant. In this manner the beams maintained their presence pointed toward the ice. The warriors knew victory waited for them with each noise from the mountainous ice. The young soldiers knew the moment was soon to be right, and their parents, trapped for years by Tragon's forces, would run for freedom through the subterranean cavern carved by their sons and daughters. This moment meant much to the young tunnel diggers. This time the adults would be saved by their progeny. Then the young shall inherit the land, and the land inherits the never-ceasing wind.

As the focused light loosened the glacier, a moan louder than an explosion echoed from the mountains, an avalanche soon released its energy and slid quickly and ferociously into Castlethorn. Just as the chaos exploded from the caked icy layers above, the diggers uncovered their openings. The parents then, slipped into the opening as fast as melted butter on toast. Castlethorn was soon enveloped by the avalanche and all who stood with Tragon were instantly destroyed. Tragon was buried beneath the snow with icy slabs falling in place appearing as multiple tombstones. The monster and his murderous regime were ended.

As the parents fled through the cave toward safety, all escaped, and now the former penal residence was overtaken by an avalanche, and it appeared as the earthen ice age of 10,000 years previously. Then as everyone departed the cave, the young warriors and their parents saw their escape route collapse behind them. It was all over. Tragon and his legions were now destroyed; the hostages freed. Then in a brief moment, Zollerin history found itself freed of tyranny; the ending was now its beginning.

Chapter 16

Dad recovered from his heart attack. Yet he was weak, tired and survived a close call with death. Once one survives a close call with death, the will to survive thrives.

His daughters decided to provide mom and dad with retirement, and they purchased the store. Yes, they had changed their minds, and doing so made themselves happy. Mom and dad were pleased too. The daughters moved their families to the town of their youth. Their husbands were to work beside their spouses, one became the store's accountant; the other became the store's manager.

Then much to everyone's surprise, their elusive brother Thomas stopped by the store unannounced. It was a welcomed reunion, to have all but Gordon present. Thomas scoped out the store and enjoyed a vanilla milkshake. He stayed but a few hours, but the family did have delicious ham and cheese sandwiches, made behind the ice cream counter by the young woman who worked part time, and attended college full time. Her talent for making an unusually excellent tasting sandwich was well known in Glen Iris. These sandwiches were to be an early dinner before Thomas returned to his bookstore. As usual, Tom had little to say, no travel plans discussed. All Tom mentioned were his sales numbers being good, and that a few national and local writers had book signings on weekends. However, there was a slight mention that he and his longtime woman employee, Charlotte, had more than employer-employee relationship, and their future engagement would be announced. Now this statement made an impression on his family, never had he mentioned dating before, let alone engagement. However, no further details were provided, other than Mitch dropped by monthly and made Charlotte laugh, and he, Mitch, bought lots of books.

As stated, Mitch and Thomas were more alike than Thomas and Gordon. Thomas left before dark. He hugged everyone and they thanked him for his surprise visit. Thomas did not tell anyone that he had dropped Charlotte off at the college library; that she was indeed in town; yet purposely kept from the family. It was dysfunctional behavior, as Thomas was as secretive as his 'dead' brother.

Only hours later, as he and Charlotte returned to Erie county, would Thomas realize the Paradise name had a chance of survival; however, only if he and Charlotte had a future son born to them. With Gordon's untimely demise, and any lack of male heirs in Thomas' marriage, the Paradise name would vanish from those descended by way of Walter and Nancy.

Everyone seemed satisfied in their new lives, and mom and dad rested at home and took leisurely walks every morning. They bought themselves a Golden Retriever, and discovered life with renewed reverence. Each took more time to read books. In fact, Mr. Paradise began a list of books he had been meaning to read for the last 43 years. Among those on his list: *Hawaii, The Right Stuff, The Shoes of the Fisherman, Lonesome Dove, Truman, Crusade In Europe, In the Arena, Tales of the South Pacific, The Source, Centennial, War and Peace, The Brothers Karamazov, Sketches from a Hunter's Album, This Side of Paradise, The Great Gatsby, The Sun Also Rises, For Whom the Bell Tolls,* and the entire, *Holy Bible.* Also, anything by Wouk, Singer, McMurty, and of course, Bruce Catton histories, were to be enjoyed.

Mother read murder mysteries by Margaret Truman and Mary Higgins Clark. She too read Austen's novels; the Bronte sisters as well. In her youth, Louisa May Alcott had been a favorite, having read all of Louisa's books and stories. Mom was also a member to The Louisa May Alcott Society, and attended annual meetings when she could. She also enjoyed JANSA, the Jane Austen Society. Her goal was to purchase a few first editions of Louisa May Alcott's novels, and Austen novels; yet that adventure would arrive in time. However, she asked Thomas to be on the 'lookout' for first editions of Alcott's and Austen's works. She then expressed her wish to visit Concord, Massachusetts, home to Miss Alcott, Thoreau, Emerson, and Hawthorne. Then to the surprise of all, she desired to visit England, home to the Paradise family clan, and her own family, the Morse's, and visit Austen's many sites in England. Naturally, see wanted to see the Dickens' sites as well. For was not Charles Dickens as beloved as Jane Austen?

Mom also enjoyed Margaret Mitchell's classic, *Gone With the Wind,* and Harper Lee's, *To Kill a Mockingbird.* Also, the 1850's Stowe classic, *Uncle*

Tom's Cabin, was pleasurably read in her youth. Ah youth, free time to read after chores were completed. With no husband or children to manage; did those days truly ever exist? Of course they existed, and she would not trade the present for the past for any price. The family was everything to her; a pearl priceless.

Nancy and Walt occasionally strolled downtown to the store and bought ice cream cones or milk shakes. They lived like kids some days, even flying a kite in the Glen Iris breezes of its High School football field, free of trees and other obstructions, thus perfect for a kite floating high into the sky, as if the day's purpose was merely for an elderly couple to be children once again. Naturally, their football field kite flying ended when the school's football season commenced in August. But for now, "seize the moment;' seize your enjoyment.

On other days they planned a trip to Florida or Arizona. Europe too was mentioned; possibly Hawaii as vacation destinations. Dad has been stationed in Hawaii, and it sure was beautiful compared to Iwo Jima.

Afternoon naps were a must, and daily blood pressure measurements taken. In fact, the Paradise Pharmacy purchased a blood pressure machine for customer convenience. This device made Glen Iris comparable to Rochester and Buffalo in what drugstores offered their clientele. The daughters were filling scripts and their husbands acclimated to their new work. Everyone enjoyed themselves; however, Gordon's long absence saddened the family.

A heaviness lay on everyone's hearts; yet it was rarely discussed. Reality was "too real" at times. My soon-to-be announced "death," and dad's near-death, was too much for everyone. It seemed vultures were circling overhead, waiting. My family placed frequent calls to Diana and hoped for good news. However she had only optimism to share, nothing concrete as to my return. Hope, too, was another medicine offered to mom and dad. Just a few long distance calls, and both sides broke down and sobbed. It was only natural, as tears cleanse grieving hearts. Thus crying becomes medicinal to the emotional self; thereby improving the physical self as well.

As the year passed, Diana made the decision to proclaim Gordon deceased. A memorial service was planned. Diana's parents flew in from Tulsa, and a few Paradise relatives did too.

The Pastor of Tulsa's The Church of the Resurrection said Mass without a casket present. And tomorrow, Gordon's will shall be read, as announced after the Mass.

An attorney friend of Diana's family read the simple document. It went like this: Ross became owner of the home, land, all buildings and equipment. Diana received 40% of all money from life insurance and royalties from inventions. The Paradise family received the other 40%. My car was to be sold, and the 10% was divided between Catholic Charities and Neighbor For Neighbor. The other 10% went to Dr. and Mrs. Lanier. Diana gave a fourth of her money to Holy Family Cathedral, while Anne was later given $10,000 by Diana, and Anne's parish was Resurrection. She donated $1000 to the wonderful white rock and brick Church on Fulton, near 51st and Yale Avenue.

The Paradise family returned to their rooms at the Doubletree Downtown Tulsa and rested, tomorrow they returned to New York State to resume their lives in the town overlooking the Genesee Valley, and wondered what life would be like without Gordon. Now, all realized how brief life could be on this earth.

Yet before the family departed, Diana gathered them all in one room and explained I was not with NASA at all, but a time traveler. Ross was there to explain the details so that laymen and laywomen would comprehend. Everyone was incredulous. Time travel? Science fiction! How did Ross and I devise such a thing? Anyone wishing to see Trans-17 need only walk to the lab he now owned.

Mom and dad shook their heads and grinned. Their son did what H.G. Wells dreamed of doing. The two sisters marveled, "Was their brother famous? Was he really that brilliant?"

Ross stated emphatically this information was not to be discussed. Only total secrecy protected their son and brother. If broken, the secrecy would likely cause Gordon's demise. Thus, the entire family knew Ross and Diana were not exaggerating. Therefore. Thomas and Mitch were not to be told, nor any Aunt or Uncle; secrecy must prevail.

However, Thomas did not attend. His recent visit was all he could give. Even Mitch did not attend. He and his cousin were similar, as mentioned, except for the absurd babbling Mitch constantly spoke. Thomas spoke sparingly, and disliked attending marriages and funerals, and ran his business quite well for living a monastic-like existence in his bookstore's basement. He and Gordon both liked subterranean environments; yes, family genetics! Thus Gregor Mendel was laughing from his heavenly domain, having been the first to write a scholarly analysis of genetics in the 1860s, and scientifically ignored until 1900. Yes, Abbott Mendel was delighted that his theory was now fact, and the Paradise family, and every other family, proved him correct!

Ross drove everyone to Hideaway Pizza, where everyone ate delicious pizza and drank soft drinks; telling funny stories related to the recently declared deceased, Gordon Paradise. As the night progressed, a drunken Ross was driven home by Diana, and the sisters took his truck to their hotel's parking lot.

Morning, and the entire family ate breakfast with Diana, and she bid them farewell and best wishes. Then an airport van swept away the Paradise clan to their terminal, a flight to Chicago; then onwards to Buffalo. All hugged and begged Diana to visit soon. She would always have a place to stay in Glen Iris; with a dish of ice cream at her bedside every night.

Diana's experience with Gordon's family proved to be a blessing, one she would never forget; yet treasure, as she did, all important memories. Indeed, the memories of Glen Iris, and the Paradise family gathering for this funeral Mass, had been special to her. It made her feel a 'true' member of the family, and not predicated on Gordon's presence. It was an emotional bond between her as an individual woman and the family. Few women have such emotionally intimate experiences with their future in-laws. In too many marriages, in-laws were strangers, or even enemies. Yet, these wonderful people embraced her, as she was truly a daughter to them, as if she too had grown up in their home in Glen Iris. Such a family feeling, and now grown, she had two families, one in New York; one in Tulsa.

And yes, she had introduced her parents to the Paradise family, and an immediate kinship developed. Diana's family was invited to western New York, and Diana's parents suggested they, and Walt and Nancy, share their condo in Florida soon. Hence, new friendships quickly gelled, became as adhesive in content as in feeling.

Chapter 17

Finally, I returned to the earthy pit by way of the river and found my beeper amid mud and rotting weeds. Zena did not travel with me, rather she sent two friends to assist my travel and the search for my electronic beeper. Within an hour we had found it. My delight was immeasurable and heartfelt, and a prayer rose to God from my soul; one of total thankfulness.

My wish for returning home was constantly upon my mind. I trekked back to Phillrey and Zena's location, safely by boat and by land. It took just two days as it had previously.

Zena sunbathed by the river, as her father sat besides her reading. Her partial nudity no longer made me feel immoral or lustful. I accepted the fact that Zollerin's were nudists, though I was too reserved to lay buff by the river. In one sense, they lived in "Eden" before the fall, and were more European in such matters than we puritanical Americans.

"I have some sad news and good news," I stated upon my return.

Zena immediately sat up. Phillrey looked at me with saddened eyes.

"My return trip to earth is imminent. My translator had been cleaned and re-activated. I'm now ready to depart. I feel sad for leaving you both; yet excited to return to the gardens of mortal earth."

My poetic heart burst as I spoke, and then wept. Zena placed her arms around me and Phillrey placed his palm upon my head as a patriarch blesses a son.

My departure was too abrupt; yet wasn't everything involving this trip abrupt? Answer, not really. I was in a twelve month coma just a while ago.

Immediately Zena proclaimed a festival and Phillrey nodded. Tonight we'll feast on wild boar, herbs; plant leaves for salad, roasting bird, and a type of 'vanilla ice cream' intergalactic style, found naturally in Zollerin caves.

Without a moment to lose Zena, dressed and organized the food tables with the help of dozens of her warriors. I was delighted with her "eager-to-please" attitude. Yes, Zena would make a great wife. However, I was nearly twenty years her senior. Then I remembered Charlie Chaplin and his wife Oona O'Neill. He was thirty six years her senior. Life and love rarely make sense, they just happen. Life and love happen as one river joins another, invisible and visible at the same moment. Yet such thoughts were mere amusement for me. I was returning to my beloved Diana.

By dusk a dinner fit for a king was prepared by the Zollerin youth. Soon we sat at tables in the open air and feasted on the foods before us. For entertainment, the crude; yet delightful quartet of homemade instruments enchanted our ears. Afterwards two mimes had us laughing loud and long. This meal was a cross-between Black Eyed Pea and barbeque chaos. I filled up and enjoyed each unique taste of Zollerin cuisine. A barbeque sauce made from scratch by Zena herself would make any Oklahoma barbeque restaurant proud. The poultry was superb and the salad was topped with a honey-mustard dressing that enchanted my tongue.

The third act was two standup comedians, one male and one female. They were hilarious, and even spoofed Zena and myself. We laughed like hyenas and cackled like crows. Another spoof was on Tragon and Castlethorn.

Evening came and bonfires lit. Tongues of flame leapt upwards and moved to slight evening breezes. Tonight the sky was once again studded with the jewels of distant starry fires. There above, here below, the warmth of heat, and the happiness of friendship. By this time we began singing and I attempted to teach a few folk songs to the community; yet to no avail. They however, sang their folk songs with great enthusiasm, and we had a delicious time. As we tired and said our farewells, they presented me with a necklace of pearl-like gems. It was handmade by their finest artisan. It was to be worn by the woman of my dreams. I thanked them and embraced as many as I could. They waved goodbye as they left me beside the fires, now almost extinguished, with Zena and Phillrey nearby.

"Farewell my friend, my good and gracious earth friend!"

"Surely you'll see me tomorrow, Senator?"

"No Gordon, I leave early on urgent business. A delegation of Zollerins in the north, once thought extinct, has been found. I must travel to meet them and chart the future. Zena will see you off, and anyone else you wish. I leave at sunrise for a river journey with the finest warriors to our name. This is our personal parting, our farewell to each other. Bitterness for me to bear;

yet sweet for you to return home to earth. However, I fantasize of you staying here and helping us rebuild Zollerin. Yet such dreams are selfish. Your life touched us as few others have done. Yet we dare not ask you to stay. Earth is your home and Zollerin a brief interlude in your life's experiences."

"Senator Phillrey, thank you for your help. It would be tempting to stay and assist rebuilding, for indeed. I now have two new friends; dear friends, I dare say. If not for you I'd be dead from the lizard's poison. You two have been good friends, more family really than friends. We must not forget one another. Distance often makes the heart and mind forget; yet I cannot forget. My debt to you both is beyond payment; such kindness imitates love more than mere friendship. We are not mere friends, we are truly family, you, Zena, the whole of this community, and I. My discovery of you occurred in a timely fashion, as if it were pre-ordained, which I know is true, it was pre-ordained. Nothing happens by chance, chance is simply a term for probabilities, and probabilities are providentially designed. Need I say more?"

"Say no more Gordon. You have helped me; or rather us, in a way we cannot repay either. If I had could have one other wish come true, it would be for my daughter to be your life mate. It would honor me and Zollerin to unite two planet's people in a galactic marriage. Yet I feel this event will not occur, though I see in Zena's eyes her love and devotion to you. No one has touched her heart as you. A father may not know well the heart of his daughter; however, I see the obvious, and neither wish will be ours to possess and proudly own."

I felt embarrassed, though pleased at his words. Zena glanced at me then looked downward, feeling somewhat 'put on the spot,' her father's words. Yet Zena nodded yes to her father's words, she wished to be my life's mate too, a Zollerin term.

"Your words are kindness and truth. Yet I am unable to have Zena as my mate since another waits my return. The Zollerin devotion to country and clan your daughter displays is impressive. I return to earth pleased at helping free your people from Tragon."

"Farewell Gordon Paradise, I depart for sleep prior to my day's journey." The elderly Senator departed into the quiet night, disappearing into its darkness, not light. It saddened me; reminded me of death, the death of a friend or family member.

Zena grabbed my hand and led me to recline beside her. We kissed a few times, but chose to refrain from passion. We held each other and lay in silence, looking at the stars above us in perfect majesty, burning like distant hearts; kindled by love's own passionate warmth. We fell asleep. I dreamt Diana and I were married and living in Houston. Then I dreamed of playing baseball in the park in Glen Iris, and building snowmen during winter. Then I dreamed of the Senior Prom and Zena being crowned queen. I awoke from sensing Zena's movement as sunlight quickly arrived. She chose to go swimming. I chose not to swim. Walking out from the water I offered Zena my towel, my head turned away out of modesty and respect.

Soon she was toasting bread over a fire and cooking Zollerin eggs.

We spent the morning talking of her future. She wanted to find a mate and begin a family. Yet no one seemed to interest her, except me. Indeed, I was in an awkward social position.

Then I stated, "Oh Zena, love is never simple, though we want it to be. I have no other words of wisdom, or even words that resemble wisdom. You're a wonderful young woman and I envy the young man who does win your heart."

She asked, "How does one win a heart? She looked at me with sad eyes; yet eyes aged with wisdom since our first meeting.

I spoke softly, "Having known you for the time I've spent here is a treasure; one to remember, forever."

Her reply was in a hushed tone, "I wish you'd stay. Perhaps returning to earth is not the best thing, and perhaps your mate will be a stranger to you? Gordon, I'd even live on earth as your mate, if you decided for me over Diana."

Her words astounded me, move to earth for me? Would she really do such a thing? Knowing her, yes, her heart spoke truth. She would indeed forsake Zollerin, yet I simply replied, "Zena, forget me and find one of your culture. Your future is here, Zollerin needs you."

We hugged and said little more. Then the time to return drew close, as my "Z" began buzzing, and then, with a humming noise, sounding my departure nearing. I sat in an area of low grass far from the beautiful Zollerin trees, as to have no interference from tall objects. I waved goodbye; then pressed my "Z" machine to work its electronic marvel.

She yelled out, "I love you Gordon!" just as I was caught up in the electronic sphere and placed in the time "warp." Moments later I was hurtling through the cavern of time present, heading toward earth, like a launched javelin. Zena was just a memory. There was only one direction now, homeward. Before long I was totally unconscious in my travel. Earth approached, and a dear friend it was, bringing me back, and giving me a second chance, perhaps a mystical second birth, as I headed to the blue sphere of earth so many light years distant.

Chapter 18

It may have been days, perhaps a week, before landing on earth. I had no idea how long I was semiconscious. Yet there I was, in my laboratory, being unveiled from the electronic shell surrounding me. As I eyed the familiar setting, there was Ross at the controls, excited and near tears. I stood up from the chair that was my initial exit point and return point, all in one.

"Gordon, I'm glad to see you again old man. Diana and I thought you were forever lost in this crazy galaxy, deceased as last summer's crickets."

We hugged like long lost brothers, and both of us were teary eyed. Then we shook hands and Ross spoke the words I knew intuitively were on his mind. "We truly thought you were dead.'

Little did he know that I had been so close to it, the ultimate equalizer called 'death.'

"Come; let us go inside for an Italian meal prepared by Anne."

What a coincidence that Anne was here. It caught me by surprise.

What good fortune I said to myself. I've missed Italian food, especially spaghetti!

We approached the house and Anne came running out to embrace and kiss me. Before she said a word, Ross stated with pride, "Here's the woman who has kept your place from falling apart. She kept it clean, mowed the lawn, and paid your bills with money orders. She's a real helper in time of need, a real friend to both of us, and Diana too. However, no one became as vital to your life as she."

"You befriended Diana?" I asked.

"Yes," was her reply.

I looked into Anne's eyes and said, "Thank you for your kindness."

"Gordon, I always believed you'd return. Never did I think you were dead. I could never believe it, a woman's intuition."

"Your intuition was accurate and light years away too," I mused. Then I laughed out loud and started acting silly and behaving like Zero Mostel in, "Fiddler on the Roof", dancing. As I danced, my dog Duchess raced to me, filled with excitement. What delight to see her again too! On my knees I hugged Duchess and she licked my ears as she stood up on her hind legs.

My first thoughts had been of Diana and my disappointment was immediate and intense that she was not here too. Yet I was afraid to ask where she was. In a moment though, Ross, being the direct person he was, stated point blank, "Gordo, Diana's married and living in Houston." My eyes opened in shock and disbelief. "Don't kid this long lost friend, Ross; don't tell me fabrications so soon."

"No lies, Gordo, she's married." I looked at Anne and she nodded yes, Diana was no longer mine. Mixed emotions ran through me like electricity. My shock turned to anger, anger at betrayal. Then I felt intense feelings at the joy of just being home again, here in Tulsa.

"Ross, I feel betrayed; yet I'm glad to be home."

"Hey, let's get some food into us and take it easy. You've got a little to explain too, speaking of loss and betrayal," Ross stated.

Had I been disloyal to Diana when I befriended Zena? "Yes," I said to myself. Do I understand my attraction to both women at the same time? Yes. Is love rational? No. Yet loyalty is rational, and it was no game. My flaws were mine to bear and mine to change.

I knew I was allowed one woman, one Lord, one faith, and at least a few good friends. Zena would always be one of those friends, nothing more. She was too young and too far away, light years away, farther than Houston could ever be from Tulsa. Strange to compare Zollerin to Houston, however, for a brief moment I allowed it, and allowed Zena to be a precious memory. Anne though was my future. In this realization I knew if I could change myself, my thoughts and actions, I would change my world. I would be more honest with myself, and others. I would break the pattern of denial and seek selflessness at depths few obtain. Best of all, I was not alone. No, I was never alone; my best friends were nearby, and God was always with me.

"I suppose after a year everyone thought I'd never return." Anne put her arm into mine and led me to the dinner table. I looked around my kitchen and it looked as if I'd never left. Actually, it looked better than

I remembered. Ah yes, the mystical touch of a woman's hand, a touch unequaled on earth. We ate with joy at being together again. Slowly I spoke of my life after my departure eighteen months ago. In between my stories, Anne and Ross relayed life here.

He explained how Diana and he had gone to my Memorial Mass in Tulsa; the will read, and now Ross owned my home. Diana moved to Houston, as promised; now the only analgesic was time.

"Yes, time to heal from your 'demise.' While in Houston she met an Englishman by the name of Anthony Rodger Barrister. He was, by coincidence, a Blithe corporate attorney from England, attorneys there are called Barristers. Anthony swept Diana off her feet, and in twelve weeks they married."

"She dumped me for an English barrister?"

Ross said it all, "She didn't dump you at all. We all thought you dead. Did you expect her to cling in hope for years of your possible return, while her libido was boiling over? Come on old man, you'd not be so loyal. In fact, you mention this young woman Zena in your story as if you two were a couple."

"Well, we were friendly."

"So there, you weren't exactly loyal either?" Ross said.

"Apparently not, were you Ross?"

He said nothing and I sat silent too.

Anne came in to referee the conversation. "It's not a matter of loyalty once you believe your fiancé is dead. Life goes on. Diana had a life to live and wanted it with you Gordon. Yet you left and failed to return after the promised four weeks. Diana visited your parents, and prior to departing, she felt obligated to explain your time travel. Here in Tulsa, Diana and Ross explained to your family, the best they could, what you and Ross had created for your galactic trip.

"Yet Diana knew nothing of this trip until the last moment, but felt you still might be alive, I did too. Yet the time to move forward had arrived. Do you blame her? Let me rephrase myself, I want to delete the word 'blame.' There is no need to blame you or Diana for what happened. You both made choices and now have to live by those choices. Ross kept Trans-17 turned on and was going to keep it on for decades, if needed. You were not forgotten, but darn it, we didn't know if you were dead or alive in the vastness of space. In fact, I find it hard to believe what you've just returned from, for I can't imagine traveling as you did without rockets and shuttles and all that other space stuff the news talks about. Diana couldn't fathom it either. Yet she comprehended at her level and held on for a long time.

"By the way, Diana called me when the Englishman proposed to her. She felt a deep sense of loyalty to you, but knew you may never return. She had to move on and that decision was hers alone. I supported her choice. For crying out loud, she's over thirty and wants something in life besides a corporate headquarters to call home. I even went to the Houston wedding, at her request. Ross here was indisposed and couldn't make it."

I looked at him as he mumbled, "I was drunk."

"Diana had a beautiful wedding and spoke of you before she walked down the aisle. I was with her in the preparation room and she cried for joy in her marriage, and in sorrow for your demise. She couldn't help but feel betrayed that you left just as the gears of your marriage were in action She felt betrayed that in her return from the European trip, you glibly announced your intergalactic trip. It was incomprehensible to her that you'd do such a thing. Yet she chose to give you the freedom to pursue your dreams, before and after marriage. Then when you failed to return, she felt her permissiveness slapping her in the face. She came to believe you were dead and sought the consolation of the Paradise family."

"Did she like being with my family?"

"Yes, she did, but a cousin kept harassing her."

"One of my cousins harassed Diana during her Glen Iris visit?

"Yes, the strange attorney."

"Oh yes, Mitch, he's bipolar." Yet in anger I yelled, "What is it about attorneys that appeal to her?"

"Gordon, I'd like to tan your hide; it's just coincidence, nothing more. Besides, she detested your cousin, but felt sorry for him.

"I suppose so." My angry rush to judgment calmed. Then I exclaimed, "This meal was delicious, thank you both for everything."

"Well, what a convenient way to get off the subject, compliment my cooking," said Anne.

"Yes Anne, I'm getting off the subject and complimenting you and Ross for service above and beyond duty, you both deserve a prize."

Anne stated. "I'll be glad to spend some of your inheritance from Aunt Wendy."

"Aunt Wendy died, when?" I asked.

"A while back. That's when Diana went to Glen Iris alone and was part of the will reading,"

Hearing of her demise made me realize I needed to call home, or better yet, return home and visit my beloved family. Diana had been there in the last year and I hadn't returned to Glen Iris in years. I felt ashamed. It was in that moment of shame; I realized I would fly home and visit soon, very soon. I must see my parents, my brother, and my sisters and their families. I had some serious explaining to do in person. Just the thought of returning home to the Genesee Valley provided joy to my heart, and my mind filled with things to enjoy on my return visit.

Ross didn't say much, but he ate and drank a lot. Some things never change. Yet I made the point to thank Anne over and over for keeping the place looking nice. I offered her $5,000 for her efforts, and she accepted. Her refusal would have been awkward for me.

Then I proceeded to ask Ross, "Since I'm still alive, do I get my house back?"

"Go ask an attorney. Your castle is my tipi now."

"Very funny. Now get your junk out of here and let Sir Isaac have his old shack back."

Then I started laughing and Ross and Anne joined me. I laughed raucously, my favorite way!

"You make a lot of noise when you laugh." Ross said smiling.

"Now look, let's keep my noisy laughter out of it," I replied humorously

"You come in from intergalactic travel and think you rule the roost as if nothing has happened? Well Sir Isaac, this rooster is moving over and letting you have this dump back in your possession. Besides, I'm taking a year off and traveling west. I haven't seen this country at all; besides, why should you have all the fun?" he stated bluntly.

His announcement caught me off guard. He's never been one to leave Tulsa. His staying ability was always a feature I could count on.

"May I ask where you're getting the money?" asked I.

"My patents; I've been stashing the money away, and yes, I can read your mind, and no, I didn't drink my money away."

"My return is full of surprises. Any surprises from you, Anne?"

"You'll find out Gordon. Just give me time."

"Well, I can hardly wait." I stated, "One more thing, you wouldn't be flirting with me, would you?"

She winked and ate more salad.

"Looks like your love life isn't over, Professor," Ross proclaimed.

"That is definitely good news. I'm too young and crazy not to have a woman in my life." I said.

"Young you're not. Crazy? Yes." Ross stated.

At those words Ross tossed some beer in my face and laughed wildly as he raced outdoors. I pursued this mad Indian, and Duchess joined the fun. In my hand I had a can of beer, well shaken and pointing toward Ross. As I drew near him on the other side of the barn, I pulled the tab and beer spewed, drenching him. As we turned the corner, there was Anne with two cans of beer. She pulled the pop tops and both Ross and I got a face full.

"What a waste of good beer," yelled Ross as he picked Anne off the ground into his arms. As he tried to run with her in tow, he stumbled and she flew into a clump of grass. Ross fell over laughing, while I had prepared my garden hose for an offensive barrage. Turning it on full force, I aimed at Ross and Anne and hosed them. Then I held it overhead and drenched myself. We all rolled in the grass as Duchess barked happily at the mad people. Ross grabbed the hose and watered us down more. Anne's tee shirt was soaked through and revealing. Embarrassed, she headed inside to change. I did too. Ross went into the lab. We emerged twenty minutes later in dry clothes and smiling.

"Bonfire, bonfire, bonfire!" Ross kept yelling.

"All right old man, let's do it. Anne, obtain some matches from the kitchen, please." asked I.

We gathered wood logs and crates from the barn, and old newspapers from the lab. We had ourselves a class act fire in no time. We settled into some webbed chairs and talked quietly of time past. I had yet to tell them of Tragon and how the mirrored shields had released a mountain of snow into Castlethorn. After awhile I proceeded to relate the 'galaxy game' tale; they sat there dumbfounded. Little did they know my trip would entail such excitement. As the night went darker and stars shown overhead, I ran inside to retrieve blankets in which to wrap ourselves in, for the evening was turning cold.

"Just like Zollerin," I said. "It's cold at night. Yet you should see the stars from Zollerin. The sky is so full that at times it could be daylight. It's overwhelming and beautiful."

"So you were close to the middle of the Milky Way?"

"That's what I figured, Ross. Deeper into the hub of this pinwheel galaxy, the nightly stellar display increases. Simple as that," I said.

"Gordon, will you ever go back to this Zollerin place?"

"That is what I'm asking myself now, especially since Diana's married." I paused then asked, "Shall I call her and let her know I'm alive?"

"Gordon let me do that for you. The sound of your voice might overwhelm her. Just take things slowly for a few weeks," said Ross.

I went silent. Then Anne leaned over, "Gordon, I'm here for you. You're not alone. She may be married but I'm letting you know that I care for you very much. I'll be your best friend if you'll let me, and your best girl too. Now my feelings are spoken, and I'll help Ross tell Diana."

She caught me off guard for the third time tonight. Yet it felt comforting and it made me glad. I reached out to hold her hand and looked into her eyes, eyes made visible by firelight. So we now held hands, and that in itself was romantic and pleasurable.

Sitting before the fire I knew there was a lot to catch up on, national and world news, family, friends like the Lanier's, Diana's days while I was gone, and Anne's life here next to my home, and church.

"I've missed Church and the sacraments, I stated. Though Zollerin was pagan, maybe Christianity would have a chance there someday. Maybe the seeds were already planted? I did discuss Christianity with the Senator and his daughter."

Anne held onto my hand and drew closer, it felt great. Soon we were wrapped in the same blanket and she was humming old folk songs by Woody Guthrie. Ross kept putting away beer and I knew that he had to break denial and face the beast called alcoholism. Living in denial would kill him.

Here were my unspoken thoughts. My life had to take a new course. Time travel served only as an ego trip, literally. What good had really been given to those I loved here on earth? Yet I knew the opposite side of coin to hold out as well; yes, the trip helped free a people. How many could say that in their lifetime? Yet I paid a price for it, the consequence of which saddened me.

I knew this much, that for every action we do, there is an equal and opposite reaction in human life. Life followed the rules of physics, imagine that! God planned it that way and that's the way the sciences of physics and biology merged. As I let go and drew close to Zena, and the ways of Zollerin, Diana was pulled away from me; it was, in 'a round about' way, for both of us. Yet it happened nonetheless, and it hurt. Having known Zena was fun, and Anne's faithfulness was touching and heartwarming. Yet Diana is Diana, and we had been close. To know I'll never kiss her again, or hold her close, was painful to realize. However, the reality of the former paradigm was gone. I have a new life now, the old life was over, and it's not mine anymore except in memory. It's history, and now a new future needs to be written, without her as a leading character. Yet Anne was here now and that was lovely. She was bright, good looking, loyal, warm, and friendly. How many adjectives need I list?

Ross spoke a few words that surprised Anne and me as words from Ross had rarely done. He stated in a matter-of-fact tone, "Ladies and gentlemen, I am placing myself in alcohol rehab in Arizona. Afterwards, I shall travel the roads of this nation with Kogee, my wife, that is, if she consents to my proposal. I pray to The Great Spirit she marries me, a reformed man. I have had my last beers. In a week I will be in Arizona, working my way to recovery. The Great Spirit has provided me with a host of cash from patents received, and well paying patents at that. I am no longer the drunk. I am the recovering and proud Ross Red Jacket, descendant of a famous Seneca Chief. I shall make him proud of me. I shall honor my family. Now pardon me dear friends as I fall asleep." Indeed, Ross had fallen asleep in a moment after his proclamation, and as the fire was dying out.

I hugged Anne, then told her I needed sleep. She too was overwhelmed with pride for Ross' decision to seek help; to seek freedom over alcoholism, replaced with sobriety.

As stated, I had changed too. I believed myself less selfish, less inhibited, more aware of God's plan for my life, and wanted to re-enter the sacramental life of the Church. Anne suggested we begin attending The Church of the Resurrection Parish; I consented. I knew it had an excellent reputation for its choir and its quality Pastoral leadership.

I too was sleepy, and with Anne, departed the backyard. We slipped out from beneath the blanket and placed it over Ross. He would do fine stretched out in the chaise lounge. I headed to the house with my arm draped over Anne's shoulders. She held me by the waist.

"Diana's loss is my gain" she whispered.

I didn't respond to these words except in my heart. I felt the loss of Diana; yet felt joy for my new woman. Young love, fresh on the vine is special; may this young love live long and joyfully!

We sat at the kitchen table and had an evening snack of strawberry shortcake. It was deliciously simple, especially with fresh baked biscuits Anne made earlier. I smiled at her and thanked her for her earlier statement about one woman's loss being another woman's gain. I was joyful in my new woman. I also knew it was God's guidance that led me to Anne rather than marriage to Diana. The reasons for His Will were not mine to debate. Anne proved herself priceless during my absence; she never ceased in her belief I was alive. That alone was a gift I could not pass by. Love, life, friends, and freedom, what more did I need? My friends and life were all gifts, none to be taken for granted. This realization was enhanced during my "Galaxy Game," and it was a game I had won.

However, I came to realize life was not an unending 'game,' and no other word fit my travels more consciously. I had pursued this adventure as a 'game,' and the whole incident was not conscious to me, until my return, Now I knew myself, and understood the irony of my subconscious and conscious decisions I make daily, weekly; annually.

I also realized all people, not just Gordon J. Paradise, lived their entire lives in these two realms of the knowing and hidden mind. Realizations arrived after major lifetime events, births, deaths, graduations, marriages, diseases, and the whole range of human activity. Without these events, we'd live smaller than our potential, and never be aware of what was missing.

That brings me to another thought, what realizations lie ahead? Only God knew that answer. I, and all humans, would have to wait for His divine clock to bring us around to knowing what His divine time meant, versus human time.

Afterwards Anne and I kissed goodnight, and offered to walk her home. She said no, but accepted my offer of a flashlight.

I went to my bedroom and my first night back to my queen-size bed. She disappeared into the darkness with the borrowed flashlight, and in several minutes I saw her lights turn on, and then off, in her own home. Now I was watching out for her; it felt good. I fell asleep quickly. It was delicious to sleep in my home again. As I closed my eyes and felt Duchess jump into bed at my feet, I knew I was one life among many, and that the future was as unknown, as much as the distant past had been forgotten. The past yields the present, and the future unfolded inside our hearts and minds.

Outside the clear summer night showed the starry majesty of our galaxy without Trans-17. In fact, none would see the galaxy as I had seen it with Zena, just a mere week ago. Yet few would care to, for their thoughts were stayed on earth, their home and car payments, their children's education, and the price of groceries and fuel.

I had seen another side to life, and though I respected the daily lives of my fellow citizens, this earthen village had yet to experience: the friendships of other galactic villagers, like Zollerins. Yet would I ever use Trans-17 again? I knew not. I was exhausted in happiness. Now deep into sleep I dreamed of a reunion with my best friends. We laughed and ate ice cream and barbequed ribs. We sang songs and delighted over the victories of Glen Iris High. Yet Ross, Anne, Diana, the Lanier's, Zena, Phillrey, and my parents were there too among my high school companions. It all happened in my backyard home in Glen Iris, a yard I had not seen in years. Little did I know that when I dreamed of location, the location was always Glen Iris, not Tulsa. Yet Tulsa was home and I was finally and truly home. Then in my dream I realized my good fortune to have two homes, Glen Iris, my youthful home, and Tulsa, my adult home. Both homes were precious as gold and silver; yet never were homes to be considered commodities. Home was beyond empirical wealth; rather, it possessed a spiritual and emotional quality, immeasurable; only those attuned to their spiritual selves realized not all reality was measurably and empirical in nature.

Farewell, I say to you, old and new friends, and I pray that love treats you well, and that the night sky will always fascinate you as it does me. My future will always involve watching the night sky, sitting back and watching as if nothing else mattered. In the presence of God's creation, little else does.

However, I had one wish for the multitudes of my earthly brethren, "May you find one true friend, and one true love, for each are priceless."

Now I would spend time with Anne and wish Ross the best for his future. His life and mine had been entwined for decades. Now he was free to pursue renewed health and live the life of a husband, after rehabilitation had cured his addictions. I was convinced Kogee would marry Ross, and he and Kogee would see the grandeur of our great country.

I would remain here with Anne, and such thoughts brought happiness to this inventor, poet, explorer, son, friend, and maybe, just maybe, as Anne's new husband. Her heart and mine held the answer to that question, and I hoped; I prayed that she would consent to a new live together, and return to Glen Iris to meet my family. All these thoughts were in my dreams, and my dreams seemed as real as anything else, and in fact, dreams are a reality of their own. Dreams were, in many cases, a prelude to the conscious reality of life. Yes, life, how precious it was to own it, and to realize its ownership was a gift from God.

Perhaps Anne and I would return to Zollerin, or we would dismantle the machine and keep all action secret?

Anyway, it didn't matter right now. My future was in no rush to be realized. It was time, literally, to slow my actions and live just day-to-day aware and thankful for my safe return; and night-to-night in dreams of my recent journeys, and my future with Anne.

A slower pace would be new to me, and I was ready, once again, to experience the joys and sorrows of life here in a little corner of earth, called by all, Oklahoma.

Acknowledgements

To Irene Chance, owner of "Flying Fingers-Typing and Word Processing," Sand Springs, Oklahoma, who retyped the novel onto a CD (flyingfingerstyping@juno.com). Her work is most appreciated.

To the late Dr. Leslie Fiedler, who assisted me at the very beginning of this story, and whose insights were genuine and helpful. His greatness existed in his sincerity and intellectual gifts.

Also, I wish to thank another teacher, a true gentleman; my former High School Track coach, and Art teacher, Mr. Phil Rea. I used his name for my literary character, Senator Phillrey. I trust Mr. Rea finds it to be a compliment.

In appreciation to Beth Stafford of All Saints Catholic School; Broken Arrow, Oklahoma for her careful reading of my book and in perfecting its grammar, thank you!

To Jo Ann Bly, my former spouse, who endured many years of my work on this story. And to my daughter Elizabeth, for her interest in Dad's writing, and whose comments made this novel more Christian than secular, and whose insights were mature beyond her years. God bless you both!

To the Holy Trinity, whose divine guidance was felt in the writing of this story. May the Trinity bring you, dear reader, and abundant life.

A special "thank you" to my sister-in-law, La Fonda, for her time and comments on this book.

More stories and poems of God's influence upon our lives remain to be written by this poet/writer. I ask you to look forward to reading, *Voyager Mars*, a novel already in progress, as well as my completed book of poetry, *The Seven Colors of Earth.* Two other books of poetry will appear in the upcoming years: *Rode the Four Horsemen;* and, *This House of Bread*, a collection of my spiritual poetry. All my books shall be Catholic in nature; universal, I pray, in appeal.

A special thank you to all Tulsa area Priests, Deacons, our Bishop, and Catholic laity, all of whom enhance my faith.

And to the fond memory of my late friend and fellow Church of the Resurrection parishioner, Phil Tibey, 87, who passed away on Easter morning, 2009. His examples of Christian virtues will live within me eternally. And like time with my parents, I will miss greatly Phil's and my time together.

And I have recently contemplated the possibility of writing a book entitled, *The Joy of Roman Catholicism.*

A children's book, already written and with illustrations 95% complete, will appear in the autumn of 2009 or 2010, entitled, *First Christmas for Duchess.* It's an animal story, whose audience of children, and adults with child-like hearts, will enjoy. It revolves around scripture's account of the birth of Christ in Bethlehem, and the stable animals present at that glorious moment.

In gratitude for my brothers, Lloyd and Rick, who helped and guided me over the years. I thank you both for your many kindnesses. Also, let me thank the few remaining living relatives I have, your lives prove that "character is destiny."

I also want to thank Larry and Bill Moskoff, who in 1982 hired me into the Bock Pharmacal Company, a pharmaceutical "family" once based in St. Louis, Missouri. I shall remember it all my life, and treasure it in my thoughts. In their trust in hiring me, I spent 25 years as a pharmaceutical representative. The friends I made in the industry, and in the company, live on in cherished memory and continued friendships.

To the physician offices and pharmacies I called on over the years. I cannot thank you enough for your graciousness and hospitality. The kindness each office and pharmacy provided, in their giving me valuable time to sell my medications, is a highlight in my life.

Selling medications was a way to enhance the health of the many patients your offices treated, and the pharmacies "filled." as prescriptions, and thus, it was an honor to serve in this fashion.

My passion for books derives from my Dad, and empathy for people, from my Mom. Yet from both parents I received insights into the power of human dignity, hard work, and the power of goals, and utilizing one's talents and insights. Without these insights, my ability to write fiction or poetry, and someday playwriting, would be improbable, if not impossible. The power of example is a major part of their legacy to me, their middle son.

This novel, and my poetry book, **The Seven Colors of Earth,** are available for order through your favorite bookstore, or may be purchased through any online booksellers.

To the people of Elmira, N.Y., my birthplace; Geneseo, N.Y. my home for 25 years; Buffalo, N.Y., my graduate school location; and Broken Arrow and Tulsa, Oklahoma, my home since June 1978, many thanks for your kindnesses and hospitality. Each location provided me with new friends and beloved family. Even though I have no relatives in Buffalo or Amherst, surviving the "Blizzard of 1977," made us a 'family of survivors'.

The author may be contacted at his e-mail address: *b.bly@cox.net.*

LaVergne, TN USA
13 May 2010

182522LV00003B/5/P